A Dream of Freedom

A Dream of Freedom

BY

AARON JORDAN

BONNEVILLE BOOKS™

Springville, Utah

ISBN: 1-55517-699-2
e.1

Published by Bonneville Books
Imprint of Cedar Fort Inc.
www.cedarfort.com

Distributed by:

Cover design by Nicole Cunningham

Printed in the United States of America
10 9 8 7 6 5 4 3 2 1

Printed on acid-free paper

Library of Congress Cataloging-in-Publication Data

Jordan, Aaron, 1977-
A dream of freedom / by Aaron Jordan.
p. cm.
ISBN 1-55517-699-2 (alk. paper)
1. Americans--Soviet Union--Fiction. 2. Political refugees--Fiction.
3. Soviet Union--Fiction. I. Title.

PS3610.O655D74 2003
813'.6--dc22

2003015198

To Katya

ONE

The sunshine lanced through the treetops at regular intervals, blinding him now and then as he made his way through the dense forest, pine needles and leaves crunching beneath his shoes. A gentle breeze slithered in and out of the maze of narrow trunks, gliding across the bark, rustling the branches and the underbrush, moving through the forest like fingers through hair. A light breeze caressed his face and carried to his ears the desperate, fading cry of a familiar voice that called his name.

"Meeeeeeeeshaaaaaaaa."

He stopped and looked around. A shiver traveled down his spine. The treetops swayed above him, and a burst of sunlight flashed across his eyes, warming his face. He raised his hand to block out the light, and scanned ahead. The trees all looked the same, and the sun hovered right above him. He lost all sense of direction.

He heard his name again. "Meeeeeeeeshaaaaaaaa."

He headed toward the voice. He pushed through bushes and branches, almost tripping over several fallen logs, and the sunlight glimmered through the canopy above, intermittently splashing him with light and warmth while a cool wind enveloped his face and danced across his skin. The forest unfolded before him in an endless monotony of trees and leaves and bushes and dirt.

He stopped again. "Where are you?" he yelled.

Silence.

He pushed ahead, and the forest loosened its hold on him. The trees became more sparse. The bushes disappeared. The underbrush thinned.

A few minutes later he stopped at the edge of a small clearing where the forest floor was bare. In the center of the clearing, for a radius of several meters, there were no trees, only dirt, and a single gray headstone protruded from the ground at a sharp angle.

He entered the clearing and approached the headstone with caution. The sunlight faded as he stepped forward, and he looked up. A blanket of black clouds circled ominously overhead, covering the entire sky. The eye in the center of the clouds grew steadily smaller, until the blackness had completely covered the last remnants of blue sky and swallowed up the sun.

He kept walking and stopped when he reached the headstone. Before he could take a closer look, he heard a thrashing sound above him. He looked up again. The trees were shaking violently, and their leaves, which had been a bright green, had now turned a stale, dead brown. They fell off of their branches in torrents, raining down on him in a strange autumnal blizzard. After several seconds he looked around him, only to see that the leaves had covered the forest floor and were almost up to his knees.

He crouched down before the headstone and frantically threshed the leaves in front of him with both hands, side to side, to keep the headstone from getting buried. The leaves stopped falling around him. Once the headstone was uncovered again, he put his hands on the cold, rough granite and leaned forward, squinting at the stone.

The granite was blank. He wiped his hand across it, and little chunks of rock crumbled and fell to the ground, revealing an engraved inscription. He dug his fingers into the cold stone to clear out the rock chips from the carved letters. Then he stood up and stepped back to read the name that was inscribed there.

KONSTANTIN IVANOVICH TIMOFEYEV

1872—1932

The wind grew cold and intensified, and the trees again shook ferociously. The dark clouds above converged into a black vortex that rotated in a huge circle in the sky, then emitted a low rumbling thunder. The wind reached down and picked up the dead leaves from the ground, swirling them around him in a funnel-shaped column that rose into the air, spinning the leaves so they danced about his head like large butterflies.

He again heard the distant voice call his name. “Meeeeeeeeshaaaaaaaa.”

The ground beneath his feet grew soft, and he sank into the soil until he was ankle-deep in the cold dirt, which he could feel inside of his shoes. His arms were raised high above his head and were stretched out straight, as if the wind had wrapped strong cords around each of his wrists and was trying to lift him. He tried to extract his feet from the dirt, but the ground had turned hard like concrete. He tried to pull his arms down, but to no avail. The rumbling and the wind increased until their noise became deafening.

“Where are you!” he shouted, but the noise of the wind and the storm drowned out his voice.

Now there were other voices around him, chattering and whispering, some howling and wailing, full of anguish yet muffled by the roar of the wind and thunder. He couldn’t make out what they were saying, but they seemed to be coming from the surrounding trees, as if the trees themselves were crying out to him. The fingers of the wind carried these ghostly sounds into his ears, and the trees at the edge of the clearing bent toward him, their branches reaching for him. The headstone sank down as if in quicksand, then disappeared as the ground swallowed it.

A sharp pain pierced his shoulders and his sides, then his hips and his knees. The ground beneath him was slowly moving downward, and the wind pulled up even harder on his arms, which he still could not lower. The multitude of voices grew louder, as did the thundering of the clouds and the howling of the wind.

For a brief moment, amid the voices’ sorrowful wailing, he heard someone laughing.

Intense pain shot through his body from his hands down to his feet. The ground was still moving slowly downward, and his arms were still being stretched up toward the vortex in the sky. The wailing died down, but the laughter became louder, and he discerned that it came from a single voice, a man’s voice. The timbre was deep; the tone was one of mocking.

He tipped his head back and opened his mouth to scream, but there was no air in his lungs, and all that came out was a weak cough. The pain was unbearable. Why wasn't he passing out yet? Everything around him became a blur. Blackness crept in around his peripheral vision and closed in, and he could no longer see color. At the end of the dark tunnel in front of him the world outside was spinning. The roar of the storm and the voices and the laughter were also spinning around his head, although they were growing more distant. He felt nauseated and dizzy.

With the last bit of strength he could muster, he inhaled one final gulp of air and let out a futile scream. It lasted but a moment before his voice disappeared, and although he exerted all his strength, only a mute hissing sound exuded out of his mouth as the last breath of life exited his body.

Then the tunnel closed, there was absolute silence, and everything went black.

Misha's body convulsed in a single violent twitch. He opened his eyes and sat up in bed. The phone was ringing. He looked at Larisa lying next to him. Her eyes opened, and she stared back at him in silence. They waited.

The phone rang again.

Larisa sat up and grabbed his arm. "Misha, don't answer it. They might be coming for you."

He looked at his alarm clock—2:35 a.m.

"Nobody we know would call us at this hour," she said.

The phone rang a third time.

He briefly glanced back at his wife. Her face was pale. He pulled his arm away from her and threw the covers back.

"Misha!"

He got up and walked briskly over to the table where the phone stood, then stopped and stared at it, waiting.

"Misha!"

The phone rang a fourth time.

He picked up the receiver. “Alyo.”

A horrible shriek erupted from the earpiece and sent a cold shiver down his spine. He felt the color drain from his face. A woman’s voice wailed hysterically in his ear, and he recognized it immediately. He took a quick breath to calm his nerves, then cleared his throat.

“Olga!” he said sternly. “Olga, what’s wrong?”

The hysterical wailing continued.

“Olga, calm down and tell me what’s wrong.”

He listened and waited. Several seconds passed before the wailing died down to a sob. When she finally spoke, her voice sounded weak and tired. “They’ve taken him,” she said.

“Who? What are you talking about?”

There was a pause, and he could hear her breathing. Short, shallow breaths. “Ivan,” she said. “They came tonight and took him.”

His bottom lip quivered. He pressed his free hand up to his face, covering his mouth. He swallowed hard, then started nervously rubbing his fingers across his lips.

“Are you still there?” Olga asked.

He took his hand away from his mouth and held the receiver with both hands. “You’re at home?” he asked.

“Yes.”

“Stay there and unlock your door so that I won’t have to knock. I’ll be right over.”

Olga hung up without a word.

He set the receiver down and looked at his wife. Larisa said nothing.

“I have to go,” he said. He walked over to the closet and fumbled through the clothing in the dark until his fingers recognized the familiar texture of his belt. He pulled his pants on, then threw on a shirt and buttoned it up as fast as he could.

“Misha, what’s going on? What did Olga say?”

“They’ve arrested Ivan,” he said. “I have to go over there.”

“What if they’re still there? What if they’re watching the apartment?”

He walked out of the room into the hallway and found his boots by the door.

"Misha!"

He wrapped a scarf around his neck and put on his coat, then walked back to the bedroom. "Olga's all alone," he said. "I have to go over there."

When Misha reached Olga's building, he entered the stairwell cautiously and made his way up the stairs like a cat burglar, all the while looking upward at the floors above him, hoping he would see them before they saw him. He slowed down between the second and third floors and listened closely, removing his hat to hear better. A draft from a broken window in the stairwell slithered across the back of his head, raising goose bumps on his neck and making his scalp tense up around his ears. He shivered.

But they weren't there. The stairwell was vacant. He reached the fourth floor, found the door he was looking for, and turned the latch slowly. The door opened smoothly, effortlessly, and he slipped inside, closing it behind him.

He stood with his back to the door and looked around. The hallway was pitch black, except for a little moonlight off to the right side ahead of him, which came from the main room. He felt his way along the wall until he reached the double doors that opened into the living room. Enough moonlight shone through the window on the other side of the room that he was able to make out the silhouettes of furniture. He walked over to a table against the nearest wall, almost tripping over something on the way. He turned on a small lamp.

The room was a mess. Papers and books littered the floor. Cushions had been torn from the couch. A vase lay shattered in pieces in the corner.

He turned off the light and slipped back out into the hallway. "Olga," he called out in a tense whisper. "Where are you?"

A faint voice emanated from around the corner of the wall in front of him. "I'm here."

He headed toward the sound and found her sitting in the dark on a short three-legged stool in the kitchen. Her elbows rested on the table; her face was buried in her hands. She was weeping.

He stepped into the room, and she raised her head. "Oh, Misha," she whispered, and she couldn't say any more. She pressed her lips tightly together. She closed her eyes and lowered her head, and from each of her eyes a bluish silver tear, colored by the moonlight, broke free and streamed down the sides of her face. With her left hand she covered her eyes, and with her right hand she reached out to him.

He watched her for a moment, then stepped toward her and took her hand in his own.

She stood up and pulled him closer. She wrapped her arms around him, burying her head against his shoulder to muffle the sound of her sobbing.

He held her. He put a hand around the back of her head and gently pressed her against him.

Several minutes passed before she regained some composure. She turned so that her face was no longer pressed into his coat, but she still rested her head against his shoulder. She held him tightly. She seemed afraid to let go.

"They came about an hour ago," she whispered. "They rang the bell and waited for us to answer. I told Ivan not to open the door. I told him to climb out the window and jump from the balcony and run, but he wouldn't listen. He just grabbed me by the shoulders and stared at me, and I couldn't look at him any more because he had this strange, hopeless look in his eyes, and I knew that they were going to take him from me. He said there was no way out, and then he told me that he loved me and kissed me on the forehead. Then there was a knock at the door and he walked out of the room to open it, and I knew that he wasn't even going to try to fight them or get away from them or anything. The door opened and there was all this noise, there was crashing and shattering and . . ."

She stopped. She turned her face back to his shoulder and

pressed her forehead against him. She brought her hands around to his chest and grabbed the fabric of his coat in her fists.

He felt her cry. Her body shuddered in his arms, and all he could do was hold her.

"Shhh," he whispered.

She took a deep breath and pulled at his coat. "And then I heard them beating him," she cried, her voice louder now. "And I heard him groan and cough and try to speak—"

"Olga—"

"And they just kept hitting him and throwing him around the room, and—"

"Olga!" He put his hand around the back of her head and gently pushed her face into his chest.

She screamed into his coat. It was the same horrible shriek that he had heard on the phone, only muffled. She tightened her fists even more and started to push and pull against him in a sort of rocking motion.

He held her tighter. "Olga, stop this. Please."

She stopped struggling. She leaned against him and let go of his coat. She wrapped her arms around his back, and her body went limp. She turned her head to the left again to uncover her face.

"Why did they beat him?" she asked quietly.

"Olga—"

"He wasn't trying to fight. He would have gone with them peacefully. He didn't do anything—"

"Olga, stop thinking about it. There's nothing we can do. We have to be strong."

"People are disappearing all the time, Misha. They've been disappearing for years. You go to bed at night and then you wake up the next morning, only to find out that the lady next door isn't there any more. Sometimes they take whole families. The whole world has gone mad."

"Olga."

She pulled her head away from his chest and looked up into his face. Her eyes darted back and forth between his.

"Why didn't they take me?" she asked. "What's going on, Misha? When is it going to end?"

He stared at her face. Her eyes were set deep. There were lines on her forehead and around her mouth. She was too young to have lines like that. She looked tired and frail.

He shook his head. He could think of nothing to say.

She rested her head against his shoulder again and quietly cried.

"You're not safe here," he whispered into her ear. He put his hands on her shoulders and gently pushed her away from him again so that he could speak to her face to face. She hung her head, as if she were staring at his shoes. "I can't afford to let your neighbors see me here," he said. "I have to go back home while it's still dark outside."

"Are you going to leave me?" She still did not look at him when she asked this question, but she raised her head a little. She was now staring toward his shoulder, and she seemed to have something else on her mind. Her voice was timid. She looked exhausted.

"Come to my apartment. You can spend the rest of the night with me and Larisa. You shouldn't be alone."

Olga paused for several seconds and a distant stare draped her eyes, as if she were looking at something behind him. "No," she said.

"Why?"

His question seemed to stir her out of her daze, and she made eye contact with him. "I need to stay here tonight," she said. "I'll come over tomorrow afternoon. I promise."

"Are you sure? What if they come back?"

"They won't come back."

"You don't know that. How can you be so sure?"

She reached up and kissed him on the cheek. She looked into his eyes again. She forced herself to smile, but her eyes belied her sorrow. "Ivan always said you were his only real friend. You and Larisa have always been so good to us. I want you to know that."

Misha studied her face. There was a strange, subtle change in her expression. She had been hysterical moments before, yet now she seemed calm. Maybe it was the shock. She probably wasn't thinking clearly.

"Come home with me," he said.

She forced another weak smile. "No, Misha. I'll be all right, really. I need to stay here."

He watched her for a few more seconds. "Are you sure?"

She nodded.

"Lock your door. Don't open it no matter what. Don't talk to your neighbors. Try not to let them know you're still here. Larisa will be home all day tomorrow. She'll be expecting you."

"Thank you for coming over," she said.

He couldn't take his eyes off of her. This was insane. She shouldn't stay here.

"I'll be okay, Misha, really. Don't worry about me."

He nodded slowly. "All right then," he said, turning to leave. "Until tomorrow."

"Until tomorrow."

TWO

The next day, Misha stood in a room that reminded him of a warehouse, spacious and empty with high barren walls that stretched up to a distant ceiling where an exposed network of trusses supported a dilapidated roof. The light from an impotent winter sun penetrated a row of small windows close to the top of the walls. A shaft of dust particles hung in the air above him, illuminated by a fading ray.

He wore an old brown suit. He stood in the middle of about a hundred men, similarly dressed in old suits. They shuffled into the center of the room and faced one of the walls. They stared silently ahead. This was the fourth unplanned meeting that month. He already knew who would be denounced today.

The director stood before them on a shabbily-constructed wooden stage and wrapped his fat hands around the sides of a heavy wooden podium. The podium absorbed almost a third of the stage, standing about a meter and a half tall and over two full meters wide at the base. From the hall the wood looked solid and smooth, and Misha wondered how many men it must have taken to haul the thing up there and set it in place. On the front of the podium a large hammer and sickle made of shiny brass faced the men, and on each side of these emblems of Soviet labor hung a single five-pointed red star. Above the hammer and sickle Lenin's face, engraved in a dark bronze plate, stared down at the men with menacing fury. Bald head. Keen brow. Sharp nose. Pointy chin with goatee. And the eyes—piercing Mongol-like eyes full of fire and determination that seemed to watch you no matter where you stood in the audience. The aura of the podium radiated throughout the room, calling the men's attention to it, reminding them of the awesome power and authority that stood behind it.

The director leaned his paunchy torso forward. "Comrades!"

he bellowed once he saw that the men were all in. His voice boomed, splitting the air and filling the room. Misha's ears recoiled at the sound. "Comrades!" the director repeated a moment later, making sure he had their attention. "I know that you are wondering why we are here this morning," he began. "And I suspect that you already know the answer." He looked out across the room, slowly moving his large head from side to side, scowling at them with contempt. "Comrade Malkov has an announcement."

Misha watched in silence. The director turned from the podium and sat down on an old wooden chair off to the side. Malkov ascended the handful of steps onto the platform and walked up to the podium. He grabbed the wood on each side and leaned forward, the standard stance of all true revolutionaries.

"You have been careless, comrades," he said in a loud, accusing voice. His voice was higher than the director's, and he pronounced his words more clearly. Unlike the director, whose speech was slow and deliberate, Malkov's speech was punctuated and sharp, almost artificial in the way it seemed to jump out of his mouth in short bursts. He looked around as if he were expecting a reaction. He got none. "Once again you have failed to discover a traitor in our midst."

Misha felt his stomach tighten.

Malkov continued. "Last night the Chekists arrested one of your coworkers." Again he paused and looked around the room through his thin spectacles, which sat high on his pointed nose. His upper lip was tense, as always, and the creases that stretched between the sides of his nose and the edges of his mouth were tight, so that he constantly looked as though he were sneering. He still got no response from the men.

"Well," he continued. "Aren't any of you going to speak up? I'm sure at least one person among you knows who I'm talking about."

The tension in Misha's stomach increased. Nobody spoke.

Malkov seemed dissatisfied by the silence. "Then I'll tell you. Last night the Chekists arrested Comrade Ivan Borisovich

Petrov, first assistant to the director. He had been working as a spy for a foreign government."

Nobody moved. "I can't believe it," muttered someone off to Misha's right. Misha could tell the man hadn't intended to be heard, but the man's voice somehow managed to carry enough that it was audible to those standing near him. Misha glanced at the man, then back at Malkov. Malkov had heard it, too.

Malkov faced the man squarely. "What was that, Arkadi Stepanovich? Are you trying to defend an enemy of the people?"

Misha looked in Arkadi's direction. All color drained from Arkadi's face. His body stiffened up, and he looked around him defensively, his head making nervous little jerking motions as his eyes met those of the men who stared at him.

"Are you a traitor, too, Arkadi Stepanovich?" Malkov asked from the podium.

Arkadi shook his head frantically.

"I recognize you!" someone shouted. "You were Ivan's work partner!"

Others joined in.

"You traveled abroad with Ivan last year!"

"He must be a spy, too!"

Arkadi began to panic. "No! No!" he shouted repeatedly. "It's not true! I had nothing to do with him! I swear it!"

Misha looked forward. Malkov tried to maintain a serious, disinterested face, but Misha could tell that Malkov was pleased. Malkov's eyes met Misha's.

"And what about you, Mikhail Aleksandrovich?" he asked, addressing Misha formally by his full name and patronymic. "You're rather quiet this morning."

A hundred sets of eyes turned away from Arkadi and focused on Misha. He glanced around him. The weight of their stares was unbearable, but he maintained his composure. His heart beat faster. He clenched his teeth.

"You were Ivan's best friend," Malkov said. "I've seen you two together almost every day for the past year. You of all people should have noticed something, shouldn't you? Or perhaps you were in on it as well. What can you tell us about that?"

The image of Malkov behind that massive podium, sneering at him and gloating at Ivan's demise, when just a few weeks earlier he had paraded around as Ivan's friend, stirred within Misha a hot, molten river of anger that simmered and seethed at a low boil deep within his soul, and imbued his spirit with defiance, determination, and a curious sensation of absolute confidence.

Misha looked into the faces of the men who stood around him. Several of them who knew him looked at him sympathetically. He might still have a chance.

He walked forward and pushed his way through the crowd toward the front, then climbed the handful of stairs until he was on the stage. He scowled at Malkov, who looked surprised at his boldness. Nevertheless Malkov stepped aside, and with a feigned graciousness stepped back from the podium and motioned for him to take the floor.

Misha approached the podium slowly and paused once he got there to cool his nerves. He grabbed the sides, but did not lean forward. He looked down at the wood. It was dull and dusty and dry and cracked in several places. From afar it looked so imposing; up close it was nothing more than old, rotting wood. Lenin's image flashed through his mind. He pictured Vladimir Ilyich standing at a similar podium in a street meeting, leaning forward aggressively as he appealed to the masses, pounding the wood as he denounced capitalist corruption.

Misha looked up. The men waited. "Comrade Malkov is right," he began in a calm, somber tone. "We have all been careless, and I am just as shocked as you are at Ivan's treachery. I regret that I must now stand before you and confess that I, too, was unable to discover an enemy of the people."

He looked around at the men's faces, trying to discern whether they were buying his story. Their expressions all had that cursed Russian blankness, that hopeless yet resilient look that made them all look neither guilty nor innocent, neither sympathetic nor hostile. They just stood there in silence and stared at him, waiting. To win them over, he needed something more.

"But if you recall correctly, comrades, Arkadi here was not Ivan's work partner." He paused again to watch the men's faces. He still had their attention. He raised his voice a little for dramatic effect. "Ivan's work partner was none other than Comrade Malkov!"

The men shifted their gaze to Malkov. A low, hushed mumbling spread throughout the room. Misha looked directly at Malkov, who stared back at him with wide eyes and a nervous, contemptuous look. "That's right, comrades," Misha went on, turning again toward the men, "and you all know it is true. Didn't we see them every day, walking up and down the rows of desks, talking together, joking together, watching over all of us?"

Some of the men nodded.

"And do you not remember, comrades, a month ago when Comrade Lindenbaum was arrested? It was Ivan, the traitor, who stood before you at this very podium and denounced him. It was Ivan who announced the betrayal. It was Ivan who railed against him stronger than anyone else, just as Comrade Malkov has denounced Ivan today. It seems to me, comrades, that those who do the most accusing are the ones who have the most to hide!"

Misha considered how intensely the men hated Malkov, and this speech seemed to please them very much. Several of the men vocally sounded their agreement in hushed but audible murmurs.

"Yes."

"He's right."

"That's true."

Misha lowered his voice and spoke calmly again. "Yes, comrades, we have all been careless. And now we must be more diligent than ever to protect our country against those enemies of the people who disguise themselves as our friends. Therefore, I propose that we also call Comrade Malkov to accountability."

A wave of approval swept across the crowded room. Many of the men clapped.

Misha noticed movement on his left. The director rose from his chair, apparently displeased, and turned toward him. Misha stepped away from the podium. He walked across the stage toward Malkov and the director, ignoring the director entirely so that he could keep his eyes fixed on Malkov. He wanted Malkov to see him glaring at him. Malkov needed to know that he wasn't going to just lie down and take it.

Malkov's lips were pressed together in a disdainful frown. His eyes squinted, and his head looked as though it were trembling slightly. He was visibly shaken. Misha had caught him completely off guard.

Malkov stared back at Misha with a hateful look, a look that could only mean revenge. Misha didn't flinch. He defiantly walked past him and the director, down the steps, and into the crowd. The director pounded on the podium to get everyone's attention. He announced that all of the accusations would be looked into, warned the men to be more vigilant, then dismissed them to go back to work.

Misha walked quietly out of the building with the rest of the men, thinking about what he had done. He took no satisfaction in it. What would he tell Larisa? It was a shallow, temporary victory, and it had only worsened his situation. He was no longer a nameless, faceless employee. The men would be talking about him from now on. There would be rumors and gossip. His superiors might feel threatened by him, and that could only bring more trouble. Worst of all was that Malkov, the most ambitious, petty, and envious backstabber in the institute, would now be actively seeking his demise.

He had lost his precious anonymity, and with it, his last hope for survival.

THREE

That evening, Larisa waited for Misha in the living room. She looked at the clock—half past six. He was late.

It had been a terrible day. Olga never showed up, so Larisa had gone to Olga's apartment to check on her, only to learn from an old woman that Olga had committed suicide in the middle of the night, by slitting her wrists. The old woman had found her on the floor in the bathroom, and the authorities had hauled the body away early that morning.

When Misha finally got home and entered the living room, his tie was loosened, his shirt was wrinkled, and his suit coat had dust on one of the sleeves. He had circles under his eyes, and he looked at her with that depressed, apathetic look that told her something was weighing heavily on his mind. Did he already know?

He walked over and sat down next to her on the sofa. She faced him, and perceived by the way he looked at her that he had something to tell her. She watched his eyes. He was studying her face.

"Where's Olga?" he asked.

"Oh, Misha," she said in a sad whisper. She looked away from him. "Olga is dead. She committed suicide last night."

She waited for his reaction. At first there was none. He sat motionless next to her, his hand still on her shoulder, and she could feel the weight of his stare, as if he were pleading with her to tell him it wasn't true. She felt a lump in her throat, but she resisted it. She swallowed and coughed a little and managed to push it down. She stared at the floor.

Misha took his hand off her shoulder and stood up. He walked to the center of the room and stood with his back to her for a long time, then slowly walked out of the room and headed to the kitchen. She stood up and followed him.

He sat on one of the two four-legged stools at the little table that was attached to the wall. His elbows rested on the table, his hands were clasped, and he slowly rubbed his lips across the knuckles of his thumbs. He gazed forward at nothing, and he showed no sign that he was paying any attention to her.

She pulled up the other stool and sat down at the other side of the table so that they faced each other. She tried to come up with some comforting words to say. It wasn't his fault, he shouldn't blame himself, there was nothing he could have done. But none of it seemed appropriate, so she didn't say it. Several minutes passed, and he still gave no indication that he even knew she was there. She sat quietly and watched him.

"I'm a dead man," he said at last. He started rubbing his lips slowly against his knuckles again. He still had that distant look in his eyes, as if he were watching something far away.

"What do you mean?" she asked.

He finally looked at her. "There was another meeting today."

Another meeting. Another unplanned, unforeseen meeting of the local Party committee to condemn the latest enemy of the people. It had become a regular ritual. "To denounce Ivan?"

He nodded slowly.

"Do you know who denounced him?" she asked.

He nodded again. "Malkov."

"Malkov?" She leaned back a little and turned her head slightly to one side. "I don't believe it."

"Believe it."

"You mean the Malkov who came to our apartment with Ivan and Olga for Ivan's birthday a couple weeks ago?"

"The very one."

She shook her head. "No," she muttered. "We must be talking about two different people. Malkov was so polite and friendly. I thought he and Ivan were friends."

"Malkov's only friend is Malkov."

She kept shaking her head without realizing she was doing it. "It can't be true."

Misha suddenly looked at her with a wild, ferocious look in

his eyes and slammed his hand down on the table. "Oh, wake up, Larisa!" he shouted. "Stop being so naive!"

A jolt shot through her body, and she almost fell off her stool. He had never yelled at her before.

He stood up from the table and turned away from her, then started pacing back and forth. He did this for almost a full minute, then faced her again. "Don't you see what's happening here?" he asked. His voice sounded desperate, as if he were losing his grip. "The arrests, the denunciations, people disappearing all the time? Don't you see what's going on?"

She was paralyzed. What should she say? She sat with her elbows pressed against her sides, her hands folded across her lap. He started pacing back and forth again, running his hands through his hair, rubbing his mouth with his fingers, shaking his head back and forth, muttering things to himself that she couldn't understand.

"It's not possible," he said. "It doesn't make sense. How can so many of our friends and neighbors and coworkers be enemies of the people? It seems you can just denounce anybody you like, and the next thing you know they disappear in the middle of the night. It's like calling a garbage man to come haul away the trash. Can foreign spies really be that successful? Could they really have subverted so many?"

She didn't know what he was getting at, and she didn't dare to ask. She couldn't tell if he was really talking to her and wanted a response, or if he was just venting in her presence.

Misha was still pacing. "Like Ivan, for instance. He was a Komsomol, then a Party member. He was always organizing rallies and meetings in support of the Party. I've never seen a more patriotic Soviet citizen. He denounced enemies of the people more vehemently than anyone else in the institute." He paused for a moment and stared out the window next to the stove, apparently thinking over what he had just said. "But then again, so did Lindenbaum. Ivan denounced Lindenbaum, now Lindenbaum's gone. Malkov denounced Ivan, now Ivan's gone." He turned away from the window and walked to the other side of the kitchen. "There's no logic to it. It seems the strongest supporters of the Party are the ones who always end up getting arrested. It doesn't make sense."

She watched him pace back and forth a few more times, then he looked at her again. The tension around his mouth and eyes dissipated, and he let out a deep sigh. He walked over to her and held out his hand.

She felt a lump rising in her throat again, and a warm sensation filled her chest. She reached up and put her hand in his. She looked at the back of her hand and watched as his fingers enveloped her own. He held her hand gently. His hand was warm and comforting. She looked up at his face, then arose from her seat.

He pulled her closer, and she rested her head on his shoulder. "I'm sorry," he said into her ear. "Please forgive me. I didn't mean to yell."

"It's not your fault," she said. "I understand." She felt his arms around her back and shoulders, and she relaxed a little.

They stood there for a long time without saying anything. She listened to his breathing, felt his chest rise and fall, smelled the dust from his suit coat.

"Malkov accused me at the meeting today," he finally said, almost in a whisper. "And I accused him."

She closed her eyes.

"I think I'm next, Larisa. Malkov's going to denounce me, and then they're going to come for me just as they came for Ivan."

She held him tighter. "But why?"

"I'm not sure. I think it's because Malkov wants the director's job. Ivan and I are the only two specialists in the institute who are more qualified than he is. I can't think of any other explanation."

"Misha, let's not talk about this any more. It's too much."

He ran his fingers through her hair. "I can't live like this," he said. "I feel empty inside, Larisa, and it's not just because of the fear. On a spiritual level as well, I feel empty. I need my uncle back. I need his faith. I'm not a religious man as he was, but he understood something deeper about life that gave him strength, something that I've lost since he was taken away, and I don't know where to find it."

"I can't live like this, either," she said.

"All I want is a home in a quiet little town in the country where we can raise a family and be left alone," he said.

She pulled her head back and looked up into his face. There was a deep sadness in his eyes, a hopeless, fearful expression that she had never seen before.

"We'll be all right, Misha," she said. She didn't know why she said it, because she believed the opposite to be true. But it was something to say.

He stared at her for a moment, and the anxious, worried expression melted into a serene, determined look. She was glad that she still had that calming effect on him. "I promise you," he said softly, "if I can find a way, I'm going to get us out of here."

FOUR

The next day, two men unexpectedly came to the Institute of Foreign Trade in a black government car. One of the men was large and wore a dark suit; the other man wore the military uniform of a lieutenant. They wanted Misha.

He felt sick as he rode in the back seat, and he chastised himself for yelling at Larisa the day before. So the one and only time he had ever raised his voice to her was now to be the last conversation he ever had with her. If only he had known. If only he could have just one more evening with her, one last chance to tell her how much he loved her. He noticed there were no inside door handles in the back seat, which made him even more uneasy.

The big man was friendly, but there was something untrustworthy about the man's eyes that made Misha conclude that this was the executioner. When the big man tried to make conversation with him, Misha couldn't speak because of the fear he felt. This would only take a few minutes, the big man reassured him. He'd be home in time for dinner.

Misha's heart sank when they arrived at the Lubyanka, the headquarters of the secret police.They walked down a narrow, poorly lit corridor. The floor was made of wood, and the lieutenant's boots made a monotonous clopping sound as they walked. Misha wondered if Ivan was here, but quickly dismissed the thought. Ivan was surely dead. He was likely in a shallow grave by now, somewhere in the forest outside the city limits.

When they finally entered a small room, Misha expected to see instruments of torture lining the walls, but there was nothing unique about his surroundings. Wood floor. High ceiling. A lamp on a small desk in front of him. He sat down on a wooden chair. The blandness of the room gave him a strange, inexplicable feeling of disappointment.

The lieutenant sat down across the desk from him, and the big man stood next to the lieutenant. The lieutenant pulled out a file. "Kostrin, Mikhail Aleksandrovich. Correct?"

Misha nodded, but the lieutenant didn't see it.

He looked up at Misha. "I asked you a question."

Misha almost choked. "Yes. The name is correct."

The lieutenant looked at him directly. "How do you feel about the work the Chekists are doing to root out enemies of the people?"

Misha stared back. The Chekists? He hadn't expected a question like this. This must be some kind of trick, a ploy to get him to say something incriminating so they could justify themselves in shooting him.

He cleared his throat and tried not to let them see he was shaking. "Uh, well, I believe the Chekists are faithfully carrying out their duties to protect our homeland from imperialist subversion."

He had no idea where that response had come from, but it seemed to have been satisfactory. It elicited no reaction from either the lieutenant or the big man.

The lieutenant looked down again. "You never knew your parents, who both died during the civil war. You were raised by an uncle who was repressed several years ago. You and your friend, Ivan Borisovich, studied accounting together. You were a Komsomol, then a Party member. You and your wife both speak fluent English." He looked up at Misha again. "Impressive, Comrade Kostrin. Anything you wish to add?"

The two men across the desk stared at him. The big man raised his eyebrows and was no longer smiling. The lieutenant's scowl remained unchanged. Misha felt a chill run through his body.

What did they want from him? A confession? But what could he confess to? A million things ran through his mind—events from the past week, Malkov at Ivan's birthday party, Ivan and Olga laughing together, his uncle smiling at him years ago, Larisa sitting at the kitchen table the night before.

He shook his head.

The lieutenant stared at him for a moment, then pulled out a piece of paper from the file on the desk. "We were wondering if you could clear something up for us," the lieutenant said as he laid the paper in front of Misha. "What can you tell us about this, comrade?"

Misha looked down at the sheet in front of him and leaned forward slightly. He reached out and picked up the page by the edge, holding it so that he could read it.

I, Ivan Borisovich Petrov, of my own free will, and without any compulsion or duress, do confess to the Soviet state that in October of last year, 1938, while on a professional excursion to Paris, France, led by Anton Fillipovich Lindenbaum, I voluntarily joined a group of Soviet dissidents affiliated with the French intelligence services, for the purpose of committing espionage against the Soviet Union. Upon my return to the Soviet Union, I recruited my friend and coworker, Mikhail Aleksandrovich Kostrin, to collaborate with me on behalf of the French intelligence services, for whom we have been working for the past three months. This is a true and faithful confession, made of my own free will, without any compulsion or duress, written in my own hand.

Signed this 17th day of January, 1939.

A signature followed at the bottom. The handwriting was definitely Ivan's.

Misha gently laid the paper back down on the desk. He felt unusually calm. It was the calmness that came from being absolutely helpless while in the clutches of an omnipotent enemy, the kind of calmness that reconciles a man to death so completely that there remains no will or desire to resist. How had Malkov arranged this so quickly?

"Well? Is it true, Mikhail Aleksandrovich?" the lieutenant asked.

There was no point in denying it. He was dead already. He figured they might make this less painful if he just admitted it, so he nodded slowly.

The big man walked around the desk, put a large hand on Misha's shoulder, and smiled. The man's face was calm and friendly and would have been comforting under any other circumstances. Misha hated that big round smiling face.

The big man chuckled as if he could read Misha's thoughts. "We didn't expect you to confess, Comrade Kostrin," he said in a jovial, light-hearted tone. "We know that denunciation is a lie. We just thought we'd ask you about it to see how you'd react. We don't prosecute people who are loyal to the Party."

People who are loyal to the Party. The words echoed in Misha's ears. An image of Ivan and Olga flashed through his mind.

"We'll need to speak with you again, Comrade Kostrin," the lieutenant said. "But not today. Do you live far from here?"

Misha shook his head.

"Come back tomorrow afternoon at one-thirty. Don't bother going to work. Understood?"

Misha nodded.

"You're free to go."

FIVE

When Misha got home that evening, he told his wife to put on her coat and boots and take a walk with him through their neighborhood. As they strolled between the apartment buildings, he was careful to stay away from other people. He didn't know how to tell Larisa about what had happened that day, so he started by telling her that he knew why Ivan was arrested. It all started with Professor Lindenbaum, he explained. Ivan had traveled to Paris with Lindenbaum last year, and the Party believed Ivan was subverted there by French intelligence.

Larisa listened with interest, but asked how Misha knew this. When he finally told her about the two men and the Lubyanka and Ivan's written confession, she gasped. He had to run, she said. He had to get out of the city and change his identity. Maybe they could make it to Poland or Finland. It didn't matter. But he had to leave immediately.

It took him a minute to calm her down. It was impossible, he told her. The Party would find him.

"I can't live without you, Misha," she said.

"You won't have to."

"If you go back there tomorrow, I'll never see you again."

"We don't know that."

"No one ever comes back from the Lubyanka."

"I came back today."

She forced back the tears.

He put his hands on her shoulders. "I don't know what will happen tomorrow," he said as calmly as he could. "All I know for certain is that if I don't show up, I'm dead. At least by going back I have a chance."

"But Ivan's confession."

"They said it was a lie."

"And you believed them?"

She had a good point, but he argued that maybe the two men had been sincere. Why else would they go to such trouble to meet with him, and then let him go? It made no sense.

"I'm afraid," she said.

He nodded. "So am I."

☆

The knock at the door came shortly after midnight.

Misha had been sleeping lightly, and he almost jumped out of the bed. He sat up quickly. There was an acute tension in his gut. His hands went cold and began to sweat, and his heart pounded uncontrollably.

Larisa grabbed his arm. "The window!" she whispered. "We're only on the third floor, we can make it!" Her face was white. Her eyes were wide, and her lower lip was quivering.

He grabbed her by the shoulders. "No, wait."

She shook her head frantically. "They'll be here any second. We have to get out."

He covered her mouth with one hand and held a finger on his other hand up to his lips. "Shhh."

The knocking sound came again.

He took his hand away from her mouth. "It's not our door," he said. "It's coming from somewhere else."

Suddenly there was a loud crashing sound, and a woman screamed. "Please! We know nothing! We know nothing! Please, no!" The shrill voice filled the stairwell for a few seconds, and then it fell silent. Misha heard terrible sounds coming from the stairwell—glass shattering, wood cracking, furniture and doors breaking. Thumping, crashing, knocking sounds. A man let out a long, painful gasp.

Misha grabbed Larisa and pressed her head into his bosom. Just before it was all over, there was a loud boom at their own door, and then there was absolute silence. Misha went to the front door and peered out into the hallway, but he saw nothing. It was over just as suddenly as it had begun.

He walked into their living room and sat down on the couch,

and Larisa sat next to him. "All I want is a little house in the country," he said. "I want a quiet, peaceful life so that we can have children and raise a family and live like normal people. Like my parents before the war."

Several more minutes passed in silence, then something caught Misha's eye. In the far corner of the room, a small box sat on the floor beneath a chair, partially covered by a rag. He reached over and turned on the lamp on the table next to him.

He rose from the couch and walked over to the corner where the chair stood. He crouched down and removed the rag, then pulled out the box and set it on top of the chair. "Where did this come from?" he asked.

"I was going through some of our things tonight. I found it under a pile in the bedroom closet."

It was a small wooden box, dark brown with a simple design carved along its sides, and the lid was attached by a small iron hinge at the back. A small latch in the front kept the lid closed. "I forgot about this," he said. He opened it. "Just before my uncle was repressed, he gave this to me and told me to keep it safe." He reached in and pulled out the two items it contained: a large metal key and a small black book. "I haven't opened this box since my uncle was taken. That was almost seven years ago."

It was the book that intrigued him most. He pulled it out and held it reverently in his hands, gently brushing off a thin layer of dust with his fingers. The cover was blank, both front and back. It looked as though there had once been a title on the front cover, but he remembered that his uncle had deliberately rubbed it off years ago. It was an old book, well worn, and the cover was slightly creased and bent in places. The pages were yellowed around the edges, but the book had held together well over the years. He thought of his uncle as he held it, and he recalled the distant voice in his dream a couple of nights before that had called out his name. He opened the book to a random spot and read:

Whosoever shall seek to save his life shall lose it;
and whosoever shall lose his life shall preserve it.

The passage seemed to jump off the page at him, and he read it several times. He thought about the events of the day, and a warm, peaceful feeling came over him. For that brief moment, his fears and anxiety vanished, and he was calm. He carefully closed the book and held it for another minute or so, and the words he had read repeated themselves over and over in his mind. He set the book back in the box and put the key next to it, then closed the lid and fastened the latch. He returned to the couch and sat down.

"Are you all right, Misha?" Larisa asked.

He put his arm around her and kissed her on the cheek. "We're not going to run," he said. "I know what I'm going to do."

SIX

When Misha arrived at the Lubyanka the next day, the big man was already waiting for him outside. A few minutes later, Misha found himself in a spacious, elegant room. An older man in a uniform entered the room, followed by the lieutenant whom Misha spoke with yesterday.

"Comrade Kostrin, this is Colonel Braginski," the lieutenant announced.

They shook hands, then sat down across from each other at a massive, polished wooden desk. Several seconds passed in silence, then the colonel leaned forward and clasped his hands again on the desk. "Perhaps, Comrade Kostrin, I should tell you the real reason you're here today. I want to offer you a job. How would you like to work for the NKVD?"

Misha could hardly believe his ears. "The NKVD?" he asked.

Colonel Braginski nodded.

Misha again looked at the lieutenant and the big man, searching for a clue as to what was really going on here. Any minute now all three of these government hacks were going to burst out laughing, then haul him downstairs to be shot. The NKVD—the People's Commissariat of Internal Affairs—the secret police. Either there had to be some mistake, or this was some kind of sick joke.

But no one was laughing.

Misha looked back at the colonel again, who was patiently waiting. "But I'm just an accountant," he said.

"The director of the Institute of Foreign Trade rates you as his most qualified specialist."

Misha paused. "I don't understand. I'm just an accountant."

The colonel smiled again. "Comrade Kostrin, don't be so naive. The NKVD is much more than police and military units. The Soviet Union is surrounded by imperialist nations who remain enslaved by the principles of capitalism and are constantly seeking the demise of the communist system. We need people who understand how these nations work, because we have to deal with these nations on a daily basis. We even trade with them to get the materials we need to maintain the cause of socialism and keep our government running. You don't think that police officers and military men have all the skills necessary to do this, do you?"

Misha hesitated before he answered. "I suppose not."

"Look at yourself. You're the most qualified accountant at the Institute of Foreign Trade, which means you have the skills and the education and the experience necessary to do this kind of work. And not only that, you are fluent in English. This offer to join the ranks of the Chekists should come as no surprise."

So they weren't going to kill him? "This is all so unexpected," he said. He was about to suggest that he take some time to think it over, talk to Larisa about it, but one glance at the lieutenant's sharp scowl convinced him to keep his mouth shut and go along. "Of course I accept," he said. "How could I refuse such a great honor?"

The colonel smiled a fake, hollow smile. "Good. As for this," he said, holding up the piece of paper with Ivan's confession, "I'll just put it back in your permanent file for safe keeping, so that you and I don't forget that it's in there." He put the paper back and closed the folder. "Understood?"

Misha nodded. "Understood."

"You will continue to work as an accountant, but not at the Institute of Foreign Trade. Your fellow workers will learn that you were chosen to continue your education at a special government training school. For the next two years you will deepen your studies of capitalist financial systems and markets, and you will also receive some training in state security and intelligence. You may tell your wife about this, but no one else. We'll see to it that you and your wife are moved to another apartment in a different part of the city. Do you have any questions?"

He had a million questions. "No," he said.

Colonel Braginski stood up and put out his hand. Misha arose and shook it. “Comrade Vorlakov will see you to the door,” the colonel said. Without another word, the colonel and the lieutenant walked out of the room, and the big man, now smiling again, escorted Misha outside.

“We’ll call you,” the big man said.

Misha nodded and went home.

SEVEN

"You came home!"

Misha didn't even have the door shut behind him before Larisa's arms were around his neck and her lips were kissing his face. Tears streamed down her cheeks, and he wrapped his arms around her, running his fingers through her hair, feeling her moist skin with his lips. He could taste her tears. He kissed her just below her ear lobe. "Yes."

They sat on the couch in the living room holding each other, and he told her everything that had happened to him at the Lubyanka.

"Are you sure they're not just playing more games?" she asked. "Maybe they're luring you in further so they can get more information out of you."

"They're still playing games," he said. "But they know Ivan was innocent. They know I have no information. As long as Ivan's confession is in my file, they've got me right where they want me. They have me even without the confession. They're just using it as a psychological tool to get more leverage on me. The colonel made that very clear."

"What about Ivan? If they know he's innocent—"

"Was innocent."

"You're sure he's dead?"

"He's dead."

"But you're still alive."

"I didn't go to Paris." He arose from the couch and walked over to the chair in the corner of the room, then returned with the wooden box.

She stared at the floor. "I don't understand these people."

"They aren't people." He put the box in his lap and stared at the pattern engraved around the sides, running his fingers over the grooves. The wood was old, but it was smooth, and it had a faint musty scent when he put it up close to his nose. He opened the box and let his finger glide across the soft black cover of the book, then he picked up the metal key and looked it over as it lay in his open hand. It was a large key, extending from his wrist to the tip of his middle finger, and was heavy for its size. Probably iron. He closed his fingers around it and felt it drain some of the warmth out of his hand. He held it up in front of his face and examined it closely, twirling it between his thumb and his forefinger. It smelled like iron.

Larisa sat to his left with her hands clasped in her lap, not paying attention to what he was doing. “Does this mean they’re not going to repress us?” she asked.

Misha laid the key next to the book and gently closed the lid, then secured the latch. “If they really are going to put me through two more years of school and training, then I think they’ll leave us alone for a while. We just need to go along with them and keep a low profile.”

She nodded pensively. “As we did before they took Ivan away.”

He stood up and put the wooden box back on the chair in the corner of the room, covering it with the old rag. He turned around and walked over to his wife, holding out his hands. She put her hands in his, and he lifted her to her feet. “I feel exhausted,” he said. “Let’s get some sleep.”

Misha stood in the middle of the clearing, his feet trapped in the ground, his arms held up by the wind, the blackness of the vortex looming above him, descending upon him slowly, leaves swirling around his head in an interminable fury. There was pain in his sides and in his shoulders. He opened his mouth wide, but could neither breathe nor scream.

There was an enormous tree in front of him that he hadn’t noticed before, a tree with bright white bark that looked like an aspen, yet couldn’t have possibly been an aspen because it was much too large. It towered above him and stretched high into the sky next to the vortex, and he could barely see the top of it as its upper branches scraped against the billowing underside of the dark clouds.

A low rumbling filled his ears, but it wasn't from the thunder, and the whole world trembled and vibrated, as if the forest had been hit by an earthquake. He looked down at the base of the massive white tree. The ground rippled and bulged. Cracks appeared. Several gigantic roots plowed up through the soil, and the tree started leaning toward him. Loud popping sounds punctuated the roar of the earthquake as the roots convulsed, twisted, and snapped. A weak whimper escaped from his lips, and the horror of his impending doom made him shiver. The tree was falling.

He looked up. The vortex was almost upon him, ready to swallow him up into the blackness of the sky as the ground had swallowed the headstone down into the blackness of the earth. At the last possible moment, when he could feel the cold voracious mouth of the whirlwind licking the tips of his fingers, the white trunk of the falling tree sliced through the spiraling black funnel, cutting it in half. As the tree fell, its branches shredded the two halves of the spinning black column into nothing and vanquished the power of the wind. Misha's arms fell to his sides. The swirling leaves were now suspended in the air, weightless.

The white trunk streaked past his face, missing him by a few centimeters, and crashed into the ground with a violent boom. He fell backward, ending up in a sitting position, his feet still locked up to his ankles in the concrete of the forest floor. The suspended leaves scattered in all directions from the force of the blow, then slowly fluttered to the ground.

A branch that had broken off from the fallen tree lay next to him. It was long and smooth and just slender enough in diameter that he could wrap his hand around it and get a good grip. He held it in his right hand and used it to push himself up until he was standing again. He paused to get his balance as the earth trembled beneath him, then he grabbed the staff with both hands and held it high above his head. With all of his strength, he brought it down and stabbed it into the ground in front of him.

A strange wave emanated from the point where the staff struck the soil, like ripples in a pond when a stone is thrown into the water, and as the wave spread across the ground, the tremors fell silent and the forest floor became still. The ground was suddenly soft and moist again, so he pulled his feet out of the clutches of the earth and shook the dirt off of his shoes.

"Meeeeeeeeshaaaaaaaa." The voice was growing fainter. It was no longer in the forest.

He looked up. The vortex was gone, but the sky was still overcast, covered in dark gray clouds. "Where are you?" he shouted.

The trees were thin ahead of him, so he walked along the white trunk of the fallen tree, past its massive broken roots, past the great crater that remained in the ground where it once stood. When he reached the edge of the clearing, he heard a strange hissing sound behind him. He turned to see that the tree had changed into a brown color and was decomposing before his eyes, dissolving into the ground until all that was left was a long black streak across the forest floor. A black liquid slowly trickled out of the long dark shadow, draining into the crater.

Misha turned again to the edge of the clearing and stood between two small trees, his hands on the trunk of each one. He paused and took a deep breath. The air was cool and smelled of rain. The branches of the two trees intertwined and overlapped before him, forming a gate that blocked his view of what lay beyond. He took his hands off of the tree trunks and walked forward, pushing his way through the branches and leaves.

The forest vanished. He stood in the middle of an ocean of yellow grain that grew almost as tall as he was. He could barely see over it. It stretched out to infinity in all directions, covering the landscape like a blanket. Gentle rolling hills stretched out all around him, covered in large plains of tall yellow grass, and as he stood in the middle of this strange land, he realized that he was entirely alone.

EIGHT

Mark Daniels stood on the train platform wearing the uniform of a second lieutenant in the United States Army Air Corps, a duffel bag at his side, his family surrounding him as he prepared to leave them again. He had joined the army right out of college after finishing a degree in history, and now with some basic flight instruction behind him, he was on his way to the east coast to learn how to fly a variety of aircraft, from transports to bombers and maybe even pursuit planes. It was the summer of 1941. He was twenty-six years old.

His Aunt Sue fussed over his tie while his mother brushed off his left sleeve. His father stood between his brother and sister and had a strong hand on each of their shoulders.

"All aboard!" The conductor walked down the platform, examining the cars.

Aunt Sue gave Mark a hug that almost toppled him over. She was a large woman, his father's sister.

"Take care of yourself, Mark. We'll be praying for you."

"I'll miss you too, Aunt Sue."

Aunt Sue stepped back a few feet and smiled at him, and his mom stepped in front of him. "Well, I guess this is it," Evelyn Daniels said, still staring at the brown dress uniform.

"Don't worry about me, Mom. I'll be all right."

"I know you will," she said, nodding her head. She reached up and wrapped her arms around his neck and pressed her cheek against the side of his head. "Remember what I told you about keeping the faith," she said.

"I will, Mom."

She kissed him on the cheek and pulled away from him, wiping her eyes with a small white handkerchief. He took her by the shoulders and kissed her on the forehead, then walked over to where his father was standing with his brother and sister. He kissed Mary goodbye, then turned to Kevin.

"Did Mom tell you I signed up, Mark?" Kevin asked.

Mark shook his head.

"I'll have my wings in no time, just like you."

Mark smiled. "You just take care of yourself."

"I will."

Finally Mark stood before his father and looked him in the eye. Peter Daniels was a large man who stood two inches taller than Mark and had broad, powerful shoulders. He wore a pair of thin, wire-rimmed glasses, and his eyes were always constant and steady. He had a large, square head, and his hairline had been receding for several years now. The man was like a rock. "What do you say, Son?" he asked in his deep, stentorian voice.

Mark held out his hand. His father took it. Peter Daniels' hand felt like a piece of leather wrapped around a bar of iron.

"You've done me proud," his father said.

"Thank you, sir."

"Come on over here for a minute, Son, where we won't be overheard."

His father put an arm around him and they walked down the platform a ways, and Peter Daniels lowered his voice a little. "Son, I have to be honest with you. I've got a bad feeling about how things are going over in Europe. It's only a matter of time before we're in the middle of it, too."

"You think so?"

"We're in it already. We're just not fighting yet. But I think we'll be in the thick of things by the end of this year." They stopped walking and faced each other. "Your mother and I have been pretty worried about you."

"I'm not worried."

"I know."

"You don't have to worry about me."

Peter Daniels nodded. "Remember who you are, Son. Where you came from. What you stand for. Say your prayers. And make sure you write."

Short and blunt, as always. "I will."

"I love you, Son."

"You, too."

They gave each other one last hug, then walked back to where the rest of the family was waiting.

"Last call!" the conductor yelled.

"Just where are you going again?" Aunt Sue asked.

"Newark, New Jersey," he said as he lifted his duffel bag over his shoulder.

"Oh that's right," his aunt said. "Stationed at that airfield."

"You're going to take a train the whole way?" Mary asked.

"No," he said. "Just part of the way. We'll fly most of the distance."

"Come on, folks, this train is leaving," the conductor said.

Mark picked up his duffel bag and slung it over his shoulder. "Take care, everyone," he said.

They waved and shouted their last goodbyes as he hurried to get on board. He made his way down the aisle, stowed his bag, sat down, and put his face up to the window. His mother and sister were crying, his brother looked determined, his aunt waived more energetically than the rest of them and had a big smile on her face, and his father stood quiet and stalwart, looking stern, his eyes constant and steady.

The train gently lurched forward, and Mark was on his way.

☆

Karen Jones sat at FBI headquarters in Washington, D.C., sorting through the latest load of paperwork that had been dumped on the desk that had been temporarily assigned to her while the bureaucratic wheels slowly turned. She had recently made several requests for a field assignment, and right now she was wishing that those wheels would turn faster.

"Karen, could you step into my office for a minute?" Director Robinson leaned out of his door and waited, not moving at all, his face so expressionless and still that it would have made a great stone bust.

"Hold on," she said as she shuffled some papers on her desk.

"Now?"

"Yeah, I'm coming."

He held the door open for her as she entered his office and sat down in front of his desk. She heard him shut the door behind him, then he came around on her left side and took a seat on the corner of the desk, ignoring the papers that he was now sitting on. He dropped his head down and looked at her over the top rim of his glasses, then reached up and pulled them off of his nose. "How are you feeling?" he asked.

She sat in the chair with her legs crossed and leaned back. "Good, Chief."

"Still sick of the office?"

"You could say that."

He nodded and smiled, and his eyes twinkled in that special way of his that let her know he had news for her. "How's your Russian?"

The chief was in his fifties and was bald on top, and as she watched him sit on that big desk of his, smashing official documents with the weight of his body and smiling that grandfatherly smile at her as he asked her out of the blue how her Russian was, holding his glasses in one hand as his right leg swung back and forth, she couldn't help but smile a little herself.

"What does that have to do with anything?" she asked.

He hopped off of the desk, walked around to his big leather chair and sat down, then picked up a fountain pen and fiddled with it in his hands. "Oh, nothing. I just got a call from the higher-priced help at the New York office." He put the pen down and looked at her. "They were wondering if I had an agent who speaks Russian and wouldn't mind doing some field work for a change. Someone who's good at being inconspicuous and looking innocent. You know, the usual stuff."

"And you thought of me?"

He held out his hands, then let them fall to his thighs, making a slight slapping sound. "Well, you've been hounding me for weeks about getting out of the office. You're the only woman agent I've got, and you're the only one I know who speaks

Russian. I figure you're a perfect candidate."

"So what's the story?"

"The Soviets are a real tricky bunch. There's been a lot of personnel changes recently at their Amtorg office in New York, and also here in Washington at the Soviet Purchasing Commission. Nobody really knows exactly what's going on, if anything. But we know that they're all a bunch of reds and can't be trusted. They've got their agents doing all sorts of things through their embassy and their consulates and their trading organizations."

"And we want to know what they're up to."

"Exactly."

She clasped her hands around her knee and sat up straight. "You promise this isn't just another office assignment?"

He leaned forward and looked her in the eyes, and his head was tilted down a bit so she could see the top of his bald head. "Karen, I guarantee you'll like this one. It has surveillance and everything. I'm offering it to you first, so it's yours if you want it."

Hearing these words was like taking a breath of fresh air, and she didn't need any time to think about it. "In that case," she said, "I'll take it."

☆

Harry Shipman sat on a small black chair in a dark, dusty room of the Stanton Chemical Company in New York City, scribbling down a short list of compounds on the back of an envelope under the faint light of a single table lamp.

"This is what I'm interested in," he said.

Brian Wheeler walked from the dirty little window that he was standing next to over to Shipman and snatched the envelope out of his hands. He stood still and studied the list carefully for several seconds. "Well, you sure don't ask for much," he said.

"Brian, this is really important. It's only a few chemical processes. I know you have access."

Wheeler meandered back to the window and gazed outside.

"I don't know," he said. "Do you have any idea how much I stand to lose if I get caught?"

He heard the chair scoot back behind him as Shipman rose to his feet. "Brian, I understand the risks, and I'm not trying to lecture you. But think about what's at stake. The Wehrmacht is sweeping across Europe. It isn't like it was twenty-five years ago, where both sides were in a stalemate most of the time. This is much worse."

Wheeler held his hands behind his back and nodded slowly, letting out a slow sigh.

"You're smart. You're good," Shipman continued. "And you have access. All you have to do is get one copy."

Wheeler turned around and examined the odd-looking man that stood before him. Shipman stood about 5' 10" and had droopy shoulders and a paunchy belly that pushed out his shirt, but not enough for his gut to hang over his pants. He wore thick glasses and his eyes looked like they were too close together, and there was something about the man's face that made him look like he wasn't quite normal. Wheeler could easily picture Shipman at home all alone, still playing with toy soldiers as if all of life were just some great big game and that nothing that happened in the real world had any lasting consequences.

"You've done it before," Shipman said, holding out his hand as if begging for a dollar.

"You say it will help the cause?" Wheeler asked.

"Definitely."

"Is there anything in it for me?"

Shipman smiled, revealing several spaces between his large yellow teeth. "I'll be at Amtorg this afternoon. I'll talk to Semerov. I've been working on him for months now about this, and I think he's ready to finance you."

"How much?"

"How much do you need?"

"Realistically speaking, at least twenty-five thousand. But fifty thousand would be much better."

"So you'll do it?"

Wheeler looked over the list of compounds on the envelope in his hand. “Same as last time?”

“Between fifth and sixth.”

“How soon do you need them?”

“Is Friday too soon?”

Wheeler rubbed his chin and let his fingers glide down the prickly whiskers on his neck, then shook his head. “Friday will work.”

“I’ll call you.”

Shipman stepped forward and held out a hand. There was an overjoyous smile on Shipman’s face, like that of a kid on Christmas morning who’s just received a coveted toy. How on earth did an idiot like Shipman ever get involved in this business? And what were the Soviets thinking, trusting him as much as they did?

He took Shipman’s hand and shook it firmly. “I won’t let you down,” he said.

Shipman nodded. “You’re a good man, Brian.”

NINE

Misha stood on the wooden platform, holding his two suitcases in his hands, and slowly turned in a full circle to get a panoramic first view of New York City. People from all over Europe poured out of the boat and flooded the docks while immigration officials stamped documents and looked over passports and papers. The sun was warm, the breeze was cool, and there was something almost magical about this place, something impossible to describe or define, something that made him feel lighter. He took a deep breath through his nostrils and filled his lungs with air. Never had he seen such tall buildings, or so many of them, and the city buzzed and hummed with an energetic activity that he had never witnessed in his homeland. Aside from their dress, the people looked the same as people back home, except they held their heads up, and they talked and smiled in public as if they didn't have a care in the world.

He completed his rotation, his back now to the city again, and watched the small waves in the water, the seagulls in the air, the people coming off the passenger liner. The statue in the harbor was reassuring. He had hardly been here five minutes, yet he felt there was something very good about this place.

He looked out over the ocean and thought of Larisa on the other side of this vast body of water that he had just crossed, and that strange sensation of goodness suddenly drained out him.

"Comrade Kostrin?"

He turned around. "Yes."

"Mikhail Aleksandrovich, right?"

Misha nodded.

A tall, slender man held out his hand, and Misha set down one of his suitcases so that he could shake it. "Welcome to New York, Comrade Kostrin. My name is Ryzanov, Nikolai Yefremovich. Please call me Nikolai."

"Misha."

"Let me take one of your suitcases." Nikolai reached down and picked up the suitcase that Misha had set on the ground, then turned and started walking, pausing momentarily to let Misha catch up and walk beside him. "You and I are going to be working together," Nikolai said.

Something about Nikolai was reassuring. Perhaps this assignment wouldn't be so bad.

They reached a shiny black car parked at the side of an adjacent street and put the suitcases in the trunk, then climbed in and drove off.

☆

Karen slipped the small camera into her purse, slung the strap over her shoulder, and strolled down the sidewalk for a while until she reached a small café. She walked in the front door and paused, then headed over to a table in the corner where a large, burly man in a dark brown suit sat drinking a lemonade and reading a newspaper. The stereotypical government man. She recognized her new partner immediately from the photo she had seen of him the night before. Agent Robert Howard. She sat down across from him. He didn't move.

"Are we clear?" he asked, taking another sip of his drink and turning the page of the newspaper.

"We're clear," she said, pulling the camera out of her purse and dropping it into Howard's open leather briefcase under the table.

"Quality?" he asked.

"Absolutely," she said.

"And the guy who picked him up?"

"We already know him." She stood up and adjusted her purse. "How's your drink?"

Howard kept staring at his newspaper. "Just fine," he said.

What a strange first meeting, she thought. "We'll see you around," she said, then turned and left the café out the front door.

☆

Howard waited several minutes, then gathered up his leather briefcase from under the table and casually strolled out the door onto the street. It was a warm, sunny day, pleasant in every respect, but it did nothing for his mood. Why did they give him a woman to work with? As if things weren't bad enough already.

He barely made it to the corner of the intersection when a fancy black car pulled up to the curb in front of him and a wiry man in a plush business suit hopped out of the front passenger door. Out of the back door came a large, bulky man who was about the same size as Howard. Howard didn't have time to react. They were at his side immediately. They must have been watching him all morning.

"Get in the car," the little guy said.

Howard held the leather suitcase firmly. It would be futile to make a run for it. He crawled in the back seat.

Another large man sat on the left side of the back seat. Howard squeezed into the middle, and the big guy that had gotten out of the car crammed into the right side and was barely able to close the car door. Three huge men, smashed together in the back without even room to breathe. The little wiry guy got in the passenger's seat up front and closed his door. The red light turned green, and they moved forward. Just another car in traffic.

The little guy up front turned around. "It's been a long time, Bob. We need to talk."

"I don't have it yet," Howard said.

The weasel in front of him glanced down at Howard's lap, then leaned toward Howard over the back of the seat and stretched out a hand. "What's in the briefcase?" he asked as he put his hand next to Howard's on the handle and tried to take it.

Howard gripped the briefcase tighter, and with his other hand he reached forward and grabbed the little man's tie, pulling it forward. The little man gagged, and immediately

Howard felt the barrel of a revolver at each side of his head. He didn't flinch. "This briefcase doesn't concern you," he said.

The little man wasn't gagging any more, and managed to speak in spite of Howard's grip. "I think I'll be the judge of that. Now give me the briefcase."

"You touch this briefcase, and every FBI agent in the country is going to be all over you. You'll be shut down overnight. Is that what you want?"

The little man looked into Howard's eyes. "You're serious, aren't you."

"I said this briefcase doesn't concern you." Howard pushed the little man back toward the front seat and let go of him.

The little man adjusted his tie. "Put the heat away, boys." The revolvers came away from Howard's head and disappeared into the suit coats of his two escorts. "Listen up, Mr. Howard," the little man said. "You said you'd have it for us by now, and you don't. Now when will you have it?"

"Soon," Howard said. "I'm working on it right now. I just need more time."

"You're time is running out."

"I've got a deal set up for next week. I'll get it to you sometime after then."

"You have until the end of the month." The little man turned around in his seat and faced forward, the signal that the conversation was over.

At the next light, the car stopped and the big man on Howard's right climbed out, then turned around and held the door open for Howard, who got out as well. The big man got back in and the car drove away. Howard looked around. Not too bad. They must have driven around the block, because they had let him off in the same place that they had picked him up.

TEN

Misha found himself in a spacious office inside the Amtorg building. A small, slender man stood on the other side of a wide desk and rested his fingertips on the back of a cushioned armchair. “Ah, Comrade Kostrin,” the man said with a friendly smile. “Have a seat.”

They sat down across from each other. The man looked to be in his forties and had straight black hair. His rough skin had a gray, lifeless tone, and dark circles hung beneath his eyes. His politeness seemed forced.

“My name is Semerov,” the man said. “I’m your new boss.”

Semerov looked at Misha with a scrutinizing stare that made him feel as though a powerful interrogation lamp had just been turned on and pointed in his face. “It’s very nice to meet you, Comrade Semerov,” he said.

“I’ve been reading over your file, Comrade Kostrin. Impressive. I look forward to working with you.”

“Thank you,” Misha said politely.

Semerov had an open folder on the desk in front of him and was reading from the papers inside of it. “Says here you have a wife still living in Moscow. You probably miss her very much.”

“Yes, Comrade Semerov.”

“Prove yourself to me, and I’ll arrange to have her join you here in New York. The leadership within the state security organs certainly understands the value of employee morale, as well as . . .” Semerov paused. His eyes opened wider and twinkled, and the corners of his mouth turned up slightly, but he didn’t seem to be really smiling. “Let’s just call them the dangers of distraction involved when a man is away from his wife for long periods of time.”

Misha watched the face closely. Semerov seemed to be prodding him, testing him in a way that he didn’t understand yet.

"I'm faithful to my wife," he said.

"Of course you are, Comrade Kostrin." Semerov leaned forward, resting his chest on his hands, which were clasped on the desk in front of him. "But that is merely one of the distractions I had in mind. In fact, with you it is the very last distraction that I am worried about. There are other distractions, too, Comrade, things that come from sources you never expect and sneak up on you in your weak moments and change you in subtle little ways that you don't even notice. And then one day you wake up and find that you're slacking in your duty, or you feel tired, or you just don't care anymore. It's in these weak little moments that the enemy presents himself and promises you what he can never deliver, and subverts you, tricks you into thinking you're someone other than who you really are, convinces you that you have a different purpose in life than the one you came here for. It's in these little moments of weakness that you forget why you're here."

Misha sat absolutely still and was hardly breathing. He stared at that face in front of him with its ghoulish skin color and jet black hair and dark circles under the eyes, the face of some strange little creature that was looking at him with an inexplicable expression of hunger, as if it wanted to leap up on the table and crawl inside of him. This man was eerie. "Why *am* I here?" he asked.

Semerov smiled. The eyes sparkled. "Come closer," he said, his voice almost a whisper.

Misha slowly leaned forward.

"I am a very talented man, Comrade Kostrin," Semerov said quietly. "And there is one very special talent that I have that I want you never to forget. Are you listening?"

Misha nodded.

"I can see through people. Do you understand?"

Misha slowly shook his head, fearful of offending this odd little demon of a man, yet more fearful of pretending to understand, when in reality he had no clue what Semerov was talking about.

"I can see right through people, as if they were made of glass. All I have to do is talk to them and look into their eyes from time to time, observe their behavior in different circumstances, and I gradually get a picture of what's really going on inside their heads." Semerov paused again and stared intently at him, and Misha didn't dare break the eye contact. So the two of them sat there, leaning forward toward each other across the desk, staring into each others' eyes as if playing a silly children's game. "You see, Comrade Kostrin? I'm a mind reader. I know you better than you know yourself. And that's also what makes me your very best friend."

There was another long, uncomfortable pause as Misha tried to think of something to say. Semerov seemed to be smiling at him. Misha spoke slowly in a soft, timid voice. "I don't understand how that makes you my best friend," he said.

Now Semerov was definitely smiling at him. "Soon you are going to be out in the field doing real work, and various things are going to try to distract you. But you don't have to worry about them."

"No?"

"Of course not. Because whenever you're faced with a distraction, all you have to do is remember this little conversation that we're having right now and think of me. Just remember that I'm a mind reader, that I am everywhere, that I see everything, that I am all-knowing. I have ears and eyes all over. Nothing eludes me. Absolutely everything that goes on in this country that has anything to do with this office or with any of my agents eventually comes to my attention. And since you know this now, you have nothing to fear. I am with you everywhere you go, at all times, even when you think you're all alone. So nothing should distract you. Is that clear?"

They were still staring at each other in the eye, and suddenly Semerov didn't seem strange anymore, but was just as coherent as Colonel Braginski had been in the Lubyanka a couple of years ago. Misha nodded.

"Good," Semerov said. The little man leaned back, then

stood up and began pacing slowly around the room.

Misha leaned back as well and tried not to move or make any sound, and with his eyes he followed Semerov around the office.

"Here at Amtorg you will have two principle duties. You'll spend about one-third of your time here in the office engaged in legitimate matters involving foreign trade. Stocks, bonds, foreign markets, international transactions. You have to do enough legitimate work to keep your skills up to date so that our clients will trust you as a genuine specialist in your field, and also so that you won't arouse too much suspicion. In other words, you have to maintain your cover. Understand?"

Semerov was still pacing, but glanced back over his shoulder. Misha nodded.

"The other two-thirds of the time you'll be engaged in intelligence work. Your primary responsibility is to get to know people, make contacts, find out things about them that you can use to our advantage. Find out what their political persuasions are. Earn their trust. You'll deal with all kinds of people from all walks of life. Bankers, traders, businessmen, engineers, chemists, physicists, soldiers—even politicians." Semerov returned to his chair and sat down, and Misha looked into his eyes again. "You went through two years of training with the NKVD, right?"

Misha nodded.

"Then you know this already. There are two other things you need to remember. First, you don't answer to anybody except me. Not even to the head of Amtorg, do you understand? Only to me."

So Semerov was the local *rezident,* the head espionage officer at the NKVD, probably in charge of every spy in New York.

"Second, never forget that the Americans are always watching what we do. You should have an advantage over our other agents in this regard because your uncle and your best friend were both repressed. Usually we don't let people into the NKVD whose relatives and friends were enemies of the people, and the Americans know this. So they probably won't think that you're anybody important."

"How could the Americans know about my uncle?"

Semerov frowned and shook his head. "Never underestimate your enemy, Comrade Kostrin. Americans are a naive people, but they are extremely resourceful when they want to be. I doubt there's a man in this office whom they don't have a complete file on. They probably have a file on you already." Semerov shuffled the papers on his desk, stacked them neatly and closed the folder, then put it in one of the desk drawers. "Do you have any questions so far?"

Misha shook his head.

"The best way to learn your job is to do it. Ryzanov will be your partner here in the office. If you have any questions about your job, you can ask him. There's a shipment of aluminum leaving in two days by boat to London, then it will go to Leningrad. The Soviet Purchasing Commission in Washington, D.C. has arranged for Amtorg to pay for it. I want you to finalize the transaction. As for the more important part of your work, in a few days you're going to meet a man in a bar not far from here, and you're going to arrange to pick up some extremely important documents from him."

"Will Nikolai be with me?"

"No. You'll be alone. Pay attention to your contact. He's a strange man, but he's smarter than he looks. He's been involved with the Communist Party here in the United States for the past six years, and he first approached us about three years ago with an offer to deliver information about industrial technologies. I was skeptical of him at first, and he still makes me uncomfortable, but he's turned out to be our most valuable source of industrial espionage. Whatever you do, and whatever he does, don't let him get under your skin. All right?"

"What if something happens? What should I do?"

"Nothing will happen. Trust me, this is the easiest assignment in the world."

At that moment there was a frantic knock at the door.

Semerov and Misha both stood up. “Yes!” Semerov called out in a sharp, loud voice.

Nikolai entered the office.

“Ryzanov, what’s wrong? Are you ill?”

Nikolai’s face was pale and his hands were trembling. “Comrade Semerov, we’ve just received news from Europe.” Nikolai paused, and his eyes darted between Semerov and Misha. “The Germans have invaded the Soviet Union.”

ELEVEN

Misha pulled down at the rim of his hat and stared at the pavement, watching his black shoes take turns stepping forward, left, right, left, right, left, right, counting the steps from time to time to distract himself from his nervous thoughts. Chances were they were watching him right now, following him in a car or lurking on foot behind some corner of a building next to a narrow alley. How many were probably on to him? One? Two? Five?

They could be anyone. Most likely they were the most innocuous people in the world, the type you would least expect. He couldn't let himself think in terms of stereotypes. Stereotypes were no good. Big burly men with serious faces in dark suits and trench coats, standing in corners and in shadows yet visible enough to be conspicuous. No, that was what they definitely weren't.

The black kid in a white T-shirt sweeping the sidewalk in front of a bakery. Now that was more likely. Or the young woman holding the hand of a young child, strolling toward him up ahead. Could they possibly have children working for them? Now he was being ridiculous. But what better cover than a child? Steer clear of the woman.

He stepped out into the street to avoid the broom of the black kid, who had his back to him and obviously hadn't seen or heard him. The black kid suddenly stopped sweeping and stepped back away from Misha. "I'm sorry, sir, I didn't even see you coming toward me," he said as Misha walked past.

Misha stepped back up onto the curb. He turned his head and smiled a friendly, artificial smile. "It is okay," he said, and immediately he felt his cheeks flush red. He could hear the awkwardness of his own English, his Russian accent poking through the English words. And the words themselves—

Americans wouldn't have said that. They would have said something else. Or would they?

He was approaching the woman. Slow down, you idiot. Calm yourself. Nobody knows anything. Your paranoia will give you away. Just take a deep breath and relax. Act normal. This is the easiest assignment in the world.

"Good day, miss," he said politely just as he was about to pass the woman.

She smiled back at him. "Hello," she said.

They passed each other, and he walked on. That was good, Misha, good. The woman was harmless, just a nice lady on a walk with her daughter on a pleasant summer day in New York City. He wanted to look around, just to see if he could spot something, to get a glimpse of them, see what they look like, make them real. But that would be too conspicuous. The best approach would be to go about his business as if they weren't there. They might not be there, anyway, and wouldn't that be funny, him fretting over nothing. Just calm down, Misha, relax. Things will work out.

The café was quaint, but spacious. He let the door close behind him, and he walked very slowly, looking around to absorb the place. It was on the main floor of a multi-story apartment building. Its front was all windows, and the door was basically a large pane of glass in a dark wooden frame. The morning sunlight pierced the leaves of the small trees outside and penetrated the windows, bathing the hard floor of the café in a soft, pleasant, natural light. Several tables stood around the edges of the room, especially next to the windows, with small wooden chairs around them. In the middle of the room was a small post with a circular ledge around it where people could sip their drinks standing. Farther in was a long counter with bar stools, and behind the counter stood a short stocky man with a large Roman nose and a white apron, his sleeves rolled up to his elbows. Two men were sitting at the long counter eating breakfast to his left. Behind him to his right he noticed a woman sitting in the corner with her legs crossed, reading a newspaper.

No one was standing at the circular ledge in the middle of the room.

He walked up to the long counter and sat down on one of the stools, pulling it closer to the bar. Not a good place to sit. No, he should have gone over to a corner. He looked behind to his left and saw that the other corner was occupied as well by three men who were engrossed in conversation, oblivious to the rest of the room. The counter would have to do.

"Get something for you?"

Misha swung his head around. A pair of dark eyes were looking at him. Two muscular arms covered in black hair gripped the edge of the counter, and the white apron leaned forward.

"No thank you," he said.

The bartender cocked his head. "You walk into my café and pull a stool up to the bar, but you don't want anything?"

"I'm waiting for a friend."

"I see." The man took a rag and turned away from Misha and started wiping down the counter.

Misha looked at his watch. Any minute now. He heard the door open behind him, and he instinctively turned around in his seat to see who it was. Stupid, stupid. Let him come to you. Don't be so obvious.

It had to be his contact. The man wore a tan trench coat and a matching hat. The skin on his face was pale. His eyes were large and shifty. He was a heavy-set man, but not at all muscular, and Misha could hear him breathing from across the room.

Misha faced the bar again and waited. He felt the man on his left side, and the man sat down next to him.

Misha looked over, trying to act natural, but the man was already beaming at him. His face filled the room, and his crooked yellow teeth formed a wide, discomforting grin.

"Hello," the man said. "Sure is a nice day, isn't it?"

Misha nodded.

"Name's Sam." The man held out his hand. "And you are?"

Misha shook it. "Boris."

Sam's eyes lit up, and the yellow grin grew wider. "Ah," he said.

"Get you something?" the bartender asked.

Sam turned away from Misha. "Why yes. I'd like some coffee."

"And you?"

"The same," Misha said.

The bartender reached underneath the counter and pulled out two cups and set them on two small saucers in front of Misha and Sam. "You from around here?" he asked.

Misha waited, thinking the bartender was talking to Sam, until the bartender looked at him. He shook his head. "The Soviet Union," he said.

The bartender was pouring the coffee. He raised his eyebrows. "You don't say. What brings you to New York?"

"Business," Misha replied.

"Milk?" the bartender asked.

"Yes," said Sam.

Misha nodded.

The bartender poured some milk into Sam's cup, then Misha's. "I didn't know Russians had any business here in the States."

"I'm an accountant."

"An accountant?"

"I do international trade."

The bartender nodded as if impressed, setting a couple of napkins in front of them. Just then another man stepped up to the counter a few places down. "Excuse me, gentlemen," the bartender said and left them.

Misha stirred his coffee, then nonchalantly looked to his left. The huge face still filled the room, and it was still beaming. Whoever this character was, he obviously cared little for keeping a low profile. "An accountant," Sam repeated. "Fascinating."

Misha watched as the man's eyes flickered with a sort of childlike delight.

"I have always admired the Soviet Union," Sam said. "I actually visited there once."

The scene was playing out before Misha as if he were watching a comedy film. Was it a requirement that all the people who worked in intelligence had to be quirky? Semerov sure was a hard one to figure out. And as for this guy, Misha had no idea what he should talk about, or how he should conduct himself to get on good terms with this awkward stranger. But he had never heard of an American in the Soviet Union, and since Sam had brought it up himself, he figured that was a good place to start. "Oh?" he asked, trying to sound both polite and interested without showing how nervous he felt. But his interest was genuine. "When was that?"

"Several years ago. Thirty-six, I believe. Or was it thirty-seven? No, no. Thirty-six. Yes, that's right. It was five years ago."

The man spoke in a normal voice, completely unconcerned about how loud he was, and he punctuated his speech at regular intervals, like a Brit.

"Where did you go while you were in the Soviet Union?" Misha asked.

"Mostly I was in Moscow and Leningrad. Marvelous cities, absolutely wonderful. I've never seen a nicer place in my life. The people, the buildings, the streets. Charming is a good word for it. It was all so inspiring."

Misha set his spoon down on the saucer, making a gentle clinking sound, and raised his cup to his lips. He sipped the hot coffee casually, as if he were just lounging around and had all the time in the world. But it was hard to hide his eagerness. Never had he heard a description of the Soviet Union from the mouth of a foreigner, and suddenly he didn't feel nervous any more. All he felt was a desire to listen to what Sam had to say about his homeland. "What was so inspiring about it?" he asked, setting his cup down.

"What was so inspiring? Why, everything! Your government, your people, your way of life. Simply marvelous. You know, I actually got to see one of your collective farms." The man said this with cheerful enthusiasm. "Never have I seen such a happy people. Yes, I'll remember that day for the rest of my life. They were all out in the grain fields, side by side, sickles in hand, reaping the harvest. Men and women and children, all working together under the warm sunshine, toiling for their common good. You are quite blessed."

Misha thought of the old collective farm. It must have been nine or ten years ago, just before his uncle was repressed. He could still picture that tank of a woman from his village who stood before them every day, shouting at the others to work harder so that they could fill their production quotas. And the political officer, the city dweller who knew nothing about farming and would make the most ludicrous demands that they could never possibly fill, and how some of the more stubborn villagers had killed their own pigs rather than turn them over to the collective farm. The cramped, filthy quarters, the hunger, the utter lack of any personal space, the constant decrees from some unseen central authority, represented only by the political officer, who was always yelling empty slogans and intimidating people and hauling troublemakers away, never to be seen again. Misha could still see that hard face, the vein bulging on the bright red forehead, the tongue lashing out of the lips, the eyes seething with an unsettling fanaticism, going bloodshot every time he went on one of his abusive tirades.

Misha looked at Sam, whose eyes were still bright, his face still beaming. "What do you mean?" Misha asked.

Sam let out a laugh. "My word, you astound me! Why, the Soviet Union is the way of the future. It's the last great hope of mankind. Do you have any idea how much the United States and Europe are struggling right now?"

"Of course. The war is going badly—"

"I'm not talking about the war! I mean capitalism. Just look at us. For over a decade we've been rotting in this cursed depression. Nobody can find work. People are starving and committing suicide and losing hope. How long has it been now? Twelve years? Yes, that's right. Twelve years we've been suffering, all because of our flawed economic system. You of all people should understand that."

"I'm not sure I know what you mean."

"You know what's wrong with capitalism? Selfishness. That's what. The whole system is predicated on the assumption that people should seek their own self-interest in everything that they do. Don't you see how ridiculous that is? As if every man were an island, completely isolated from all other human beings! The system encourages people to plunder and exploit each other, to step all over their neighbor and enrich themselves at everyone else's expense. The whole arrangement begs the powerful to exploit the weak, the rich to manipulate the poor. It turns people into materialistic animals. Disgusting."

Sam paused to take a sip of his coffee, then continued.

"You know, I read a book several years ago that changed my life. Can't remember the name of it. But it was a novel, written a few years before the stock market crashed and started this mess that we're currently in. My, that was a brilliant book. It depicted the rich in a way that made everything clear to me. Their pomp and decadence and self-indulgence." Sam's face grimaced. "Made me sick, thinking about all that money they were wasting on fancy parties while the rest of society was struggling just to get by, and it made me realize that capitalism couldn't last."

"Why is that?"

"Because of it's basic premise."

"Selfishness?"

"Of course. You see, I realized that these rich people were not necessarily evil. Or maybe they were evil, but it really wasn't their fault that they were evil, because society made them that way."

"How is that?"

"Well you see, I realized that people more often than not are products of the culture and society in which they are raised. Children grow up believing what they are told to believe. So the decadence of the wealthy class of society is not really their fault, because they too are simply products of their upbringing. The reason these people are so selfish and wasteful is because the economic system here in the United States and in Europe has encouraged them to be so. All they're doing is fulfilling their societal role. And when they grow up, they realize that their whole station in life is dependent upon their exploitation of the working class, and that the only way for them to preserve their way of life is to keep the masses under their thumb. But of course this makes them feel guilty, because people have a conscience, you know, so they have to cope with this constant guilt. And you know how they do it?"

Misha shook his head.

"By escaping from reality. It's ironic when you think about it. Their lifestyle produces guilt, yet they cope with their guilt by indulging in their illegitimate lifestyle even more. They feel guilty about repressing the masses, but they deal with this guilt by pushing the masses down even further. Does that make sense?"

Misha shook his head again.

"I really shouldn't be using this word, I suppose."

"Which word?"

"Masses. It makes it sound like all of society is just a lump of dirt. But society is about people. And people deserve more than exploitation. Don't you agree?"

Misha stared into the murky brown coffee. He shrugged his shoulders.

"But the Soviet Union has escaped this pitfall," Sam said.

Misha's head was swimming, and he noticed that the bartender was listening in as he dried a couple of glasses with a towel. "In what way?" Misha asked.

"Because communism is not predicated on the dark side of human nature. On the contrary, the communist system embodies the higher values of humanity. Hard work, generosity, rational thinking, taking care of the poor and the weak, looking out for your neighbor. Indeed, I would say that it is a much more Christian way of life than capitalism. Are you Christian?"

Misha took another sip of his coffee. "I don't know."

"Don't know? What do you mean, you don't know? Are you an atheist then?"

Misha shrugged his shoulders. "I'm not sure."

"Well, I suppose it doesn't matter, anyway. To tell you the truth, religion is not all that it's cracked up to be. I was raised in a religious family. Good parents. We had the Bible and all that, and we even went to church at least once or twice a month. And I've read the New Testament. You know, it's shameful the way religion exploits people. The Bible is full of noble ideals, yet I've never seen so much exploitation of the common people as what goes on in your average church. And it doesn't seem to matter which religion you're talking about, either. They're all about the same. But communism has solved that problem, too."

Misha couldn't think of anything to say. All he could do was look over at Sam and wait for the man to go on. Sam made eye contact with him and leaned forward a little before he continued.

"Communism takes all of those noble Christian ideals of service and brotherhood and taking care of your neighbor and puts them into action, but does so without feeding people's heads full of fairy tales. That's what the Bible really is, you know. Just like the Greek gods or the Roman gods or the Hindu Trinity or the Great Spirit of the American Indians. You fill people's heads and hearts full of fear, and they'll do what you tell them to do. Religious leaders know this, and that's why they're always in league with politicians, because politicians know that if you get yourself on good terms with clergy, then you've got the average man in the palm of your hand. You see how this works? But communism's brilliance lies in the fact that it has preserved the charitable side of religion without using it to dominate people. You see, that's what's so great about the Soviet system."

The more Sam spoke, the more excited he seemed to become, and the harder it was for Misha to follow what he was saying. This must be what Semerov had warned him about when he had said that this guy was odd. But Misha hadn't expected this.

"In the Soviet Union, the whole political and economic systems are built upon the good side of human nature. The Soviet system itself encourages people to turn away from their selfishness, to work for the common good, to participate in something greater than themselves. That's why it will triumph in the end. Because the average man is not stupid. He'll see this, and once he realizes just how much he's been exploited and held back, he'll throw off his shackles just as your people did twenty years ago, after the Great War." Sam picked up his cup and gulped his coffee as if it were orange juice until he finished it, then set his cup down on the saucer with a timely clink and let out a satisfied sigh. He looked at Misha again. "Didn't you have any religion in your life?"

Misha didn't feel like drinking any more. "My uncle was a priest."

"A priest? So you're Catholic?"

"Russian Orthodox."

"Baptized and everything?"

"Yes."

"Do you believe in it?"

"Believe in what?"

"In Russian Orthodoxy."

"I don't know what I believe in."

"Well you must believe in something. I mean, here you are serving your country in a foreign land, right? You are a communist, aren't you?"

The bartender glanced over at Misha, and from the look on the bartenders' face, Misha knew that the man had already concluded that Sam was crazy and was now trying to figure out if Misha was crazy, too.

"You belong to the Party, don't you?" Sam asked again.

Misha looked away from the bartender and thought of Ivan. "I am a member of the Party, yes."

Sam smiled that wide yellow grin and patted Misha on the back. "Absolutely marvelous. I tell you, Boris, these are exciting times to be alive."

Misha felt a strange heat rising up the back of his neck, and he was sure his ears were turning red. He could see the bartender shaking his head, and suddenly he had an urge to grab Sam by the coat and shake him hard. Hadn't he heard? The Germans were wiping out his countrymen, and all Sam could talk about was the blessings of communism.

Calm down, Misha. Professionals don't get angry. Semerov said not to let him get under your skin.

The bartender walked over to them and jumped in. "If the Germans have their way, there won't be any Soviet Union left at all," he said. He then looked at Misha. "Do you have family over there?" he asked.

Misha watched the Roman nose, the hairy arms gripping the counter, the dark eyes leaning forward. "My wife is in Moscow with our son, who was orn in May of this year. He is our first and only child."

The bartender shook his head. "I'm sorry to hear that. I'll tell you what. Coffee's on me."

Misha looked at Sam, puzzled. "He means we don't have to pay for it," Sam said.

"Oh. Thank you," Misha said to the bartender.

The bartender nodded, then walked over to his other customers.

Enough of all this chitchat. It was time to get down to business. "You have some papers for Semerov?" Misha asked in a quiet whisper.

Fortunately, Sam got the hint and answered in a quiet voice that was barely audible. "Yes. But they're not ready yet."

"When?"

"Soon."

"How soon is soon?"

Sam became jittery, but tried to keep the smile going. "I'm not sure. My friend has had a hard time putting them together. He just needs a little more time."

"How much?"

"At least a few more weeks. Could you give me a month?"

A month? A whole month? Would Semerov agree to so much time? “All right. You have exactly one month.”

The jitteriness vanished instantly. The smile beamed. “And financing?”

“Fifty thousand is a lot of money.”

Sam nodded his head anxiously. “But it’s worth it. My friend can do a lot of good for you.”

“Semerov is still not convinced.”

“I swear it. Tell him he won’t regret it.”

Misha sat up straight and looked Sam in the eye. “Semerov doesn’t like to wait. A month is a long time.”

“I know. I know. But I promise you, it will be worth the wait. And the financing, too.”

“One month, no more. We’ll go along this time, but only this once. Don’t let us down, Sam.” He had barely met the guy, and now he was talking to him as if he had known him for years.

Sam nodded. “I promise.”

“Just name the time and place.”

“Exactly one month from today. Two o’ clock. Between fifth and sixth. You and me alone.”

Misha nodded. His stomach was gnawing at him with an anxiety that he hadn’t felt for a long time, but he kept his face as stern as possible. Sam was obviously weak, a pushover in spite of his long experience with Semerov. And Misha had done well. Suddenly his English was flowing as it usually did, the accent almost not even there. Sitting in that café, playing it cool, finishing strong—it gave him a satisfying feeling of power. For the first time in his life, he felt that he was in control of something.

“Take care of yourself, Sam,” he said in a softer tone of voice, then patted the man on the shoulder. “I’ll see you in a month.”

Karen watched the Russian leave, but stayed in her seat in the corner of the café. The other man lingered around for about five minutes, then left as well. Once both men were gone, Agent

Howard, big and burly and wearing a dark brown suit as always, who had been sitting at the far end of the counter, finished his breakfast and wiped his mouth with a napkin. He stood up, paid the bartender, then walked casually over to her corner.

"Well, what do you think?" she asked as he sat down across from her.

"Hard to tell. This new Russian guy doesn't fit the typical description of an NKVD agent, but he's obviously involved in intelligence."

"Maybe he's just a pawn," she said.

"Meaning?"

"Maybe Amtorg just has him doing pick-ups and small errands because he's harmless. Maybe he doesn't know what he's doing."

"I don't know . . ." Howard trailed off, rubbing his chin and looking down at the table.

"Who's the other guy?" she asked.

"No clue. Never seen him before."

"Do you think he's important?"

"I doubt it. The man is a buffoon. I can't believe someone that stupid could have any real clout. Makes me nervous."

"Nervous?"

"Yeah. The way he strolled on in here and shot his mouth off about the Soviet Union. It was like they wanted us to notice them. Maybe they're setting us up, or trying to distract us."

She nodded. "I have to admit, I've never seen such sloppiness from the Russians before."

"My guess is that he's a go-between."

"They went quiet there at the end. Did you hear what they were saying?"

"No. Did you?"

"No."

"Did you get pictures of them?"

"I took about ten shots," she said. "The angle might be a little weird on some of them, but I got both of their faces."

"And this is the same Russian that came in on the boat?"

"Positive."

Howard had a stern, serious expression and looked as though his face would crack if he ever smiled. He looked down at the table. "How was your orange juice?"

"Good." She smiled, thinking he might be opening up a little, but he didn't smile back. He looked like he had something on his mind, but his face remained stoic. "You look worried about something, Howard."

His eyes were fierce and uninviting. He shook his head. "Just thinking about the Soviets," he said. "That's all."

Something about Agent Howard wasn't quite right. He was much too serious. Too uptight. Certainly there were plenty of that type in this business, the cold, tough guys with indecipherable poker faces, iron men who did their jobs and did them well and didn't care much to talk about anything that wasn't work-related. Howard projected that kind of exterior, but she sensed that somehow this stereotype didn't quite apply to him.

"What's the matter, Bob?" she asked in a deliberately coy voice. "Don't you like the idea of working with a lady?" She smiled, trying to keep it light and sound as chummy as possible, but Howard's expression remained indecipherably dispassionate. Tough guy. Poker face.

"Let's get one thing straight," he said, his tone bland and humorless. "My relationship with you is strictly professional. I don't care to make friends with coworkers, and I don't flirt."

"I wasn't flirting. Just trying to get to know you better."

"Don't. And just call me Howard."

She looked into his eyes—cold, unfriendly, stern. He wasn't just jostling her to test her wits; this guy genuinely disliked her. This guy genuinely disliked everybody. She set down her paper and gathered up her purse. "Are we going to be working together in the future?" she asked.

He nodded slowly, his expression unchanged. "Most likely."

He couldn't get to her. No one could. She felt relaxed and poised, eager to whittle him down or at least get under his skin. If he really was the unpleasant type, then her enjoyment would be that much more complete. She smiled a confident grin. "Good," she said, then got up to leave.

He didn't respond.

She made a mental note to herself as she walked out the front door onto the sidewalk. His coldness had only solidified her determination to find his buttons and push them. Sooner or later, she was going to figure Agent Howard out.

TWELVE

It was a sultry afternoon in late August, and no one at Amtorg was wearing suit coats. It was hard to believe that two months had passed since the meeting in the café. The pick-up at the end of July had gone flawlessly. Misha had walked down the street going one way and sat down at the bench by the bus stop, and Sam had come from the other direction and sat down next to him. The bus came a few seconds later, Sam got on board, and Misha walked away with the small folder tucked under his arm that Sam had left on the bench. All without looking at or talking to each other.

Misha found Semerov in his office.

"I wanted to congratulate you, Comrade Kostrin," Semerov said, "on a job well done." Semerov walked around his desk and sat down. "Have a seat, please."

Misha sat down. "I'm not sure what you're referring to, Comrade Semerov."

"Those documents you picked up from your contact a month ago—you know, the man you met in the bar back at the end of June. You've done well, Comrade."

"Thank you, Comrade Semerov."

"I've been thinking a lot about that pick-up, Kostrin. If you recall, I never gave you permission to extend the pick-up by a month."

"I apologize, Comrade Semerov. It was my first assignment. I didn't know what to do."

"Don't apologize, Kostrin, you did well. You see, this is what I like about you. You know what I expect, but you're a decision-maker. Do you know how frustrating it is to work with agents who can't think for themselves, who always come running into my office sucking on their thumbs, asking me what they should do about every little thing? It's maddening. On the other hand, it's just as frustrating to have agents who think they know everything, who go out thinking they see the big picture, when all they have is a little piece of the puzzle, but their heads get so big that they mess everything up. Do you have any idea what it's like to run a place like this? Do you see the paradox? I need to delegate in order to get things done, but at the same time I'm afraid to delegate out of fear that I'll lose control of the whole organization."

Misha nodded.

"But your little operation with the document pick-up went so smoothly that I didn't even have to think about it. That's how I like it. That's the way it should be. Do you have any idea what was in those papers you picked up?"

Misha shook his head.

"Rubber."

"Rubber?"

"And plastic." Semerov smiled and laughed. "That Harry Shipman is a real mystery. He's one of the stupidest men I've ever met, yet he's extremely intelligent at the same time."

"Harry Shipman?"

"The man you met in the bar."

"Sam?"

"Yes."

Misha thought about it for a second and realized that he hadn't used his real name at that meeting, either.

"Those documents he handed you contained the latest in American chemical research on rubber and plastics. There were even detailed blueprints of how to build a complete rubber factory. You've done a great service to your country, Comrade Kostrin. You probably had no idea just how valuable your work would be when you came over here."

"Thank you, Comrade Semerov."

Semerov stood up and walked over to the window, peering out as the sunshine blanketed him. "How have things been going for you?"

Misha shifted in his chair and crossed his legs. "All right, I suppose."

"Are you comfortable with your work?"

"Yes."

"And your contacts?"

"I don't feel that I'm getting much done, Comrade Semerov. I go to these cocktail parties and socials and I talk to all sorts of people, but nothing seems to be coming of it."

"Be patient, Comrade. Your name is going around the social circles, and people seem to have a good impression of you. It may not seem like you're doing much, but you're actually doing exceptionally well. Remember that this type of work requires tremendous patience and a keen sense of discretion. Right now you're laying the foundation. The fruits of your labors will come later."

Semerov turned from the window and walked back over to the desk. He stood there for a moment without saying anything and drummed his fingers on a stack of papers. He studied Misha's face. "Patience and discretion," he repeated, saying the words slowly, methodically, hanging on them. "Qualities that you seem to have, Comrade Kostrin. Which is why I have chosen you to work on a special little project, something that Moscow is getting more and more interested in." Semerov sat down in his chair again and leaned back. "What do you know about atomic physics?"

Misha watched the dark eyes with the black circles under them, as he always did whenever he talked to the *rezident*. "I've never heard of it. I don't even know what that is."

Semerov nodded. "We've received a request from the Centre to keep an eye out for any information regarding uranium. Are you familiar with it?"

"No."

"Neither am I. All I know is that it's the heaviest metal on earth and that it's radioactive, and both the United States and England seem to think that it might prove to be valuable as a source of energy, maybe even as a weapon. Of course, this means that we're interested in it as well. The Soviet Union enjoys much sympathy within American universities, so that might be a good place to start. I want you to make contacts with any American physicists or chemists that you can find. See if you can find any leads. Talk to Shipman, too. See if he can get something as well. Do you have any questions, Comrade?"

Misha shook his head.

"How is Ryzanov treating you?"

"Very well."

"Good. Pay close attention to him. He can teach you a lot."

"Yes, Comrade Semerov."

"That is all."

Misha stood up and turned toward the door, then paused and looked back at his boss. "Comrade Semerov."

"Yes?"

"Have you heard anything from home?"

Semerov deliberately did not look at him, but shuffled papers on his desk instead. "It's bad, Kostrin."

"How bad?"

Semerov looked irritated. He set down the file he was holding. "Do you really want to know?"

Misha nodded. One thing that he had learned to like about Semerov was that the man didn't paint a rosy picture of everything, as the Party radicals always did back home. When you asked the man a question, there was a good chance you'd get a straightforward answer.

"The Germans are slaughtering us," Semerov said. "There are so many dead that I can't even guess at the number. Their army is sweeping toward the east as if they were unopposed, and if something doesn't change soon, they'll have Moscow in a month or two, maybe even less. Don't worry about your wife, though. The families of all overseas personnel will be relocated to the Urals if the Germans get too close. That's why we need to keep working. Understood? Keep your focus, Comrade."

"Yes, Comrade Semerov."

THIRTEEN

The power was out, the apartment was dark, and the silence filled the room like a fog. Larisa paced through the apartment for several minutes, listening for any sounds that came from the neighbors. She thought about her husband. He had left in June, just before the Germans invaded, barely a month after she had given birth to their first child. Now it was October 1941, and the Germans were laying siege to the city. June to October. Four months. It was hard to believe he had really been gone that long.

She walked over to the crib and rested her hands on the railing. She looked down at the infant lying on his back, his blanket draped over the front of him, his hands poised above his head and his fingers curled into little fists. She could hear the faint sound of his breathing and could see his tiny chest moving. He had Misha's face. She reached down into the crib, and with the back of her forefinger she gently caressed the soft, thin hair on the baby's head.

There was a quiet knock at the door.

She left the room and walked down the short hallway to the entrance. "Who's there?" she asked.

A woman's voice answered. "It's Elya."

Larisa opened the door and let the woman in, then peered out into the hallway to scan for signs of her neighbors. No one was there.

Elya was a young woman in her mid-twenties. She was shorter than Larisa and had a round, plump figure—although she had become quite gaunt recently—and she had beautiful black hair and green eyes like emeralds. Elya removed her boots and her coat in the doorway, then picked up the bag she was carrying and took a few steps down the hall. "How's the baby?"

"Sleeping. But you may go in there if you like."

Elya walked into the baby's room and hovered over the crib

for a moment. “He’s beautiful,” she said.

Larisa sat down on a small bed next to the crib. “Do you have any news?” she asked quietly so as not to wake the baby.

Elya turned away from the crib and sat down next to her. “It’s bad, Larisa. The Germans cut off the railway between Moscow and Leningrad a few days ago, and now they’re on the outskirts of the city. People are panicking everywhere. They’re trying to flee. The roads are jammed and some people are fighting each other. There’s looting. I’ve never seen anything like it.”

“What do you plan to do?”

Elya stared down into her lap as if she were about to confess a sin. “I have an aunt who lives in Perm. If I can get out of Moscow today, then I have a good chance of getting to her.” There was a long pause. When Elya finally looked up, she looked anxious.

Larisa put her hand on Elya’s knee. “You don’t have to worry about me,” she said.

“I feel guilty about leaving you.”

“Do you really think you can make it?”

Elya looked down again and started picking at her fingernails. She nodded.

“Elya, listen to me. If you think you can get out, then go. I’ll be taken care of. My husband is overseas with the diplomatic corps, so I know the government will take care of me. Why do you think I live in this nice apartment and have so much food? But you, you’re just . . .” She stopped herself. How could she finish that sentence without sounding condescending?

“A nobody,” Elya said.

Larisa reached out and took Elya’s hands in her own. “Have you heard anything from your father or brother?” she asked.

Elya shook her head. “They’re still at the front. That’s all I know.”

Larisa let go of Elya’s hands and stood up. “Then you should go. Right now. I have a bag for you in the kitchen.”

Elya looked up and pushed her black hair to one side. There

were tears in her eyes that made her emerald pupils sparkle. She stood up also. “Larisa, I don’t know what to say.”

“Don’t say anything.”

“If it weren’t for you, I don’t know what would have happened to me.”

Larisa took her gently by the arm and led her out to the kitchen, where she pulled a cloth sack out of her cupboard and handed it to Elya. “Take this,” she said. “There should be enough in here to get you to Perm. But be careful. Don’t let anybody know that you have this food. If the government finds out that I’ve been sharing my rations with you, I could get into serious trouble.”

Elya nodded, then put her arms around Larisa’s neck. “Thank you so much,” she said, and her voice broke slightly. “I’ll never forget you.”

They stood in the hallway in silence, and once Elya had put on her boots and her coat, she looked into Larisa’s eyes and forced herself to smile. She then grabbed Larisa’s hand and pressed a heavy, wadded-up piece of cloth into Larisa’s palm, pushing Larisa’s fingers closed over it.

“What’s this?” Larisa asked.

Elya was still forcing herself to smile, and her eyes glistened. She leaned forward, still holding Larisa’s hand closed around the wad of cloth, and kissed Larisa on the cheek. She then picked up the sack of food, opened the front door, slipped out into the hallway, and hurried down the stairs without saying another word.

Larisa closed the door and stepped back into the hallway. She opened her hand and looked at the wad of cloth in her palm. She walked back into the bedroom and sat down on the small bed next to the crib, then peeled back the edges of the cloth with her other hand. In the center of the cloth there was a small necklace. She pinched the thin metal chain and slowly lifted it up out of the cloth until the necklace gently swayed in front of her face.

Hanging from the bottom of the chain was a tiny silver cross.

A single kerosene lamp cast its warm glow upon the bedroom as Larisa put Kolya back to bed. It was after midnight. She had been sitting in the dim lamplight for only a minute or two when she heard the distinct sound of knocking at her front door. It must be Elya, she thought as she walked down the hall and opened the door a crack.

She was startled to see a large man in the stairwell. He had a friendly smile, but there was something dark about his eyes that put her on guard. “Comrade Kostrina,” he said.

“Who are you?” she asked.

He introduced himself as Comrade Vorlakov, and to convince her that he was legitimate, he told her all about Misha working for the NKVD in New York. He said he had orders to relocate her to Sverdlovsk.

She didn’t need to pack. She knew that other diplomatic families had been evacuated, so she had been expecting to be relocated herself for several weeks now and had wondered why no one had come by to get her. She had two suitcases and a handbag ready to go. She made sure that Elya’s necklace and Misha’s brown box were in her handbag, then took Kolya and went with Vorlakov, who carried the two suitcases to a black car that was waiting for them outside. When she got in the back seat, she noticed there were no inside door handles.

Roadblocks were going up all around Moscow to prevent people from fleeing, but the car that Larisa rode in was allowed to pass through. They drove well beyond the city limits, then got on a train and rode slowly for almost two full days. Finally they arrived in Sverdlovsk and drove immediately to an apartment building at the edge of the city.

Vorlakov knocked and someone inside opened the door for them, but Larisa didn’t see who it was. She followed Vorlakov down a small hallway into a quaint little bedroom where a crib and a small single bed stood side by side, and Vorlakov set down the suitcases.

After putting Kolya to bed, she went back to the kitchen. She walked in and stopped just inside the doorway. Vorlakov and another man were sitting at a table on two small stools, and they stood up when they saw her. The other man looked familiar. He had dark black hair and a large head, but he was much shorter than Vorlakov and his face was more square. He wore a small set of spectacles that made his eyes look like they were too close together, and his nose pointed downward. He had broad shoulders and no neck, and his cheeks sagged down off of his jaw bones in a way that made him look old and fat.

Suddenly she recognized him, and it made her feel ill.

"Hello, Comrade Kostrina," the man said with a fake smile. "It's been a very long time. Do you remember me?"

She nodded slowly but said nothing.

"This is Comrade Malkov," said Vorlakov. "He's temporarily in charge of the families here in Sverdlovsk that were evacuated from Moscow and Leningrad. If you'll excuse me for a few minutes, I need to speak to the lieutenant out in the car."

Larisa wanted to say something to Vorlakov, to tell him not to leave her, but he stood up and walked past her and out the door so quickly that she couldn't think of anything to say.

Malkov got up, too. He stood in the middle of the kitchen floor with his right hand resting on the back of his chair. "How is your husband?" he asked. "I hear he has been working in New York City."

"That's right."

"Do you know when you might be allowed to see him again?" he asked.

"No." He looked older and fatter and uglier than he had been when he had come to her home for Ivan's birthday party almost three years ago. He seemed to have the same politeness, but this time she wasn't fooled. Looking at his eyes made her feel dark inside. This was the man who had killed Ivan and Olga. This was the man who had tried to kill her husband.

Malkov stepped toward her slowly, cautiously. "The nights are getting colder now here in the Ural Mountains. They can be very lonely." He stopped about a meter in front of her and gazed into her eyes as if he were admiring a sculpture in a museum. "Have you received any letters from your husband?" he asked.

"No."

Malkov shook his head and made his face look as though he were both surprised and genuinely sympathetic. "That's too bad," he said. "It's unfortunate that this happens so often when men go overseas. They get so involved in their work. And there are so many young women around them, competing for their attention. It's easy to get distracted."

His words cut her to the core, but she knew he was lying. He didn't know what kind of man Misha was. "What do you want, Comrade Malkov?"

He slowly reached up with his right hand and touched her softly on the cheek. She stepped back. He smiled at her. "You are a very beautiful woman, Larisa," he said. He stepped toward her and tried to touch her face again.

She was trembling, but his insolence had stirred up enough disgust and rage within her that she gathered up the confidence to resist. Before his fingers reached her face, she grabbed his arm by the wrist and held it. "Don't touch me, Comrade Malkov. And don't call me by my first name."

He smiled again. "You're all alone here, Larisa," he said in a quiet, soothing tone. "You're young. You're beautiful. You're lonely and afraid. Your husband has forgotten you. I know. I have connections with our network in New York. But I can help you, if you'll let me. I'm in charge of all the families here in Sverdlovsk right now. I have connections all over. I can get you almost anything you need. Why don't we establish a relationship? You can give me what I want, and I'll help you get what you need."

His smugness was unbearable. Impulsively, she leaned forward and spat in his face.

His head jerked back, and he pulled his wrist out of her grip.

He took off his glasses and wiped his face using a towel that was lying on the table, then wiped his glasses as well and put them back on. His warm smile was gone. He scowled at her with a viciousness in his expression that made her stomach go hollow.

He stepped toward her and raised his hand as if to slap her, but she refused to cower before him. "Go ahead, Comrade Malkov!" she shouted. "Do it! Strike me! Show me what kind of a man you really are!"

He froze. The fingers of his open hand curled into a fist, and he slowly let his hand down. Deep lines cut into each side of his nose as he glared at her with a hateful sneer. His mouth was tight, and his eyes flickered like a black flame. He stepped back and took a breath to calm himself. "If I were you, I'd take some time to reconsider my offer," he said. His voice was quiet and low, but he still didn't quite have complete control over it, and the biting edge of his tone sent goose bumps down her back. "Don't deny me, Larisa. You are all alone, and I am a powerful man. One way or another, I'll get what I want. I can make your life very comfortable here, or I can make it miserable. It's your choice."

At that moment the front door opened behind her, and she turned. Vorlakov entered. "We need to get going," he said to Malkov. "The lieutenant is waiting for us in the car." Larisa looked at Vorlakov. He looked at Malkov, then at Larisa, and his expression changed. "What's going on here?" he asked.

Larisa grabbed his sleeve. "Comrade Vorlakov, please. You have to protect me."

Vorlakov looked down at her for a second as if trying to ascertain whether or not she was serious. Then he looked over at Malkov, and his face turned mean and cold. "Get out of here, Malkov," he said. "Go wait in the car."

Malkov hurried out of the apartment, and Vorlakov turned to Larisa again. "Did he harm you, Comrade Kostrina?" he asked.

"No," she said. "But he tried to touch me." She was shaking all over, and she started crying. She looked up into Vorlakov's eyes. "He threatened me. I'm all alone here. I have no one. He's going to take advantage of me here. Please, Comrade Vorlakov. Please keep him away from me."

Vorlakov's eyes were black as coal, and his face was unusually severe. He looked cruel. She was thankful that he was angry at Malkov and not at her.

He put his massive hands on her shoulders and lowered his head so that he was looking at her more directly. "Don't you worry about a thing, Comrade Kostrina. I'll have him transferred back to Moscow tonight."

She was almost as afraid of Vorlakov as she was of Malkov, but she believed he meant what he said, and the sheer power that she felt in those hands as they rested on her shoulders was reassuring. She was sobbing uncontrollably now, and she put her hands up to her face. She couldn't speak, so she just nodded in acknowledgment.

He let go of her. "Are you going to be all right?" he asked.

She kept nodding, then she took her hands away from her face and cleared her throat. "Yes," she said. "Thank you."

Malkov was standing by the car when Vorlakov came outside. Without hesitating, Vorlakov immediately stepped up to him and planted his large hands on Malkov's chest. He lifted Malkov off the ground and shoved him against the side of the car. "What do you think you were doing in there?" he asked.

"Nothing that you haven't done yourself," Malkov answered.

"You've got to learn to control yourself. We have strict orders to keep her safe. You want a woman to prey on, go find some local girl." He lowered Malkov back to the ground and let go of him. "Get in the car. You're coming back to Moscow with me tonight."

"But—"

"Shut up and get in the car."

FOURTEEN

In the United States, time passed both slowly and quickly during that first year of the war. The days were long but the weeks were short, and the months seemed to fly by. The year 1942 was almost over.

In November, Mark Daniels stood at attention in the colonel's office in Newark, New Jersey, his heels together, hands at his sides, back straight, eyes forward. He heard the colonel close the door behind him, and then old Eagle Eye marched around him and stood on the other side of the small metal desk that stood between them.

"At ease, soldier," the colonel said. "Have a seat."

Colonel Griggs was a tall, slender man in his mid-fifties with a broad forehead and a stern face. The top of his head was completely bald, and what hair he had left on the sides was already white. He had been one of the first army aviators during the last big war in Europe, a triple ace with fifteen kills to his name, and had been shot down himself once over France. He got his nickname from the fact that he could see the enemy planes coming over the horizon before anyone else could, which gave him a significant advantage in air-to-air combat. The man was a legend. Just being in his presence gave Mark a feeling of confidence.

"Well then," Griggs said, "let's get down to business. How long have you been stationed here at Newark?"

"About a year and a half, sir."

"Like it?"

"Yes, sir."

"You were a second lieutenant when you came, weren't you?"

"That's right, sir."

"And now you've made first lieutenant."

Mark nodded.

"A full-fledged pilot, got your wings and everything. You could fly anything we told you to fly, couldn't you. And I bet you're all excited to see some action."

Old Eagle Eye had a way about him—maybe the twinkle in his eye, or the confident edge in the older man's voice, or just knowing that under that ram-rod surface was a guy who truly cared about you—that made Mark swell up inside. "Yes, sir."

Griggs opened up one of the desk drawers and pulled out a piece of paper and handed it over to Mark. "Your orders, Lieutenant Daniels." Mark took the piece of paper. Griggs folded his hands on the desk, leaned forward, and stared at Mark in the eye. "Go ahead, son. Read it."

Mark looked down at the little piece of paper that could determine his fate for the rest of the war, maybe even the rest of his life. He skimmed it quickly until he found the only part of the document that had any real importance, the one line that said where he was going.

All of a sudden a sinking feeling filled in his chest, and he let himself fall back against the back of his chair. He scanned the paper several times over, double-checking the name, rank, and serial number, rereading the location in the hope that he had misread it the first time. When it finally sank in that this little piece of paper was authentic and that it really did contain his orders and that he really was the person it was intended for, all he could do was look back up at the colonel and stare.

"I knew you'd like it," Griggs said.

"There must be some mistake," Mark said.

"No mistake, son. Those are your orders."

"But I've been training to fly bombing raids over Europe."

Griggs leaned back in his chair. "Are you complaining, Lieutenant?"

"No, sir." Mark glanced over the orders again. "Permission to speak freely, sir."

"Denied." Griggs stood up and walked over the hardwood floor to the small window where a beam of light illuminated a cascade of dust particles in mid-air. "I already know what you're going to say, son, and I don't want to hear it. I know what you're thinking. What you wanted to say was, 'but Colonel, it's already November and it's been almost a whole year since the Japs bombed us at Pearl and I've been stuck at this worthless airstrip for a year and a half training to fly heavy bombers from England to Germany.' That's what you were going to say, wasn't it? And for the past year and a half you've had your heart set on getting into the action, right? That's what you were thinking, isn't it."

"Yes, sir."

"And flying C-47 cargo planes stateside is beneath you, isn't it."

Mark said nothing.

Griggs started pacing slowly across the floor, and with each step his shoes made a mild clopping sound. "Now listen, son, I know exactly how you feel, but I'm the last person on this earth to whom you should be complaining about this, because the truth is that you've got nothing on me." Griggs' shoes were clopping behind him now. "Do you think I like the idea of sitting out the war up on some high plateau in the middle of nowhere when I could be leading a squadron of guys like you over that goose-stepping maniac in Berlin? What I wouldn't give to be in England myself right now. But I'm afraid that's not to be. We've both been relegated to the back burner, so to speak."

Mark folded the piece of paper in half.

Griggs came around the left side of him and perched himself on the corner of the desk. "Daniels, I know you're disappointed. And I promise you that I won't keep you there forever. But I need you to help me get things going up there. I gave this a lot of thought, and when I looked over my list of candidates, I knew that you were the best man for the job."

"You don't think I'm as qualified to fly bombing missions as the other guys?"

"That has nothing to do with it. I chose you because, number one, you're an excellent pilot. And number two, I know you'll give this assignment everything you've got, even if your heart isn't in it. Am I right about that?"

Mark sat up and looked into the colonel's face. "Yes, sir, that's right."

"That's the spirit." The colonel leaned forward and slapped Mark on the shoulder, then got off the desk and went back to his chair. "Actually, Daniels, this assignment involves a little more than just flying cargo planes. You ever hear of Lend-Lease?"

"It sounds familiar, sir."

"Lend-Lease is a program that President Roosevelt signed into law almost two years ago. The legislation authorizes the United States to send aid to our allies all over the world to help out in the war effort. Ever hear of the Alsib Pipeline?"

"No, sir."

"One of the countries we're helping out through the Lend-Lease program is the Soviet Union. The Russians have been taking quite a beating for the past year and a half, and right now they're basically the only ones fighting the Germans on the ground in Europe. If the Soviet Union falls, then all those German divisions will be freed up to come fight our boys in the west. I know we're fighting the war mainly on the sea and in the air right now, but we'll be on the ground eventually, and we definitely don't want to face more Germans than we have to. Now you're probably asking yourself, what does this have to do with me, right?"

Mark nodded.

"I've been stationed here at Newark for about six months, and I'll bet you've noticed that there are a handful of Russians running around here all the time, haven't you."

"Yes, sir."

"Well, those Russians are the main reason I'm here. Now I've got to tell you, these Russians are just about the most pigheaded bunch of people I've ever worked with, but for some strange reason my superiors felt that I was the best man for the job, so here I am. I personally don't like the Russians very much, but I respect them and they respect me and we've reached a level of understanding that allows us to get along. Any questions so far?"

"No, sir."

"Alsib stands for Alaska-Siberia. We used to supply the Russians mainly by sea, but the Germans caught onto us and started sinking a lot of our boats in the Atlantic. So we tried flying in supplies to them across Africa, but the sand kept damaging the planes. Finally we convinced Marshall Stalin to open up a direct flight route across the North Pole between Alaska and Siberia. This allows us to get supplies to them without being harassed so much by the Germans. The Alsib Pipeline started operating out of Gore Field, Montana this month. Whenever we need to send the Russians something by plane, we'll send it through Gore Field to Alaska. Once our pilots land the planes in Alaska, Soviet crews will take over and fly the planes to Siberia. From there the Russians can ship the supplies wherever they need them."

"So my job will be to ferry Lend-Lease shipments between Montana and Alaska."

"That's right. There are usually two or three Russians that accompany every shipment, so you'll be working with them as well. Do you speak any Russian?"

"No, sir."

"Neither do I. But that's never been too much of a problem. Most of the Russians I've worked with speak English well enough to communicate with me." The colonel put his hands on the desk and leaned forward again. "That's all I have for you right now, Lieutenant. Do you have any questions?"

Mark folded the piece of paper once more and slipped it into his pocket. "Not really, sir. When do I start?"

"You'll be in Montana before the end of the week. Oh, yes. One more thing, Daniels. Since you'll be my number one pilot up there, I've already put you in for promotion to captain. I know it hasn't been long since you made first lieutenant, but there's a war on, and I can't have you running things like I need you to if you don't have some more rank. Maybe we'll even get you up to major sometime."

So there was a silver lining behind the rain cloud after all. Maybe going to Montana wouldn't be so bad. "Thank you, sir."

It was December of 1942 already, and Misha didn't know where the time had flown during the last year and a half. He was proficient at his work now with enough experience under his belt to give him a sense of confidence about what he was doing. For over a year he had focused most of his efforts on establishing contacts with various people who might have some information on why the Americans felt that uranium was so special. So far he had not enjoyed any tremendous success, but he had put together a few reports and made some pick-ups from Shipman and was getting more information all the time. And he was still keeping his eyes and ears open for industrial secrets as well. Overall, Semerov was pleased with his work and considered him one of the most valuable intelligence gatherers at Amtorg. He missed Larisa terribly, but at least their letters had finally started reaching each other earlier that year. He couldn't say that he was happy, but considering all the circumstances, things were going rather well.

On the other hand, he hated the constant deception involved in his work. If only the Americans knew what he really was. He always lied to them, not so much with his words, but with the pretenses he made. Sure, I'm a foreigner, but you can trust me. I'm a nice, friendly person, just like you. What am I doing here? Oh, I'm just an accountant. You know, nothing exciting. I have a regular job. I'm just an average guy.

And when you're not paying attention, I'm stealing every one of your technological and military secrets that I can get my hands on.

He hated the hypocrisy. He did the work because he had to, but he still hated it. And he was getting tired. He had thought that Larisa would be with him by now, but Semerov still hadn't brought her over yet, and he was beginning to wonder if the little demon ever would.

There was another thing bothering him, too, something that he tried not to let himself think about too much, but couldn't help it because it nagged at him all the time. During the past year and a half, he had come to the conclusion that the United States was a better place to live than the Soviet Union, and the more he was here, the less desire he had to spy on the Americans. Other than seeing his wife again, more than anything he wanted to understand what it was about this nation that made it so great.

But he couldn't let himself think about that right now. He had to stay focused. If he wanted to see Larisa and Kolya again, he had to prove himself to Semerov.

At the next meeting with Shipman on a side street not far from Amtorg, Misha told him that the Centre wanted the real thing now. Blueprints and documents and photographs were all very good, but now the Centre wanted uranium. Uranium oxide, uranium nitrate, uranium metal, that kind of thing. Misha asked if Wheeler could come up with some.

Probably not, Shipman told him. Wheeler wanted out of the espionage business and was mad at Semerov for not funding him. Wheeler gave Shipman some documents in exchange for money, but that was all.

This wasn't what Misha needed to hear. The chemistry professor at Harvard had backed out, and his business contacts didn't have access to that kind of material, so Misha was running out of leads. What he needed was a person like Wheeler: someone with influence and access inside a major chemical company.

"Well, it might not be that important, anyway," Misha said. "Semerov thinks the Roosevelt administration will give it to us if we ask for it. The Soviet Purchasing Commission is going to place an order for some of these things next month. We'll see what happens."

"You're going to raise some eyebrows at the War Production Board," Shipman said.

Misha didn't look directly at Shipman, but kept his eye open for eavesdroppers. "We'll see," he said. "But just in case the order falls through, stay alert for these kinds of materials. If you find a way to get hold of some of them, let us know immediately."

Shipman's nod seemed exaggerated, as did most of his body movements. "Right," he said.

Misha turned and walked away.

On his way back to the office, Robert Howard took a short detour down a narrow alley between several large buildings, where a tall man in a black trench coat and hat waited next to a short cement staircase. Howard approached him, glanced around, and without a word handed the man a cigar box. In turn, the man handed Howard a sealed white envelope.

"This is the last time," the man said. The Austrian accent was barely noticeable.

"But I need more," Howard said.

"Then you'll have to shift your focus. I want information on uranium research."

"I can't do that."

"Then get yourself another client." The man turned and started to walk.

Howard knew that if he didn't want to lose this contact, he would have to act now, but he doubted that it would prove fruitful in the future, so he let the man go. He opened the envelope, slipped his fingers inside, and pulled out a couple of bills, which he pushed down into his pocket. Then he started walking back to the street.

Five minutes later he handed the envelope through the back window of a fancy black car that had pulled up to the curb. "And the rest?" the voice from inside asked.

"I'll get it," Howard said.

"When?"

"Soon."

"You're pressing your luck, Bob. Don't disappoint us."

The car drove off, and Howard fished through his pocket, fingering the few bills that he had left. It was more than enough. He looked around, searching for the nearest establishment that sold hard liquor.

FIFTEEN

The black circles under Semerov's eyes looked wider and darker than usual, and Misha found it hard to pay attention to the trivial pleasantries that they were exchanging as they greeted each other in Semerov's office. The shiny black pupils sparkled within the white circles, and the white circles radiated against the backdrop of the dark black circles that surrounded the eye sockets. Such a look couldn't be healthy, Misha thought. Semerov must have some kind of liver disorder.

"When did you last meet with Shipman?" Semerov asked.

Misha counted the time in his head. It was now early February 1943. "It was about six weeks ago, Comrade Semerov. Just before Christmas."

"Has anything come of it?"

"Not yet. Wheeler resigned his position at the Stanton Chemical Company right after the New Year's holiday, and a couple of days later he told Shipman that he wouldn't see him any more. We haven't heard from him since."

"What about your other contacts?"

Misha reached up and wiped his forehead with the palm of his hand, letting his fingers push his hair to one side. "Well, I've been working on this for over a year now, and still no one can get me any uranium. We've collected a lot of technical data, but no samples."

Semerov watched Misha closely for a minute. "You look tired, Kostrin. Are you feeling okay?"

Misha nodded. "I've just been having a hard time sleeping the past few days. It's nothing serious."

Semerov opened up a file on his desk. "You've been doing excellent work, Comrade. The intelligence you've collected during the past year has proven to be among the most valuable that we've sent to Moscow. Of course, you wouldn't know that.

You just make the contacts and pick up the goods. But I know what comes through your hands, and I am very pleased with your work. You seem to have a knack for getting people to open up to you."

"Thank you, Comrade Semerov."

"As I said before, you have good discretion, and you have patience." Semerov closed the file in front of him. "As I recall, you have a wife and son back in Moscow, correct?"

"Yes, Comrade Semerov."

"Tell me, how long has it been since you last saw them?"

Misha thought back. It had been an eternity. "Since I started working here," he said. "Just before the invasion."

"June of 'forty-one? And now it's February of 'forty-three. That would make a year and eight months, right?"

"Yes."

"And how old is your son?"

"A year and nine months."

Semerov nodded slowly, and his whole upper torso rocked gently back and forth in his chair as he did so. "I'm sure you miss them very much."

"Yes."

"Tell me another thing, Comrade Kostrin. During the past year and eight months, have you been romantically involved with any women here in New York?"

"No."

"You've been absolutely faithful to your wife."

"Yes."

Semerov propped his elbows on the desk, then picked up a pen in front of him and rolled it between the thumbs and forefingers of his hands, staring at it as if he were inspecting it for blemishes. "Do you remember what I told you during our first meeting in this office?"

"You said that if I prove myself, you could arrange to have my family join me here in New York."

"That's right." Semerov set the pen down and leaned back in his chair. "In the time that you've been here, you've been absolutely faithful to your wife, and so far you've been absolutely faithful to me. I give you assignment after assignment, and you always manage to pull through and get results." Semerov looked up at Misha as if searching for a reaction, but Misha didn't move or speak. "Of course, you're not the only faithful agent in the NKVD, nor are you the best. But you are very reliable. You've proven yourself to me in almost every respect."

Misha didn't feel tired any more, and he sat up straighter in his chair. "Does this mean I'm going to get to see my wife again?"

Semerov smiled his standard, fake smile, the one where the lips curved upward slightly but the eyes belied the outward pretense of sincerity. Misha doubted if Semerov had ever smiled a genuine smile in his life. "I have two more assignments for you, Comrade Kostrin. Once you've completed them, your wife and child will join you here in New York City."

Misha put his hands on the arms of the chair. "What are they?"

Semerov stood up and walked slowly around Misha's back. "Have you noticed anything odd about Comrade Ryzanov lately?"

Misha turned his head to the left and thought back on everything that had happened in the office during the past week. "It seems that he's been a little jittery, I suppose."

"Yes? Go on."

"Well, he looks like he hasn't been getting much sleep." Misha shifted in his seat. "He isolates himself at his desk for several hours every day, and there have been a couple of times that I've seen him muttering things to himself."

"And you don't think that's odd?"

"Not really. He's been working on that nickel deal for the past month, and he hasn't been able to find a supplier willing to sell. He's under a lot of stress."

Semerov walked around Misha's right side to where Misha could see him again, and he was shaking his head back and forth. "No, no, no. You disappoint me, Comrade. I think there's more to it than that."

"Like what?"

Semerov stopped where he was and turned around so that he faced Misha. "I don't know. But I think something is wrong, and I want you to find out what it is."

Semerov stepped over to his desk and rested the fingertips of his right hand on the base of the lamp. Misha's shoulders were tight, and he still gripped the sides of the chair. "You mean, follow him around and find out what he's up to?"

"Precisely."

"But I didn't think we were supposed to spy on each other."

Semerov raised his hand, then brought it down hard and slammed it against the desk, hitting it in just the right spot so that a loud booming sound reverberated throughout the office. "Well you'd better start thinking about things like that!"

Semerov's voice was cold and sharp, and it made Misha's scalp twitch around his ears.

Semerov walked over to the window sill, where he sat down and faced Misha again. "Have you heard the news from Stalingrad?" he asked.

"I heard that we defeated the Germans there last month and that we're on the offensive now."

"The war may have taken a turn for the better, but that doesn't mean that it's over, and it doesn't mean that we can get lax in our efforts. And it doesn't mean that we should kid ourselves into thinking that everyone in the NKVD is a loyal patriot."

"Do you think that Nikolai is a traitor?" Misha asked.

"I don't know. But he's acting strangely, and I've got a bad feeling about it. Maybe it is the stress. Maybe all he needs is a new assignment or some time off. But maybe there's something that's distracting him from his work, and if there is, then I need to know about it."

"What do you want me to do?"

"Keep an eye on him. Pay attention to his schedule. Take notice of where he goes and who he talks to. Follow him around if you have to. Then report back to me." Semerov stood up from the window sill and walked back to the desk.

"What's the second assignment?" Misha asked.

"A few days ago the Soviet Purchasing Commission placed an order with a local chemical company here in New York City for a couple hundred kilograms of uranium compounds. So far it looks like Lend-Lease will probably approve it, which means we shouldn't need an export license for it. If everything works out, we'll ship it to Montana as soon as we get it, then send it by plane up to Alaska and from there to the Soviet Union. I want you to go with it."

Misha raised his eyebrows. "Go with it?"

"Yes. I want you to accompany it all the way to the Soviet Union. Then you can meet your wife and son, and after a few days we'll have you fly back to the United States by the same air route."

"And my wife and son?"

"We can't send them by military cargo plane, but we'll bring them right over shortly afterward, probably by boat. How does that sound?"

For a brief moment, Misha actually felt affection toward the *rezident*. "It sounds wonderful," he said. "Thank you, Comrade Semerov."

Misha stood in the Amtorg building, staring outside. A monotonous gray arched across the sky and cast a soft, melancholy light through the window. He searched the overcast haze for some inkling of blue, but found none. He put the back of his hand up to the pane of glass and held it there for a few seconds until his flesh tingled and started to go numb. It hadn't snowed in several days now, and the days were getting longer, which gave Misha at least something to be optimistic about, but the temperature outside was still cold enough to make life lethargic and uncomfortable. But what was he so despondent about? February in New York City was nothing compared to the winters back home.

He pictured Larisa walking down some narrow pathway between a cluster of apartment buildings in Moscow, wearing a dark fur coat and a fur *shapka* on her head and black gloves on her hands and a handbag slung over her shoulder. Her hair would be tucked up under the *shapka* and her soft cheeks would be a bright pink from the frigid outside air. At least that's how he pictured her. She said in her last letter that she was being well taken care of, that the government had people meeting her every need, that she had plenty of food and warm clothing and that the baby was well taken care of, too. She wrote that little Kolya was speaking now and trying to walk on his own, and that the other day he pointed to an old photograph of Misha and said the word "papa."

But then again, such an image of his wife and son had no logical connection to reality. Moscow had almost fallen to the Germans a year and a half ago. There were estimates coming into Amtorg from the Soviet Union of horrendous numbers of Soviet dead. Although the official press was touting the stunning virtues and miraculous victories of the Red Army, thanks in particular to the new TU-34 tank, Misha knew better than anyone except for old Semerov himself that the entire Soviet nation had teetered dangerously close to military collapse. Even now his people were on the brink of starvation, and the one lifeline that the Soviet people had was the Lend-Lease program, which he was exploiting and manipulating and leeching for all it was worth.

But he should feel no qualms about his espionage work against the United States—at least he told himself that he shouldn't. The billions of dollars that the Americans were spending on Lend-Lease was nothing compared to the millions of dead soldiers and peasants that the Soviet Union had already lost. Yes, he would continue to exploit and extort and bribe and corrupt the Americans all he could if it meant the war would end sooner and bring him and his family back together. He knew all this talk of being allies was nothing more than hot air, anyway. He knew what Soviet life and society were like, and now he knew what American life and society were like, and although he didn't consider himself much of a political philosopher by any stretch of the imagination, the one thing he had convinced himself of during the past year and eight months was that the two ways of life were absolutely incompatible. He had already figured out what everyone with any real power already knew—that once the war was over, the United States and the Soviet Union would stop being allies overnight and would immediately be at each other's throats.

What did he care about the Americans, anyway? They were his enemies. They were the ones watching him and resisting his efforts all the time and imposing export restrictions on certain materials and technologies that his people needed to beat the Germans. The Americans cared for the Soviet Union only so long as the Soviet Union kept the Germans tied up on the eastern front. If every Soviet citizen were to die off, the Americans wouldn't even care. The Americans were just biding their time, hoping that the Germans and Russians would kill each other off so the Americans could sweep in and clean the place up and become the next great world power.

No, that was too harsh. He was lying to himself, and he knew it. He was lying to himself because he couldn't bring himself to terms with what he knew to be the truth. Scapegoating the Americans was too easy, and he couldn't allow himself to do it just so he could go on living this ridiculous lie. It wasn't the Americans who killed Ivan and Olga and his uncle Konstantin and his father and mother. It wasn't the Americans who forced him onto the boat that brought him over here. It wasn't the Americans who were exploiting him and blackmailing him and holding his wife and son hostage in their own home to ensure that he continue to serve the Party. No. The Americans represented everything he believed in.

He looked outside at the New York City skyline and took it all in—the sky, the buildings, the streets, the pedestrians on the sidewalks. Everything was better here. Here was prosperity, progress, law and order, democracy, freedom, religion and family and business and people walking around pursuing their own interests without that omnipresent fear that someone was going to put a bullet in the back of your brain for doing so. And yet the Americans were just coming out of the worst economic depression in their history! He couldn't even imagine what this place would be like in good times when the economy was thriving and there was no war going on. It would be the closest thing to utopia that the world had ever known. No wonder this was now the most powerful country in the world, the sleeping giant that most of the world had ignored until the Japanese dragged it into this latest world conflict. No, this country could not be his enemy, because this country was fundamentally good.

He turned around and looked over the office at the rows of desks and piles of paperwork. Everyone here was just like him. They were like hamsters in a cage. Slaves to an all-consuming, self-serving dictatorship, a rotten Party apparatus that sucked every bit of hope and happiness out of all aspects of life and turned men into animals. And Semerov, that rotten piece of trash, that horrid little worm, what he wouldn't give to storm into that office right now and strangle him by the throat until those demonic little black eyes popped out of his head. Yes, admit it! Admit it to yourself! His only real enemy was the Party. His enemy was the very country that he was working for.

And he was one of them.

He turned to the window again. He put his hands on the window sill and leaned forward, lowering his head. Calm down, you fool, take it easy. You can't lose it now, not when you're so close! He took several deep breaths and cleared his mind. He had to get a grip. He had to hang in there. Larisa would be here soon. He would do what Semerov told him to and he would keep playing the little games without complaining and he would keep his cool. Larisa would be here soon.

He heard someone get up behind him, so he stood up straight and turned around to see who it was. Nikolai had risen from his chair and had gathered up some papers from his desk, which he now shoved into the upper left drawer. He turned around and caught Misha's glance. "Misha," he said as he walked toward him. "I'm going out. If Comrade Semerov asks where I am, tell him I'm meeting a contact, will you? I shouldn't be gone long."

Misha nodded, but he couldn't look Nikolai in the eye. "Sure," he said.

Nikolai patted him on the shoulder. "Thanks," he said, then walked away, and Misha watched the back of him. Even from behind, the tall skinny figure looked frazzled, and Misha saw a little wisp of hair bouncing up and down on Nikolai's head as he walked out of the office.

Well, this is it. Don't think about it. You don't have any other choice, anyway. Get it done and it will be over with, and Larisa will be here soon.

Misha walked down the corridor and picked up his coat along the way and put it on without breaking his stride. He reached into his pocket and pulled out his scarf and wrapped it around his neck, then put on his hat and started buttoning up his coat as he made his way out onto the street. He paused momentarily on the sidewalk and looked around until he spotted the slender figure with the familiar gait moving away from him. Then he headed after him.

They walked for a long time, and Nikolai was moving fast, so Misha had to trot now and then to keep up with him. The grid of streets was like a labyrinth that never ended, and they turned down this block and that one, down a narrow alleyway, around the back of an apartment building. At one point Nikolai ducked into a small fruit market, but just as Misha was thinking that this was the contact point, the lanky figure was back on the street again with an apple in his hand, which he slid into his coat pocket. It went on for several more blocks like this, Misha always staying at least half a block behind Nikolai, and he had to be careful not to lose him. They ended up in a section of town where Misha had never been before, and finally Nikolai stopped at a street corner in front of an old brick building.

Misha ducked behind the corner of a bakery shop and

watched. Nikolai looked around and waited, and about thirty seconds later he was approached by a woman wearing a long black overcoat. They spoke to each other briefly, then Nikolai went down a small stairway into the basement level of the brick building, and after glancing around her in all directions, the woman followed him. Misha looked around, worried about FBI men, but figured he probably wouldn't recognize an American agent even if he saw one, so he came out from behind the bakery and ran the half block or so to the intersection, where he crossed the street and cautiously approached the old brick building. As luck would have it, there was a pile of boxes and wooden crates and construction materials on the sidewalk just outside the basement window of the room where Nikolai and the woman were, and Misha hid himself amid the pile in such a way that he was invisible to passers-by from the street, yet he could still see through the window.

The sun had set and the sky was growing dark, which made his job all that much easier. It would be harder for people both inside and outside to see him hiding among the boxes and crates, yet at the same time it would be easier for him to see what was going on in the room. He crouched down and put his hand on the one of the crates and made sure that he wasn't cutting off the circulation to his right foot. The scent of dust and plaster from the old wood entered his nostrils and lingered there.

Nikolai and the woman sat across from each other at a small card table in an otherwise empty boiler room, and there was another man with them, a tall imposing man with a somber face who was wearing a dark trench coat and matching fedora. This tall figure came over to the window and peered outside, which made Misha's heart jump up into his throat. He ducked quickly, and the man didn't see him. Then the man pulled the blinds closed so that Misha couldn't see what was going on.

Misha let out a faint gasp of frustration, then leaned forward and repositioned himself so that his head pressed against the brick, and from this new position he could barely see through the crack between the blinds and the side of the window. He couldn't see Nikolai any more, but he could see the woman still sitting down with her hands clasped on the card table, and he could see the legs of the large man who was standing next to her. The woman's lips were moving and her eyes were focused ahead of her, so he figured she was talking to Nikolai.

The woman looked vaguely familiar, but nothing rang a bell. She had straight blond hair that she had combed back and tied behind her head, and she wore a small pair of black glasses. Her skin was smooth and had a healthy color to it, and her black overcoat made her fair cheeks and light blue eyes stand out. Her lipstick was a deep red.

Her demeanor was relaxed and confident. She listened for a while, then spoke, then listened again, then spoke. Most of the time she sat in a reclined position, but at one point she leaned forward and tapped her finger on the table as if to emphasize whatever it was that she was saying. At another point in the conversation the large man behind her leaned down and put his hands on the table and seemed to be looking directly at Nikolai, whom Misha still could not see, but it gave Misha a good view of the large man's face.

The man's expression was serious. Not once did he ever crack a smile or show the least bit of discernable emotion. And he really was a large man. He was not only tall but stout, with broad shoulders and a straight back, and even though he wore a suit with a trench coat over it, Misha could tell that the man had a solid build. The man wore wire-rimmed glasses and had a round chin with no dimple. His face was broad and smooth, and his nostrils seemed to flare when he spoke. Then the large man stood up again and Misha could no longer see him, and it was back to the woman at the card table.

It went like this for about fifteen minutes, the whole scene playing out before his eyes in a profound silence. Then the woman stood up from the table and Nikolai stood up, too, because Misha could now see Nikolai's back and Nikolai was blocking his view of the woman and the large man. Then the light went out, and Misha could see nothing.

Misha made sure he was well covered and kept himself absolutely still, careful not even to let his breathing make any noise. His lower back was starting to ache, but he didn't dare move, not even just a little, and his nose and cheeks were going numb from the cold. He heard a door open and shut, then there were shoes climbing up cement steps to the sidewalk, and through another crack in the pile of boxes and crates he caught a brief glimpse of the three silhouettes in front of the building. Then they all walked away from where he was. The large man and the woman turned left at the street corner and disappeared behind the building. Nikolai crossed the street heading in another direction and started back the way he had come.

Misha was paralyzed. He waited for several minutes, and when he finally got to his feet and slipped out from between the crates, his toes were so cold that he could no longer feel them. But at least it was done. He took a different route than the one Nikolai had taken, and he walked deliberately and slowly as he made his way back to the Amtorg building.

SIXTEEN

The next morning Misha was in Semerov's office.

"Did you recognize the woman?" Semerov asked. The black circles were as dark as ever.

"No. She looked familiar, but . . ." He shook his head.

"And the man?"

"The man looked familiar, too, but as I said, I can't remember ever seeing these people before. It's as though I'm having déjà vu. I feel that I've seen their faces before, but I don't remember where or when."

Semerov leaned back in his chair as he always did, and he rubbed his chin with his left hand. His eyes wandered up to the ceiling for a moment, then focused back on Misha. He put his hands on his desk and stood up. He pulled a key out of his pocket, turned around, and opened a drawer to a metal filing cabinet. He rummaged through the files for a few seconds, then pulled one out and closed the drawer. He opened the file, his back still to Misha, and studied something for a moment. Then he turned around again and handed over a black-and-white photograph. "Is that her?" he asked.

Misha held the picture close to his face and examined it carefully. It was taken at an odd angle, and the woman in it was holding an umbrella that partially covered the side of her head, but her face was clear. The eyes, the lips, the cheek bones, the straight blond hair—he nodded slowly. "I'm not a hundred percent sure, but I think that's her." He handed the photograph back. "Who is she?"

Semerov put the print back and laid the folder on the desk. "We don't know. Not yet, anyway. These FBI people try very hard to blend into crowds and look like normal people, but when the same faces repeat themselves at the very times and in the very places that our agents are doing their work, we start to pay attention. This photograph was taken about a month ago. It was snowing that day, and that's why she's holding the umbrella. She was on her way into a fancy hotel here in New York and had just walked under the canopy that shades the entrance when one of our people managed to get this shot off. Not bad, don't you think? Not a single snowflake on the film." Semerov sat down again.

Misha heard Semerov's words, but he was only partially paying attention. In his mind, he saw the yellow teeth, the bulbous nose, the wide smile. The bartender had been off to the right.

"What about Nikolai?" Misha asked.

"I want you to stay away from Ryzanov," Semerov said. "I'm going to send him down to Washington tomorrow with some documents we've received from Tennessee."

No, behind Shipman, on the far side of the bar, the man eating breakfast who hadn't taken his hat off.

"Do you think you can trust him?" Misha asked.

"No, but I don't want him to know that, do I?" Semerov clasped his hands on the desk. "Besides, he'll have another agent with him. The documents will arrive at the Soviet Purchasing Commission without any problems."

Misha pictured the three men over his left shoulder at the table in the corner who were talking loudly. And over his right shoulder . . .

"What will he do in Washington?" Misha asked.

"That's where we're preparing the next big shipment of documents," Semerov said. "He'll spend his time packing them into black suitcases for transport to Great Falls, Montana."

In his mind, Misha saw the person over his right shoulder behind him in the other corner, sitting at a table alone with a newspaper, her face hidden.

"When will the shipment be made to the Soviet Union?" Misha asked.

"This one will go out immediately, but Comrade Ryzanov won't be with it. I'm going to have him stay a few weeks at the

Soviet Purchasing Commission to keep him out of our way. That will give me a chance to see if I can find out some more information on these people he was meeting with. That area of town you found him in has a lot of Jews in it. It's a haven for Trotskyites and other dissidents. That's why I don't allow our people to go there without my express permission."

Misha could see the newspaper as she lowered it to turn the page. Her head was down. The page turned, her head came up, and she started to raise the newspaper. There were the eyes, crystal blue.

"And the uranium?" Misha asked.

"The deal is going through right now. It will ship toward the end of March, and you'll be with it. I'm going to put Nikolai on that plane, too, and I want you to keep a close eye on him. Don't let him out of your sight."

Suddenly it all clicked, and Misha's mouth dropped open as he stared at Semerov's face.

"What is it?" Semerov asked, his expression puzzled. "Is something wrong?"

"The woman."

"What woman?"

"In the photograph. I know where I've seen her before."

"Where?"

"The first time I met with Shipman, just after I got here. I was sitting on a bar stool at a counter in a café, and there was a woman behind me to the right who was reading a newspaper all alone at a table in the corner. I didn't think anything of it at the time—"

"And you think that was her?"

"Yes. And the large man she was with last night . . ." Misha raised his finger and started shaking it in front of him. "He was sitting at the counter eating breakfast, and the reason I remember him is that he didn't take his hat off, and I thought that was strange."

"Are you sure?"

Misha put his hand down and shook his head. "I can't be

absolutely certain, but I think that's where I saw them before."

"That was a long time ago, Comrade Kostrin. Memory can play funny tricks on us."

"I remember that day as if it happened yesterday." The more he thought about it, the more confident he felt. "That's where I saw them, Comrade Semerov. It was in that café with Shipman. I'm sure of it."

Semerov pressed his lips together, held his fist up to his mouth, and stared at the desk for a moment as he thought things over. "If that's the case, then these people have been on to us for a very long time," he said. He took his hand away from his mouth and looked up again. "This matter certainly deserves looking into. You've done a good job, Kostrin. I'm very pleased."

"Thank you, Comrade Semerov."

"You look tired, Kostrin. Why don't you finish up those purchase orders I gave you yesterday and go home a little early. You need to relax. Make sure you get a good night's sleep."

"Yes, Comrade Semerov."

Misha stood in a vast field, and the wind blew gently all around him. The sky was still overcast, and as far as he could see in all directions there was nothing but gently rolling hills covered in a swaying yellow tapestry of grain that rustled softly as the wind stirred it. He held in his hands the small wooden box with the fire-branded engraving around the edges, and when he lifted it to his face, he could smell the mustiness of the old wood. He undid the latch and opened it, checking for the little black book and the key, but the box was empty.

He heard his uncle's voice carried by the wind. "Meeeeeeeeshaaaaaaaa."

He looked around him again in all directions, but saw nothing. "Where are you?" he shouted.

No answer.

He started running. The ground was rough and lumpy, and several times he stumbled and almost fell. The wind was getting stronger and felt cold against his skin, sending chills down his neck and back as he trudged through the endless fields. The sky above was growing darker, and after several minutes of running, he felt a few small raindrops on his cheeks. His thighs and calves were growing weaker; his muscles were starting to burn.

In the distance up ahead he saw a single silver cross rising up out of the horizon, and this gave him the incentive he needed to keep on running. The rain was still very light, but the wind was cold, and each gulp of air sent a freezing pain through his lungs. He paused for breath. His skin was tense all over his face, and goose bumps covered his arms. He closed the wooden box and shoved it up under his shirt to keep it out of the rain, then tucked his shirt into his pants and started running again.

The cross stood atop a small brown dome that was pointed at the top and bulged at the sides—an onion dome, common for the towers on Russian Orthodox churches. Beneath the brown dome was a small white bell tower with several oval windows that faced all directions, and beneath the bell tower was the main roof, also brown. The walls of the church were made of white stone, and as Misha got closer he saw a large wooden door.

He stopped running when he reached the door and looked around him, but he saw only endless fields of yellow grain, swaying in the wind. The door of the church was enormous and was made of old wood that was splintering everywhere, and a huge iron ring hung from the front of the door about a meter and a half above the ground. Above the ring at about eye level Misha saw a large iron key hole. He ran his finger across it. The metal was like ice. He grabbed the ring with both of his hands and pulled. He leaned back and put all of his weight into the effort, but the door wouldn't budge.

He stepped back away from the door several paces and looked up at the bell tower windows, but saw only darkness. Just then there was a bright streak of lightning behind the church accompanied by a loud crack of thunder, and the flash illuminated the silhouette of a man standing in the window. The man wore the long black robes of a Russian Orthodox priest, and on top of his head sat a tall black hat—not a top hat, but a cone-shaped hat, the hat of a priest. A scraggly black beard, graying from old age, clung to the man's face.

"Uncle!" Misha shouted. "Uncle, it's me! Let me in!"

The figure stepped forward out of the darkness, and his image filled the window. The old man looked down on him rigidly.

"Uncle, it's me, Misha! Don't you recognize me? Why do you look upon me with such contempt?"

His uncle stared at him for a moment, then answered in the same voice that Misha had heard in the forest, only now the voice was strong and clear. "I know you not," the old man said.

"But uncle, you called my name! I need you!"

The old man pointed down at a small table in front of the church that Misha hadn't noticed before, and Misha saw the little black book resting on top of it, open. "Read," came his uncle's voice.

Misha picked up the book and read:

Whosoever shall seek to save his life shall lose it;
and whosoever shall lose his life shall preserve it.

A dark, poignant tension filled his chest, and he looked back up at his uncle. "But what does it mean?"

The old man stretched out his arm and pointed a scathing finger down at him. "You have failed," he said.

"I don't know what you mean!" Misha shouted. "How have I failed?"

The book in his hands started to shake, the wind intensified, and one by one the pages started to tear out and fly away. They flew rapidly out of the book until they were all gone, and at that moment the wind reached down and snatched the black cover out of his hands, and it fluttered up into the sky, twisting and swirling until he couldn't see it any more.

He ran to the door and wrapped his hands around the metal ring again, pulling with his arms and pushing his left foot against the wall, but the door was solid and wouldn't budge. His hands slipped off the cold metal and he staggered several steps backward until he tripped and fell on his back.

He was stunned for a moment, but when he came to, he raised himself up on his elbows and shook his head to regain his senses, then looked up. His uncle stood in the window of the tower with a spear in his right hand, and his right arm was raised above his head, poised to throw. "Now you are dead to me," his uncle said, and lunged forward, thrusting the spear downward with a mighty heave.

The sharp point of the heavy spear slammed into Misha's chest with inexorable force, pounding his torso into the hard dirt beneath him, pinning him to the ground. Unbearable pain shot through him, and he couldn't breathe. Strange clicking sounds forced their way out of his throat as he tried to cough, and he grabbed the iron spear with both hands, pushing with all his might to release himself, but to no avail.

The voice again came from the tower. "Redeem thyself," his uncle said, "and return with the key."

SEVENTEEN

A gentle March breeze swept across the airfield, chilling the back of Mark's neck just above the collar and making a low-pitched, hollow whistling sound as it blew across the fuselage and wings of the C-47. But the sun was shining warmly, and only a few isolated cirrus clouds glided across the vast expanse of blue that arched overhead and seemed to go on forever. No wonder they called this place big sky country. It was a bright, clear flying day. It almost always was at Gore Field.

Mark held the clipboard in his left arm and made little notes with the pencil in his right hand as he trudged around the outside of the aircraft. He looked over the wings and the propellers and the engines and walked the full stretch of the fuselage lengthwise from nose to tail, visually scouring the surface for anything out of the ordinary, as was his routine before each flight. It wasn't a bomber, nor did its nickname, "gooney bird," carry an elegant ring to it, but to Mark it was a beautiful airplane nonetheless. The late morning sunshine glistened off the silver skin of the C-47, adding the perfect touch to an already near-perfect flying day. The aircraft was supposed to be repainted green, but for some reason nobody had gotten around to it, so it was the only C-47 at the airfield colored silver.

He climbed up inside the aircraft and had to stand still for a moment to let his eyes adjust to the dim reflected sunlight that permeated the plane. He blinked a few times and squinted. When he could see again, he counted two burly Russians off to his right in the cargo hold who were stacking wooden crates in one corner of the plane, and sure enough, just in front of the wooden crates stood a pile of black leather suitcases bound with white cords and sealed with red wax. He looked to his left toward the front of the plane and saw Lieutenant Paulsen coming out of the cockpit.

"Hey there, Captain Daniels," the young man said, stretching out a hand for Mark to shake.

"What's the story, Paulsen?"

Paulsen nodded in the direction of the Russians. "See for yourself."

"More black suitcases?"

"Just like last month."

Mark held the clipboard at his left side and pointed with the pencil in his right hand. "And what about those crates? Any idea what those are?"

"Couldn't tell you, Captain. I just fly the plane."

"What do you make of all this, Paulsen?"

"I don't know, Captain. All I know is that these Russians are shipping more and more stuff all the time, and I don't think it's all war supplies. They've been acting really funny about those crates and suitcases."

"What do you mean?"

"They just seem real touchy all of a sudden. Usually when we load the planes, they let us help out and they don't care what we see, since it's all just food and weapons and ammunition. But this time when I offered to help unload those crates, they just about had a fit. 'Oh, no, no,' they said. I think they're moving something that they don't want us to see."

"What do you make of the suitcases? We've been seeing a lot of them the past little while."

"Well, they say it's just luggage, but that doesn't make sense. I could understand one or two suitcases, but fifty at a time? Not even generals carry that much stuff with them, and these guys sure aren't generals. Luggage my eye. I mean, if thousands of your countrymen were dying and needed supplies to fight a war on your own territory, would you take up half a cargo plane with personal luggage? And if all you're doing is flying back and forth between two remote locations to ferry military supplies, would you need much luggage, anyway? All I take with me on these missions is one little bag."

The two Russians had their backs to them for the most part

and paid no attention to the two pilots watching them. "I don't like it," Mark said. "Something's going on here." The two Russians disappeared for a moment, then returned carrying another wooden crate, one man on each side of it. "I want to know what's inside those crates, and especially what's in those black suitcases."

"You have something in mind, Captain?"

The Russians started to set the crate down, but one of the men lost his grip and dropped it. The crate landed on its side with a loud crash, and the force of the impact dislodged the lid, which toppled over onto the floor, leaving the crate standing on its side, open.

"Hold this," Mark said and pushed the clipboard into Paulsen's chest. He walked over to where the accident happened, ignoring the two Russians as they righted the crate, and stood over the lid. A metal box had fallen out of the crate and was sitting upside-down on top of the lid, and Mark stooped down and set the box upright. There was no lock on the latch, so he opened it up and looked inside. The Russians were so occupied with getting the crate back up straight that they didn't notice what he was doing.

All there was in the metal box was a strange-looking pile of dirt. Mark put his hand down into the box and scooped up a handful of the stuff, then turned his head and looked over at the Russians, who were now staring at him. Both of the men's faces went pale.

"No touch! No touch!" one of the men yelled as he scurried around the crate to where Mark was. The man crouched down opposite Mark and slapped Mark's hand so that the dirt fell back into the metal box.

"Hey, what's the big deal?" Mark asked. "What is this stuff, anyway?"

The Russian, who was short and round and stocky and had a scraggly beard and whose face was now red and flustered, grabbed Mark's wrist with one hand and brushed the remaining dust off of Mark's palm with the other.

Mark pulled his hand away from the man and wiped it on the side of his hip.

"No touch!" the man said. "Burn hands."

"What do you mean 'burn hands'?" Mark said. "It looks like dirt to me. What is this stuff?"

The Russian closed the metal box and latched it, then picked it up and set it back inside the wooden crate. Then he picked the crate lid up off of the floor and put it back in place. "No touch," he said. "Very special chemicals."

Mark stood up and walked to the other side of the crate and put his hands on the lid, and the Russian standing across from him kept his hands on the lid as well. "Oh yeah?" Mark asked. "What kind of chemicals?"

The burly, bearded face looked confused and panicky, and the red forehead wrinkled up. The dark brown eyes were fixated on Mark, and this little standoff went on for several seconds. The Russian was speechless.

"What's your name, anyway?" Mark asked.

"Dima."

"Dima? Now listen up, Dima, are you going to tell me what all this stuff is or am I going to have to search these myself?"

Dima didn't answer.

Mark tried to lift the lid off of the crate, but Dima kept his hands on it and leaned down with his body weight to keep it shut. Mark looked at the frightened, determined expression on Dima's face and let go of the crate lid, then walked over to Paulsen. "Do you have a sidearm, Lieutenant?"

Paulsen looked surprised but calm. "Yes, sir."

"Good. Throw that clipboard in the cockpit, then come back and cover me. I'm going to find out what's going on here, and I don't want these guys trying anything funny."

"Yes, sir." Paulsen disappeared for a few seconds into the cockpit, then returned with his flight jacket open, and Mark saw a holster strapped to Paulsen's side.

Mark pulled a pen knife out of his pocket and walked over to the pile of black suitcases. He grabbed one by the handle and set it up on its side, then sliced through the white cord and opened it up.

Dima started yelling hysterically and rushed over to where Mark stood with the suitcase. "No touch! No touch!" He tried to pull Mark away from the open suitcase, but Mark pushed him away with his right hand.

"Hey!" Paulsen's voice pierced the air of the cargo hold. Mark looked at the Russian, who had temporarily frozen and was staring at something, terrified. Then Misha looked over his shoulder at Paulsen, who was standing with a pistol drawn, holding it up with his right hand so that it pointed toward the ceiling. With his left hand Paulsen pointed at Dima and motioned for him to back away.

Dima looked over at the other Russian, who all this time had been standing motionless against the wall, and shouted something in Russian. The other man, who was still white as a sheet and had sweat appearing on his forehead, nodded frantically, then hurried out the open door and down the steps.

Dima then turned around and tried again to pull Mark away from the suitcase. "No touch! No touch! Please no touch!"

Mark pushed him away again, then Paulsen put his left hand on Dima's chest and shoved him backward. "I told you to back off!" Paulsen pushed Dima back against the wall of the cargo hold and held him there with his left hand gripping Dima's shirt, his left forearm pushed up against Dima's neck, the pistol still in his right hand, pointing upward. Dima got the hint and stopped struggling. "No touch," he said quietly, resigned to his helplessness. "Please no touch." Then he put his hand up to his forehead.

Mark looked through the suitcase and saw tightly bound stacks of folders, all containing papers and photographs. He pulled one of the folders out and set it down on another suitcase, then opened it up and looked over one of the pages. All sorts of unfamiliar words jumped out at him: uranium, polonium, deuterium, thorium, Oak Ridge, Manhattan Engineering Project, sodium uranate, cadmium, radium, and dozens of others. He put the paper back and looked through another folder. He saw maps of almost every city in the United States, ordinary road maps that you could buy at filling stations, and other maps of train routes and distances between points of destination, and he found topographical maps and mileage tables and charts and blueprints of buildings and a whole host of technical engineering documents with designs on them and equations and things he couldn't understand.

"Daniels!" Griggs' voice boomed throughout the cargo hold.

Mark turned around. Old Eagle Eye stood inside the plane just a few feet away, and several panicky Russians rushed in through the door, stopping to see what was happening. Griggs looked over at Paulsen with his pistol drawn and Dima pushed up against the wall. "Let him go, Lieutenant. And put your weapon away." The Russians walked over to where Mark was and pushed him aside. They gathered up the files, put them back in the suitcase and closed it. "Follow me, Captain," Griggs said, then turned to exit the plane.

In Griggs' office, Mark stood in front of the desk and stared straight ahead.

"Captain Daniels, you should have come to me before attempting a search like that."

"I thought you told us to be on the lookout for suspicious activity, sir. You said these Russians can't be trusted and that we had the right to inspect whatever cargo they brought aboard our planes."

Griggs was standing with hands clasped behind his back and his head bowed. "I know that's what I said, and that's why I'm going to go easy on you this time. Don't get me wrong, now, I'm not angry at you. You've got a good head on your shoulders, and if I had been in your position, I probably would have done the same thing. But that's not the point. The point is that I was wrong when I gave you authority to search cargo, and I'm rescinding that authority. From now on there will be absolutely no searches of any cargo on these planes."

"But I believe these Russians are spying on us, sir. I'm sure of it. If you'll just go take a look at what's in those black suitcases, you'll see—"

"Captain Daniels." Griggs held up a hand for Mark to stop. "Captain Daniels, I don't know how to tell you this any other way." The colonel put a hand on Mark's shoulder and looked him in the eye. "You and I are both in over our heads on this one. I've had the same impression myself about this operation here, so yesterday I called around to see what I could find out. You know what happened?" Griggs took his hand off of Mark's shoulder. "Last night I got a phone call from the War Department and was told in no uncertain terms that we are not to hinder these Russians in any way. Understand? I just haven't had time yet to spread the word to all you pilots."

"But sir—"

"Let it go, Daniels."

"But they're spying on us."

"I said let it drop." Griggs put his hand on Mark's shoulder again. "Daniels, you're awfully young to be wearing those captain's bars, and if there wasn't a war going on, you'd still be a lieutenant, just like Paulsen. But I expect you to understand that when people higher up tell you to get your nose out of something, then you'd better get your nose out of it. Now I don't pretend to know what's going on with this Alsib Pipeline, but whatever these Russians are taking home with them, it seems to me that for whatever reasons, our government is giving it to them. You understand? When I called around, the most I was hoping for was that some one-star general would get back to me in a week or two and fill me in. The next thing I know I'm getting a call directly from the War Department in Washington, D.C. telling me to stop asking questions immediately. What does that tell you, son?"

Mark didn't feel like saying anything, so he pressed his lips together and stared at the wall.

"No matter what it looks like to us, you have to remember that down here in the field we're only seeing one small piece of the puzzle. If you're ever going to make it in this man's army, you're going to have to learn to exercise faith in your superiors, no matter what. You just have to trust that someone up the ladder a few more steps than you can see the big picture and where you fit in it, and that it all makes sense. Understand?"

"Yes, sir."

"Dismissed."

Mark turned to leave, but as he reached the door, he heard the colonel call after him.

"Oh, Daniels, one more thing."

He turned around. "Yes, sir?"

"If I were you, I wouldn't go apologizing to those Russians any time soon." A broad smile stretched across Griggs' face. "I actually think it did them some good to have a little scare like that. Helped remind them who's really in charge here."

A light breeze tousled Misha's hair, blowing several strands across his forehead, and the sun bathed the skin on his face, radiating through his overcoat and warming him, a pleasant contrast to the chilly air and the wind.

He stood on the airstrip off to the left side of a large American cargo plane, its silver skin shining in the reflected light of the sun. Several of his countrymen were still going in and out of the plane, carrying the last items on board and securing what they had already loaded. He looked all around him, but could see no one that he knew.

A short, stocky man who looked like a wrestler and had a dark beard came down the steps from the plane and walked over to him. "Comrade Kostrin?" the man asked.

"Yes."

"We're ready for you to come on board."

He looked around him again, searching. "Where's Comrade Ryzanov?" he asked. "He and I are supposed to accompany the cargo to Alaska together."

The stocky man nodded. "Yes, yes, he will join you on the plane in a few minutes. We have orders not to let him on board until the engines are running and the plane is ready to take off."

"But I was hoping to speak with him before we got on the plane."

"I'm sorry, Comrade Kostrin, that won't be possible. I have my orders."

Misha wanted to say more, to push a little harder, to bargain and coax, but he thought better of it and bit his tongue. "I understand," he said.

"Come, I'll show you to the plane."

Misha walked behind the stocky man across the airstrip, then marched up the steps to the open door of the cargo hold, where he paused again and turned around, scanning the area for any sign of Nikolai. An American in a flight jacket was walking toward the plane from one of the little buildings adjacent to the airstrip. He was a younger man with dark hair, handsome and athletic, and looked like he was in his twenties. Must be the pilot.

"Comrade Kostrin." The stocky man's voice came from inside of the cargo hold. Misha turned around and stepped inside the plane. "Comrade Kostrin, you will be here." The man pointed to a short metal bench against the side of the wall that had a couple of seats on it with harnesses. "It gets a little noisy back here, but it's not too bad."

Misha walked over to the bench and sat down, putting his small bag at his feet. "Thank you."

The stocky man sat down next to him and leaned closer. "I assume you know how important this cargo is," the man said in a quieter voice. The man's eyes were sharp and penetrating, and his face had such a serious expression on it that it made Misha feel uncomfortable.

"Yes," Misha said.

"It is your responsibility to make sure that this cargo makes it to Kuybishev undisturbed. You understand?"

"Yes, I know. I know my assignment."

The man grabbed Misha's forearm and squeezed, leaning even closer. "Listen," he said, his voice still hushed, his face still stern. "The Americans are suspicious. You can't trust those two pilots." He nodded in the direction of the cockpit. "They tried to search our cargo just before you arrived."

Another unexpected detail that he had to worry about. "Do they know?" he asked.

The stocky man let go of his arm and leaned back, wrinkling his lips and shaking his head. "The pilots don't know anything. One of them opened a suitcase, but he looked like he didn't understand anything that he saw. I sent for their commander, and he put a stop to it."

"Has this ever happened before?"

"No. That's why you have to be extra careful with these pilots. They might try something on the flight."

"Do you know them?"

"I've seen them both before, but we've never had problems with them until today. I don't know what made them so bold all of a sudden, but it makes me nervous."

The young pilot that Misha saw on the runway stepped inside the open door. He immediately stopped and turned toward them, staring at them with a sort of cold scowl. Misha and the stocky man stared back. The three of them were all frozen, and for a brief moment it seemed that time had stopped. The young American had his pilot's hat on his head now, covering his hair. He had a smooth forehead and high cheek bones that made his eyes look deep-set and serious. Then the American stepped toward them. "Who are you?" he asked.

"I'm accompanying the cargo," Misha said.

The pilot looked over at the stocky man. "What do you say, Dima, are we ready to fly?"

The stocky man looked irritated, and Misha could tell by the look on Dima's face that Dima was holding himself back. Misha sensed an acute tension between these two men, and it felt fresh, as if they had just ended a fistfight and were now thinking about going at it again. "One more passenger," Dima answered in English with a thick Russian accent.

The American looked back at Misha again with the same disdainful scowl, then turned his back to them and marched off to the cockpit at the front of the plane. Dima looked back at Misha. The cold look on Dima's face reaffirmed his distrust. He slapped Misha on the shoulder. "Be careful," he said, then left the cargo hold.

☆

Mark wiggled his way into the pilot's seat and locked himself in, then started his routine pre-flight checklist. Paulsen sat to his right. The radio man, Burns, was standing outside on the ground talking to another officer.

"So what did the colonel say?" Paulsen asked.

Mark shook his head and chose not to look at his co-pilot. "He said we're not to hinder the Russians in any way. He has orders straight from the War Department."

"Man, it figures. This whole thing feels eerie. I'm telling you, there's something going on with these Lend-Lease flights. Something just ain't quite right."

Mark looked over the dials and gauges and switches, then leaned back in his seat and turned his head to the right. "It's none of our business," he said. "Someone must know what's going on."

"Yeah, like the Russians." Paulsen looked over the controls for a second. "So what was in the suitcase?"

Mark turned in his seat toward Paulsen as best he could. "They've got maps of the whole United States in there, with bus routes and railroad routes and everything. There was also a list of strange chemicals, and all kinds of engineering diagrams. And you know what's in those crates back there?"

"What?"

"Some kind of weird-looking dirt. That burly Russian guy said it would burn my hands."

"How can dirt burn your hands?"

"I don't have a clue. Must be some kind of chemical."

"Is that Russian guy flying with us?"

"No. They've got two other guys coming along on this flight. One of them's back there already."

Paulsen leaned to his left and looked behind him, trying to see the Russian in the cargo hold, then sat up straight again. “Boy, when I joined up, I thought I’d be flying over Europe by now. Did you ever think you’d be doing stuff like this when you finished flight training?”

“Nope.”

“It’s kind of funny when you think about it. I signed up thinking I’d go serve my country, and now it feels like I’m working for the Soviets.”

“I know how you feel.”

“I don’t trust these Russians, Captain.”

“Neither do I.”

At that moment, Burns stepped into the cockpit and took his seat at the radio, and Mark told his co-pilot and radio man to make their final preparations for takeoff.

EIGHTEEN

The engines were running and a low droning sound reverberated throughout the fuselage. Two men walked in through the door on Misha's left, and Misha recognized one of them as Nikolai. The other man was much smaller, with black glasses and a pale face. The little man motioned for Nikolai to sit down next to Misha and watched carefully while Nikolai took his seat and strapped himself in, as if he were trying to see if Nikolai was hiding something from him. The man didn't smile at all, and scowled at them even worse than the American pilot had. When the little man was satisfied that Nikolai was in his seat, he walked to the front of the plane and ducked his head into the cockpit briefly and yelled at the pilots that they were ready to go. Then he came back their way, looking at Nikolai one more time before exiting the plane.

One of the pilots, not the one that Misha saw before, came back to make one final check of the cargo hold and see that the door was securely shut. "Do you speak English?" he shouted at Misha over the roar of the engines.

Misha nodded.

"We're ready for takeoff," the co-pilot said, then went back to the cockpit up front.

Misha looked over at Nikolai, who sat somberly and stared down at his hands, not paying attention to Misha at all. He was twiddling his thumbs and nervously rubbing his fingers. Misha said nothing and looked toward the front of the plane. He could barely see the two figures inside the cockpit, their hands flipping switches and their heads looking around. Then the engine noise grew louder, and Misha felt the plane start to move. They taxied for a few moments, then the engine noise got even louder. He could feel the plane barreling down the runway, bouncing and shaking and creaking, and it made all the muscles in his abdomen tighten up involuntarily. Just when he thought the plane would break apart, there was no more bouncing, he felt his body weight pressing into his seat, and he had to open his mouth and yawn to get the pressure in his ears to equalize. Within a few minutes the plane leveled off. The noise was not nearly as bad as it had been at takeoff, and there was a steady humming drone throughout the cargo hold.

He looked over at Nikolai again, who was still sitting in the same position that he had been in before takeoff, only this time he looked back at Misha, and their eyes met. Nikolai's face looked drawn and worn, as if he hadn't slept in a week and had something on his mind. His cheeks were gaunt, circles bulged under his eyes that made Misha think of Semerov, and his hair was uncombed. Maybe he already knew.

Misha wanted to smile and act friendly, but he couldn't bring himself to do it, not after what he had done. And the fact that Nikolai looked so terrible made it even worse.

"Hello, Misha." The voice was tired and apathetic.

"Nikolai, I have to tell you something." Misha's mind was suddenly full of images of Larisa, her soft cheeks, her brown hair, her beautiful eyes that always made him feel calmer inside. He looked away from Nikolai and pressed his eyes shut for a moment. He had to get those thoughts out of his mind.

Nikolai was looking down at his hands again. "I think I know what you're going to say."

The more Misha looked at him, the more tension he felt in his chest, and the harder it was to bring himself to say it. "Nikolai, I—"

"I have a bad feeling about this flight," Nikolai said, then looked over at Misha. Nikolai's eyes looked like they were about to shed tears, and his lips were pressed together so that it looked like he was frowning. The crease in the skin below his bottom lip deepened, and his chin quivered. "I think I'm under suspicion, Misha," he said. "Semerov was acting peculiar when I left, and there was no reason for him to send me down to Washington. The people at the Soviet Purchasing Commission behaved oddly around me, too, as if I had some kind of disease, and no matter where I've gone the past few weeks, there's always been someone following me around, watching everything that I do. They won't let me out of their sight."

"Nikolai, I'm sorry. I—"

"Like that guy who brought me onto the plane. He's been hovering over me all day. Usually they try to act friendly, you know, to keep you calm so that you don't think anything is wrong. But this guy didn't even try to pretend. He made sure I knew that he was watching me and that I'd better not try anything, and he always had his hand in his pocket where I couldn't see it." Nikolai put a hand up to his forehead and ran his fingers back through his hair, then let out a long, deep sigh. "I'm a dead man, Misha."

Misha recalled Larisa sitting on a stool at the kitchen table a few years ago when he told her about Malkov denouncing him. He remembered her sitting with her hands clasped in her lap, looking at him with that frightened, uncertain expression on her face. "Nikolai, I've been doing a lot of thinking the past few weeks, and I've decided that I need to talk to you."

Nikolai looked over at him. His eyes had an apathetic, desperate look of hopelessness in them. "About what?" he asked.

Misha's throat tightened. "I already know about Semerov. I already know that he's suspicious of you." Misha pressed his lips together and waited for a reaction.

Nikolai looked puzzled. "What do you mean?"

Misha swallowed and coughed into his hand, then took a deep breath to calm himself. "Last month Semerov called me into his office. He said you were acting strangely and that he wanted me to keep an eye on you for him. I didn't want to do it, but I didn't know what else to do." Misha couldn't look into Nikolai's eyes, so he stared at Nikolai's hands and took another deep breath. "So I followed you one day down to that Jewish part of town that we're not supposed to go to, and I saw you meet a man and a woman there. I didn't know what you were doing, and I didn't hear what you were talking about, but I told Semerov about it the next day."

Several seconds passed without a word, and the droning of the engines swelled inside Misha's ears as if the sound was swallowing him whole. Finally he couldn't stand it any more, so he looked up at Nikolai's face.

Nikolai stared at him with a pained look, as if Misha had just informed Nikolai that Nikolai's mother was dead. Nikolai's eyes pierced Misha to his soul, and it was agony to hold the eye contact, but he kept staring at Nikolai anyway. He owed at least that much to him, to look him in the eye after making the confession.

Nikolai maintained the eye contact for several seconds, and his eyes darted back and forth between Misha's, as if he were looking for some indication that what Misha said was not true. Then he turned his head away and covered his mouth with his hand and stared blankly forward at the wooden crates.

"I'm sorry, Nikolai." Misha had to say something, but nothing he could say would have sounded any better. The apology was weak. Was there a right way to apologize for such a betrayal?

After several seconds, Nikolai dropped his hand back into his lap and lowered his head, which he slowly shook back and forth, as if he couldn't quite comprehend what Misha's words meant. Then he put his elbow on his knee and rested his forehead in the palm of his right hand. "It's all right, Misha," he said. "I don't blame you for what you did. If you had done anything else, Semerov would have suspected you, too." Nikolai put his hands on his knees and raised his head. "It's all right. Really. Don't worry about it."

Misha had a lump in his throat and he couldn't bear to look at that tired, anxious face any longer, so he leaned forward and rested his forearms on his thighs and stared at his shoes. "I had wanted to talk to you before now, but there was no way I could have contacted you in Washington. I tried to get that stocky guy to let me talk to you before we got on the plane, but he wouldn't allow it and I didn't want him to get curious about anything."

"Don't worry about it, Misha. Honestly. I don't blame you for it."

"I wanted to warn you, to give you a chance to run."

Nikolai reached over and put an arm around Misha's shoulders. "Misha, there's nothing you could have done. You know that. You and I are in the same boat. We do what we're told. We have to. Otherwise . . ." Nikolai couldn't finish the sentence. It was better not to talk about such things. "Misha, turn the whole situation around and look at it from a different perspective. If Semerov had told me that you were acting strangely and that I should follow you, I would have done the same thing you did."

"Would you?"

"Yes."

"I don't believe it."

"Well, I would have. And you know why."

Misha imagined Larisa sitting on their bed, a pillow propped up behind her, the newborn baby cradled in her arms. The baby whom he hadn't seen in almost two years.

Nikolai took his arm off of Misha's shoulders, then unstrapped himself and stood up. He walked over to one of the wooden crates and leaned against it, studying it, holding it in his hands with reverence, as if it were the Ark of the Covenant or some great artistic masterpiece.

Misha arose and walked over to Nikolai. He leaned against the same crate and faced Nikolai on the opposite side. "What are you going to do?" he asked.

Nikolai looked up at him. "What *can* I do?"

"We're not in the Soviet Union yet."

"What is that supposed to mean?"

Misha looked around the cargo hold at the suitcases and crates and other boxes. "Well, this plane is going to land in Alaska before it goes on to Kuybishev."

"You think I should make a run for it in Alaska?" Nikolai laughed. "It would never work, Misha. Think about it. The instant this plane touches the ground, it's going to be surrounded by Soviet troops, and these three Americans up front are going to be replaced by Soviet pilots. If I was going to run, I should have done it back in Washington or New York."

"There has to be a way," Misha said.

"Like what?"

Misha let go of the crate and walked by the black suitcases, running his finger across the top of one. He stopped and noticed a piece of paper at his feet, which he leaned down and picked up. It was a shipping label. *Director, Institute of Technical and Economic Information*, it read. It must have fallen out of one of the suitcases when that American opened it.

He slipped the paper inside the white cord of another suitcase, then headed over to a small window at the right side of the plane. A vast blue sky stretched out in all directions as far as the eye could see, and several white clouds sailed beneath the plane against a backdrop of earth. He stood there for several minutes and thought of Larisa and the baby back home. Did she even know he was coming? Would she even recognize him when she saw him?

He turned around and looked back at the wooden crate where Nikolai was standing, and it took a few seconds for his eyes to readjust to the dim light inside the plane. Nikolai walked back to his seat. The tall, slender figure sat down and leaned back, resting his head against the inside of the cargo hold. Misha made his way back past the suitcases and crates and sat down next to him.

"Any ideas?" Nikolai asked.

"Just one."

"Well, let's have it."

Misha nodded toward the front of the plane. "What about those two pilots and their radio man?"

"What about them?"

"Maybe they could help us."

Nikolai leaned forward and looked toward the cockpit. "I doubt it."

"It's worth a try, isn't it? You've got nothing to lose."

Nikolai started nodding slowly, and Misha could tell that he had him thinking. "You've given me an idea," Nikolai said. "If I can get one of them to make a phone call once we're on the ground, then I might have a chance." He turned toward Misha. "Don't you think you're taking an awfully big risk?"

"What do you mean?"

"What if they don't go along with it? What if they talk? It'll be your head as well as mine."

"I know," Misha said. "But I could never live with myself knowing that you were repressed because of me. You'd do the same."

Nikolai gave him a blank look. "Yes. Of course I would."

"Then let's do it."

Misha made his way to the front of the plane and stuck his head into the cockpit. It was open, and he knocked on the side of the door to get the Americans' attention. The young man in the seat on the left turned around and seemed surprised to see him. "Take over, will you, Paulsen?" the young man said. "I'll go back and see what they want." The pilot got out of his seat and followed Misha back to the cargo hold, where the young captain stood in front of Misha and Nikolai. "What's the problem?" the American asked.

"I know you're going to find this hard to believe," Misha said. "But we need your help."

NINETEEN

Mark looked at the two Russians standing before him. The one on his left was about the same height as he was, with dark hair like his own. The one on the right was tall and skinny, and it was this one that really caught his eye, because the man's skin was a sickly gray color, as if he were anemic, and his cheeks were sunken in. His eyes had circles under them and he looked as though he hadn't eaten a good meal in at least a week. They both watched him, waiting for some response. Neither spoke a word, and Mark looked back and forth between them a couple of times, scrutinizing their facial expressions and body language. Something felt very wrong about all this.

"What do you mean, help?"

The two men paused and exchanged glances between themselves as if they weren't sure what to do, as if they hadn't really thought through whatever it was that they were up to and were now trying to think of something on the spot. Their hesitation made him nervous. If you're a couple of Russian spies and you're going to pull something, are you more likely to stand around looking like idiots while you try to come up with a plan, or would you have already carefully thought it through? What if it were him? Yes. Definitely. He'd have it all planned out so that no decision-making would be necessary, only the execution. But these guys obviously hadn't. Could they be sincere?

He looked at their eyes closely as they glanced back and forth. These two Russians looked serious, and if that wasn't fear that he saw in those eyes, then he didn't know what fear was. But they're Russians! You can't trust a Russian, especially not these two, not with all these sealed black suitcases and crates of chemicals heading for the Soviet Union. Colonel Griggs' words echoed in his ears—the most pigheaded people he's ever worked with. That's right. The only way to deal with the Russians is to take the hard line.

It took him only a few seconds for these thoughts to pass through his head. He saw that the tall skinny one was about to speak, so he decided to pre-empt him. "Look here," Mark said in the most authoritative voice he could muster. "I don't know what you guys are up to, but I have better things to do than stand around waiting for you two to figure out what it is that you want to tell me. Now if you need help with something, then tell me what it is. You do speak English, don't you?"

The skinny man nodded.

"Is there something wrong with the cargo?"

"No, no. Nothing like that," the man said.

"Then what is it?"

The man glanced over at the other guy momentarily, as if waiting for permission to speak or asking for reassurance, and the other guy nudged his head toward him as if telling him to go ahead. The man looked back at Mark. "It's a long story," he said. "And it's hard to explain. I don't know where to start."

"Well if this doesn't beat all," Mark said. "Don't test my patience. And don't try to pull anything."

The man looked anxious all of a sudden and held up his hands in front of his chest. "No, of course not. We're serious. We need your help. It's just that . . ." The man looked over at his buddy again, who nodded his head at him. "It's just that–well, what we have to say is a very sensitive matter, and we're not sure how we should begin, especially since we don't know you."

The man's English was flawless. Either these two guys were really in some kind of trouble, or they were very good actors. "Well," Mark said in a softer tone of voice, "why don't we start with your names."

The man put his hands down and said something to the other man in Russian that Mark couldn't understand, and the other guy answered back in Russian. "My name is Nikolai," the man said to Mark. "And this is Misha," he said, pointing to the other guy.

Mark pointed to the tall skinny guy. "Nikolai." He pointed to the other one. "Misha."

They both nodded.

"And you speak English, too, right?" he asked, still pointing at Misha.

"Yes," Misha said.

"My name is Captain Daniels." There was another long pause, and the two Russians still looked like they didn't know what to do. There was no color in their faces, and the one guy, Misha, was biting his bottom lip, while the skinny guy, Nikolai, was wringing his hands. The spectacle of these two Russians standing here in his cargo hold on his plane, wanting to tell him something but scared to death to do so, swept away all the nervousness and fear that he himself had just felt a moment ago. "You don't know if you can trust me, do you?" he said.

Nikolai held his hands up in front of his chest again, only this time they were clenched into nervous fists, and then he pushed his right fist into his left hand and started squeezing it. The other guy, Misha, put his hand up to his mouth and started running his fingers across his lips, and it was obvious that neither of these two had any idea what to do next.

"Tell you what," Mark said. "Why don't you two have a seat."

Misha and Nikolai sat down on the bench with the seats on it, and Mark grabbed a couple of parachute packs off the wall and sat down on them in front of the Russians. This was a good arrangement, because the two parachute packs were farther up off the floor than the little bench that the Russians were sitting on, so it allowed Mark to sit higher up and look down on them, and it forced them to look up at him. He didn't know what psychological effect the arrangement might have on them, but it gave him a strange and pleasant feeling of reassurance, letting him know that he was in command here, like a judge seated behind a raised bench or a king sitting on an exalted throne.

"I don't know what I need to do to help you two trust me," he said, "but perhaps I should start out by letting you know where I'm coming from." He leaned forward and made sure his voice was strong and sharp and clear, and he pointed a scolding finger at them. "I don't trust you people. You understand? I don't trust you Russians, or you Soviets, at all." He kept his eye contact with them, but swung his arm around the back of him and pointed at the cargo. "You fill my planes with fifty black suitcases a pop and say that it's luggage, when I know very well that those things are full of documents and diagrams and scientific papers and who knows what else, and now you've got my plane loaded with crates full of some dangerous chemical substance, and you won't even tell me what it is. I'm a pilot, you see? I'm responsible for the safety of every person on board, and I don't like it when I have to fly stuff around that could explode or start a fire if I make a wrong turn in flight or something. My safety's on the line too, you know. So if you don't trust me, that's just fine, because I sure don't trust you." He sat up straight and put his hands on his hips. "Now that we've got that out of the way, what is it you want to tell me?"

He waited for their response and was a little worried about his approach, but he thought of Griggs and his own father and decided that he didn't care. He looked carefully at the two men's faces and noticed that they were calmer now, less agitated.

"You're right," Nikolai began, and he moved his hands as he spoke. "We're spies." Nikolai looked over at Misha, whose face was so white that he looked like a ghost. Nikolai's face was still gray, but he didn't look nearly as paralyzed with fear as Misha did. "Well, we're not exactly spies. What I mean is, we're spies, but we're really accountants."

"You're spies, but you're accountants."

"Yes."

"How does that work?"

Nikolai leaned forward and looked into his hands as he spoke. "You see, we're not really professional agents. We're not military men, we're not with the secret police, we never chose to work for the government at all." Nikolai looked a little frustrated, and he bobbed his head back and forth a couple of times as he tried to figure out how he wanted to phrase things. "Okay, so we actually do work for the secret police, but we're not really with the secret police, because we're really just accountants. Does that make sense?"

"No."

Nikolai nodded. "All right, let me explain. You see, in our homeland, we were just ordinary citizens, and we worked as accountants. But in the Soviet Union, the government controls everything. And the government decided that it needed accountants who understand international financial systems to work for the NKVD overseas."

"What's the NKVD?"

"The People's Commissariat for Internal Affairs. It's basically the secret police, but it also does espionage in foreign countries. A couple of years ago its name was changed to the NKGB, then back to the NKVD after the Germans invaded the Soviet Union, and a couple of months ago it became the NKGB again."

"Which stands for . . . ?"

"The People's Committee for State Security. But that's beside the point. The point is that we were recruited into this organization against our will and forced to come here to work in America to help the Soviet government gather intelligence."

Mark put his hands on his knees and started shaking his head. "Recruited by force?" he asked. "I don't believe it."

"No, it's true."

"But that doesn't make any sense. How could the government trust you, especially with matters of national security, if it knew that you don't really want to be here?"

"They know they can trust us because our families are still in the Soviet Union. We have no control over what might happen to them."

Mark put up his hands. "Wait just a minute. You're telling me that the Soviet government is holding your families hostage so that you will spy for the Soviet Union?"

"Yes."

Mark watched Nikolai's eyes closely. The man looked sincere, but the story was hard to buy. "I've never heard of anything like that before," he said.

Nikolai nodded. "I know. But you have to believe us."

"If what you're saying is true, then doesn't that mean you shouldn't be talking to me? Won't you be arrested, or shot, if your government finds out?"

Nikolai nodded again. "Please, you must trust us. I'm begging you. We're telling the truth."

"All right, all right. So let's assume that what you're saying is true. Why are you telling this to me? And why now? Just look around. We're on an airplane that is heading to the Soviet Union as we speak. It seems like you've picked a pretty bad time and place to come out with this. I mean, you're going to be home in a day or so, aren't you?"

"I know, I know. You are right. Absolutely right. Everything you are saying is the absolute truth. But I can explain. You see, a few months ago I made contact with an American agent. A woman. She and I were working on a deal." Nikolai glanced over at Misha, then hung his head lower and stared down. "She said the American government might let me stay here if I give her information about Soviet operations here in the United States."

Mark noticed a change in the facial expression of Misha, who perked up at this and was looking at Nikolai as if this was news to him. Mark pointed at Misha. "Were you part of this deal, too?"

"No," Misha said. "I know nothing of this."

Mark turned back to Nikolai. "I thought you said your family was being held hostage back in Russia, and that if you ever squeal, something bad will happen to them."

Nikolai sat there for a long time without saying anything, and when he finally lifted his head a little, tears were streaming down both cheeks. He tried to speak, but his voice cracked. "A few months ago . . ." He couldn't say anything for a few more seconds, and he cleared his throat a couple of times to get hold of himself. "A few months ago, I found out that my wife and two sons . . ." He pressed his eyes shut and his whole face tensed up, and crease lines appeared around his eyes and on his forehead and around his mouth, and he put both hands up to his face. He coughed a couple of times and started to cry out loud, and then he lost all control of himself for several seconds, and Mark and Misha watched without saying a word. Finally Nikolai breathed in and blurted out in a voice that was barely audible over the drone of the engines, "They starved to death during the siege of Leningrad."

Nikolai sat hunched over with his face buried in his hands and cried for at least a minute or two, and his body shook. From the look on Misha's face, Mark could tell that Misha hadn't known about this, either, for Misha turned his head away and put his hand up to his chin in a pensive pose and was blinking over and over again to keep himself from crying. As Mark watched Nikolai's pathetic figure literally writhing before him, he felt a lump rising in his own throat, and the tension drained out of his shoulders. This was too real. These guys couldn't be faking it.

Finally Nikolai calmed himself down enough to sit up again and wipe his eyes. "I'm sorry," he said. "I'm sorry."

"It's all right," Mark said, and suddenly he felt guilty for taking the hard line against these guys.

"This is the first time that I have told anyone about this," Nikolai said.

Misha put a hand on Nikolai's shoulder.

"Are you okay?" Mark asked. "Can I get you anything?"

"No, I'm fine. Really." Nikolai took a deep breath through his nostrils, then pulled out a handkerchief and wiped his eyes and nose. "Anyway, it was after I received the news about my family that I decided I had nothing to go back to in the Soviet Union. I started meeting with an FBI agent, an American lady named Rose Petersen, and she was going to arrange for me to defect. She wanted to know why the Soviet Purchasing Commission in Washington, D.C. was so interested in uranium chemicals, so I told her that I would find out what I could."

"Uranium chemicals?" Mark interrupted. "Is that what that dirt is?"

"Yes."

"So that stuff is radioactive?"

"Yes."

So that's what Dima meant when he had said it would burn his hands.

Nikolai continued. "The problem with my defection is that the United States and the Soviet Union are officially allies right now, so the American government was worried that if it granted me asylum officially, it would offend the Soviet government and hurt the war effort. So we were going to stage an accident and fake my death so that the Soviet government would never know. We were planning to do this sometime in April or May, but then Semerov got suspicious and the next thing I knew, I was at the Soviet Purchasing Commission packing documents into all these black suitcases."

"Who's Semerov?"

"He's the NKGB resident in New York City. He's the head of a huge spy network, and he's very good at what he does. He has a sixth sense about who is loyal and who isn't, who is reliable and who can't be trusted. I was too careless. I spent too much time in the office. I didn't smile and laugh and joke enough when I talked to other people, and I guess he noticed it. I did a good job of pretending that everything was normal, even after I learned about my wife and sons, but it was making me crazy. The more I pretended, the more I could feel my own mind slipping away from me, until finally I reached the point that not even my fear of Semerov could keep me going on in that artificial state of denial that I was living in. I guess the strain started to show, and he picked up on it like a bloodhound on a scent."

"And all this was going on in New York City."

"Yes. In the Amtorg building."

"Amtorg?"

"It's a trading organization that does business for the Soviet Union in the United States. It's where we do most of our work. Anyway, the point is that Semerov is sending me back to the Soviet Union because he thinks I'm a traitor. If the NKGB in Moscow gets a hold of me, they'll kill me."

"Why didn't you run? Why did you let yourself get on this plane?"

"Because I didn't know. I thought this was just another assignment. I noticed that people were acting strange around me, but it wasn't until this morning when I was with that little guy who never smiled that it all came together. That's when I started to think that I might be in trouble. But by that time it was too late to run, and I still wasn't a hundred percent sure that I was under suspicion until I saw Misha on the plane. I added everything up and started to get very worried, and my guess was that I had been denounced. Then Misha told me about Semerov right after takeoff, and my worst fears were confirmed."

Mark looked over at Misha. "So how do you fit into all of this?"

"Semerov assigned me to keep an eye on Nikolai during this flight and keep him at ease so that he wouldn't get suspicious. I have to see that he arrives safely in Kuybishev."

"In the Soviet Union."

"Yes. If he's not on this plane when it arrives, then I'm dead, too."

This was unbelievable. He had heard some tall tales from his father that cowboys used to tell around campfires back in the old days, but this beat them all. "Well, you sure don't seem to be doing your job very well. Why are you helping him?"

"Nikolai is my friend."

Mark put his hands up to his forehead. "I just can't believe this," he said. He dropped his hands to his lap. "So now you want me to help you escape once we get to Alaska."

"No." Nikolai leaned forward and looked almost panicky. "No, we can't do that."

"Why not?"

"Two problems. First, we'd never make it. You've flown these flights before, haven't you? You know what it's like. Soviet troops will surround this plane the moment it lands. There's no way we could evade them."

"Well, we could put you in a crate or something and haul you off before the Soviet flight crew takes over. We might be able to give you a five- or ten-minute window of opportunity, maybe even longer."

"It's not possible. There's another problem. Even if we make it, Misha's wife and son are still in the Soviet Union."

"So what you're saying is that you can't make a run for it all by yourself because Misha here will get shot if you do, and the two of you can't make a run for it together because Misha's wife and son will be punished."

"Yes."

Simply unbelievable. "What's your plan then? What do you want me to do?"

Nikolai pulled out a notepad and a pencil from his pocket and started writing. "I need you to make a phone call."

"That's it?"

"Yes. Call this number and ask for the Chief, or Director Robinson. They're the same person. This is a direct line, so he should answer the phone himself. Then tell him that you need to speak to Rose. He'll ask you which Rose you want, and you'll say you want Rose Petersen. He'll say she's unavailable and he'll ask to take a message for her, and you'll tell him that Rose's cousin Alfred is sick and would like to see her."

"Are you writing all this down?"

"Yes. It's very important that you follow these instructions exactly. Otherwise he might not trust you. The only problem you might have is that you are an American, and he might be expecting someone with a Russian accent. But don't worry. He'll just ask you if this is Alfred calling, and you'll say no. After that you can have a normal conversation with him."

"A normal conversation?"

"Well, what I mean is that there are no more code words or anything like that."

"Who's Alfred?"

"I'm Alfred."

Mark just nodded. Nikolai wrote for a few minutes and filled several pages of the notepad, then handed the whole thing over to Mark. “Just tell him what I’ve written in this notepad.”

Mark looked over the pages to make sure that he could read everything that Nikolai had written, then tucked the notepad into his shirt pocket. “Is that all I have to do?”

“Yes. Please make sure that no one sees that notepad. Don’t tell anyone anything about what we’ve discussed, not even your commanding officers. My life is depending on it.”

They all stood up and shook hands. “I’ll make the call just as soon as we land in Alaska,” he said.

“Thank you,” Nikolai said.

“Yes, thank you,” Misha added, and Mark could see the desperation and gratitude in their eyes.

“Try not to worry too much,” he told them. “I believe your story. You can trust me.”

He put the parachutes back, then returned to the cockpit and took his place behind the controls.

“Man, I was beginning to think that you were never coming back,” Paulsen said. “I thought those Russians might have done something to you. What did they want?”

“Nothing,” Mark said, and he could feel the little notepad in his breast pocket pushing against his chest, right over his heart. “Just worried about their cargo.”

TWENTY

After Misha watched Captain Daniels disappear into the cockpit, he turned to see that Nikolai had been staring at the young American as well. "What do you think?" he asked. "Can we trust him?"

"Do we have a choice?" Nikolai put his pencil back into his pocket and sat down.

Misha sat down next to him. "Are you going to tell me what your plan is?"

Nikolai leaned back and put his face in his hands and stretched for a moment, then clasped his hands around his belt line. "The way I see it, my only hope is to convince Semerov and the NKGB that I'm not a traitor. Would you agree?"

"Absolutely."

"If this American pilot can get through to the FBI, then Rose Petersen can go to Semerov and pose as a dealer in nickel. Have you done any work on the nickel deal?"

"No."

"The Americans have put up a trade barrier to prevent the Soviet Union from purchasing nickel for some reason, so nobody will sell nickel to us. All Rose Petersen has to do is go to Amtorg and tell Semerov that after meeting with me, she has agreed to sell nickel to us. Once she delivers the goods, Semerov should be convinced that she's legitimate, and that will explain why I was meeting with her and that other man on the night you followed me."

"But Semerov thinks she might be an FBI agent," Misha said. "He told me so himself."

"That's still not a problem, as long as he believes that the reason I met with her was to purchase nickel. Who knows, maybe this will convince him that she's not an agent. You see, Misha, this is why Semerov has the advantage. He has you and me so paranoid that we don't even talk to each other about our work, even though we might have information that we could use to help each other."

"What if Rose Petersen doesn't get the message, or decides not to go to Amtorg?" Misha asked. "And even if she does, what if Semerov doesn't take the bait?"

Nikolai leaned back and stretched out his long torso again. His face looked more placid. He was definitely calmer. "Then I'm dead," he said.

Misha leaned back in his seat as well. It was easier to relax now. There was something reassuring about having a plan, even though he didn't know if it would work. It was much better than fretting over what to do.

"You've taken a big risk for me, Misha," Nikolai said.

"I betrayed you."

"You did what you thought you had to do."

"I betrayed you, Nikolai. I got selfish. I had a weak moment, and I betrayed you."

"But you've atoned for it. I don't blame you for what you did."

"You're a gracious man, Nikolai. Thank you."

"You must realize that you and I are different now, Misha."

"In what way?"

"You still have something to lose. I don't. I know how much you want to see your wife and son. How long has it been for you, two years?"

"Almost."

"And you were willing to take the risk that you might never see them again, just to try to save me."

"I'm not a hero, Nikolai. I did an evil thing, and now I'm living with the consequences. At best, I'm just a prodigal."

Nikolai chuckled softly. "A prodigal. Do you know where that term comes from?"

"Yes."

"Are you a religious man?"

"I don't know."

"You want to hear something funny?"

Misha looked over at Nikolai, who was smiling. "What?"

"I'm a Baptist."

Misha leaned forward and turned himself toward Nikolai. "A Baptist? You're joking."

Nikolai was still leaning back, looking up at the ceiling, his head resting on the back of the seat. He was still smiling. "No, it's true. But don't tell that to Semerov. My parents were the most religious people I knew, and they raised me in the faith until I was twelve years old. They were murdered by the Bolsheviks during the civil war, and I was raised by my grandmother until she passed away. By then I was almost an adult, so I took care of myself from then on. How about yourself?"

This was a strange conversation to be having, and Misha wondered for a moment if Nikolai had snapped under the stress, but it was better than thinking about the trip ahead of them, so he decided to go along. "My uncle was a priest."

"Orthodox?"

"Yes."

"Tell me about him."

The one solid rule that had kept Misha alive during the past decade and a half was that he knew how to keep his mouth shut, and Nikolai's request took him off guard. He thought it over for a few seconds, then decided to go ahead and answer. "He was repressed eleven years ago because he refused to deny his faith."

"How did it happen?" Nikolai asked.

"We lived in a village back then, not far from the Ukrainian border. The censorship squads were burning books in the village square and decided to burn all the books and records in my uncle's church. I was watching the people fuel the bonfires by throwing books on them, and I overheard their intention. So I ran to the church as fast as I could and told my uncle about it. He took the key to the church door and put it in a little wooden box along with a small black book, then he put the box in my hands and told me to run into the forest and hide. 'Take this book and guard it with your life,' he said. 'Carry it with you and follow its precepts, and it will guide you to peace and happiness.' Those were his words. Then he hugged me and told me that he loved me and that he would always remember me, and I ran to the forest and cried. I climbed a tree and stayed close enough to the edge of the forest that I could see the front of the church when the mob came.

"My uncle had closed the door and barricaded himself in the church's tower, and I could see his figure in the window. He watched the mob quietly and made no resistance, and it took the people over an hour before they finally were able to take a log and bust through the entrance. They pulled my uncle out of the church, and they beat him as they went. They threw him to the ground and dragged him across the dirt by his beard, and little children kicked him in the face while some of the older boys from the village jumped on him. He disappeared in the mob for a few minutes and I couldn't see him, and then he was visible again as they picked him up and lifted him over their heads. They threw him in the back of a horse-drawn cart and made him stand up in front of the people. One of the political leaders of the censorship squad demanded that he denounce his faith in front of the villagers, and promised that if he would do so, his life would be spared. But he refused, so they took him away."

"The villagers turned against your uncle?"

"Only some of them. The villagers followed along and watched because they were afraid of what would happen to them if they didn't, but most of them respected my uncle and belonged to his congregation. It was only a few of them who joined the censorship squad in the mob." Misha leaned forward and rested his elbows on his knees and picked at his fingernails while he stared at the floor, and he sensed Nikolai sitting up and leaning forward next to him. Misha was tired of talking and didn't want to say any more about his uncle, so he turned toward Nikolai and changed the subject. "That's interesting that you're a Baptist," he said. "I didn't think the NKVD would ever recruit a Baptist." He sat back in his seat again. "I didn't think a Baptist would ever agree to serve in the NKVD."

"Well, I guess I'm not a real Baptist," Nikolai said. "Not like my parents were. But it probably explains why I've decided to defect to the United States."

"Why is that?"

"Because of the religious culture in the United States. Haven't you ever looked around some of these old American towns? Many of them were built around churches. The church was the center of the community."

"There's nothing unique about that, Nikolai. You could say the same thing about Europe or the Soviet Union, too."

Nikolai continued without responding to this. "Or have you ever read American history books and noticed how much of a role religion played in the people's thinking? Especially in the thinking of their leaders. It's astounding."

"Semerov would repress you for sure if he caught you reading an American history book."

Nikolai smiled. "The thing that impresses me the most about the United States is how much Christianity has influenced American culture."

"The same is true of Europe and the Soviet Union."

"But there's a difference. In America, there were many different Christian groups. The was no single state church."

Misha thought about the Russian Orthodox Church, the Church of England, and the Catholic Church. "All right," he said. "But what's your point?"

"The point is that the United States was the first Western nation that did not use an established state church in order to exploit the people politically. Yet at the same time, the United States preserved a general national religion."

"Christianity?"

"Yes. Don't you see what the Americans did? They abolished the state church, but preserved the national religion. In this way they preserved their political freedom, without losing their Christian virtues. And even though the dominant religious culture was Protestant Christianity, there was still tolerance toward Catholics, Jews, and other religions as well."

"I never thought of it that way," Misha said.

"Notice also the irony in the fact that the Americans, without a state church, took Christianity more seriously—unlike the Europeans, whose religions were so full of pomp and ceremony and tradition. The Americans treated their Bible as if it were really true. That's why morality was always so much more protected in the United States than in Europe."

Misha shook his head. "You're a dangerous man, Nikolai. I had no idea you thought about all this. If the Party knew what goes through your head, you'd be repressed immediately."

Nikolai nodded. "True. And that's the other thing that impresses me about the United States. The whole country is founded upon the idea that individuals should be free. I think that's why there is so much prosperity and happiness in America."

Misha thought of the communists' red banners parading down the streets of Moscow with the words "freedom" and "equality" emblazoned on them in white, visible from a kilometer away. "I don't know," he said. "I still can't figure it out."

"Figure what out?"

"What went so wrong in the Soviet Union. Why so many people are slaughtered all the time like animals. The communists did it for years before the Germans started doing it to us, but only the Germans are labeled our enemy. The Soviets, on the other hand, can do no wrong. Communism is based on the idea of freedom, too, but as far as I can tell, it's all empty slogans and meaningless banners and ignorant people repeating the Party line."

Nikolai squeezed Misha's shoulder. "But don't you see the difference? Communism promises freedom to the people as a group, whereas the American idea of liberty promises freedom to the people as individuals. Any group, without individuals, doesn't exist. It's a vague, meaningless entity. But an individual, with or without a group identity, is still an individual. In the Soviet Union, who has all the power and privilege and rights?"

"The Party."

"But who is the Party?"

"I don't even know any more."

"Exactly. The Party is whoever has the power and privilege and rights, but the individuals who make up the Party are changing all the time. The Party today is the same Communist Party that existed ten years ago, when you look at its basic creeds. But the Party, as a group of individuals, is made up of different people now than it was ten years ago. Some individuals who had rights when they were members of the Party back then don't have those rights today, because they were excluded from the Party. And other people who didn't have any rights back then, because they weren't members of the Party, have rights today because they joined the Party. Does that make sense?"

"I'm not sure."

"Didn't you and your wife get a better apartment once you joined the Party?"

"Yes. It even had a telephone."

"And when you became a member of the NKVD?"

"We got an even better apartment."

Nikolai got up and walked over to the wooden crate again. In spite of the energy that he exuded while he spoke, he still looked ragged and pale. "It makes me depressed to think that I'm going back there," he said. "How about you?"

An empty, depressing feeling settled over Misha, as if a dark, heavy vapor had permeated the entire aircraft. "I just want to see my wife and son again."

The time passed slowly, and it was dark outside when the plane finally landed. Mark and Paulsen and Burns got off, and a Russian crew went aboard. The two Russians in the cargo hold never even had a chance to get off the plane. The aircraft was refueled and was back in the air almost immediately, and now that it was piloted by a Soviet crew and headed toward Siberia, Mark headed for the nearest phone.

He made sure he was alone, then pulled the notepad out of

his pocket, picked up the receiver, and had the operator put him through to Washington, D.C.

"Hello." The connection was a little fuzzy, but the man's voice was strong and clear.

"Yes, I need to speak with the Chief," Mark said.

"The Chief?"

"Uh, yes. Director Robinson."

"May I ask who is calling?"

"Uh . . ." Mark rubbed the back of his finger against his forehead. "Could you please just put me through to Director Robinson? It's very important."

"You're speaking to him."

"Oh. Good. Yes." The paper, the paper, look at the paper. "I need to speak to Rose." For several seconds there was no response, and Mark couldn't tell if the noise he heard was the rustling of papers or just static on the line. "Hello?"

"I'm still here. Could you please give me a second to close the door?"

"Sure."

Several more seconds passed, and the voice was back on the line. "Which Rose did you want?"

"Rose Petersen."

The man on the other end of the line cleared his throat. "I'm sorry, Rose Petersen is not available to take your call right now. Could I take a message for her?"

"Yes. I was calling to let her know that her cousin Alfred is sick and wants to see her."

"Is this Alfred calling?"

"No."

"Who are you, then?"

A name. Was it safe to use his own? A name, a name, a name. "John."

"Where's Alfred?"

"He's on a plane to the Soviet Union right now, and he's in a lot of danger. But he gave me a message that I need you to pass on to Rose Petersen."

"How about I send Rose Petersen to meet you."

"No, there's no time," Mark said. "We have to do this over the phone, and we have to do it right now."

Mark could tell that Robinson was thinking. "All right, John," the voice said. "I'm listening."

TWENTY-ONE

Misha felt that he was living in a dream when the driver dropped him off in front of the apartment building in Sverdlovsk where Larisa and Kolya were living. A minute later he stood in front of the door and held the key in his right hand, palm up, examining the little piece of metal that would now give him access to everything he loved and held dear. He was trembling. He stared at the keyhole in the door for a moment, then quietly inserted the little piece of metal and turned it gently. He opened the door as quietly as he could and slipped inside, closing the door behind him with great care. He set his bag down on the floor, and when he turned away from the door, the first thing that caught his eye was a familiar fur coat with a rich brown color and magnificently soft texture that hung on the wall in the entryway. He reached out and touched it.

The apartment was silent. He tiptoed down the short hallway and glanced into the kitchen on the right, but it was empty, so he took a few steps further to where two glass doors with curtains on them opened into a living room on his left. Only one of the doors was open, and he hid himself behind the door that was closed. He gently gripped the side of the door with his hand and put his face up to the white paint, then slowly peered around the edge of the door to see what was in the room.

Larisa sat on a small sofa against one wall. Her head was turned slightly away from him, and she was gazing with a melancholy stare toward the windows on the side of the room opposite the two glass doors where Misha stood. The late winter sunlight from outside illuminated the room through the thin white curtains of the large windows and cast a soft light on everything it touched, and the glow it cast upon his wife made her look like an angel.

She wore a simple dress that hung lightly from her round

shoulders. Her skin was bare a couple of centimeters below her collar bone, and he could see how pure and healthy her skin tone was. Her hair was light brown, lighter than he remembered it, and it shined. It was parted in the middle and flowed around the sides of her head in large, radiant waves. Her skin looked soft and smooth and milky white and had no trace of even the slightest blemish. Her lips were supple and full, and her high cheekbones highlighted her dark brown eyes. The lashes were long and black, and as he stood there admiring her, he felt a tension in his chest that rose to the bottom of his throat, and his lips began to quiver. He blinked several times, then stepped out from behind the closed door.

Her head jerked around and she looked terrified for a moment, then her eyes grew wide and her mouth opened and she put a hand up to her lips. He stepped inside the room and stood in front of the doors. She stared at him for a second as if she didn't recognize him, then she looked like she didn't really believe it was him, and then she jumped up and rushed over to him. She threw her arms around his neck and pressed the full length of her body against him, and he wrapped his arms around her and could feel her shoulder blades with his fingers.

He felt a tear escape from his left eye and stream down the side of his face. It hung on the skin at the edge of his jaw for a moment before it finally broke free and plummeted downward, and a tear from his right eye broke free and flowed down to where their cheeks were pressed together. Their faces were wet. He ran his hands through her hair and kissed her repeatedly. He felt her hands on his back and in his own hair and her soft lips on his chin and on his mouth, and every little movement they made accentuated the softness and smoothness of her skin and the agility of her body, and he was kissing her earlobes and smelling the gentle fragrance of her hair. And then she was shaking, shivering, trembling in his arms and he had to close his eyes but the tears kept coming and he could tell she was trying to say something but couldn't stop crying, and he knew that he couldn't speak yet himself because the tightness in his throat was so intense that it was painful. He held her tightly against himself and wished that they could die right then in each other's arms and never be separated again.

They held each other in silence for several minutes, and neither one could speak. When the tightness in his throat finally started to subside, he put his hands on her shoulders and gently pushed her away from him so that he could see her face again. She looked back at him into his eyes and there were still tears streaming down her cheeks. Her skin was so luxuriously white and smooth and her hair radiated and her eyes sparkled and she was so irresistibly beautiful that he put his hands up to her cheeks and caressed her face and stroked her scalp with the tips of his fingers. He kissed her softly on the lips again, and he felt her hands on the back of his. He held her there for the longest time until they were back in each others' arms with their cheeks pressed together and his lips close to her ear and he was smelling the fresh scent of her hair.

"Oh, Misha," she whispered, and the sound of her voice made his ears tingle and sent goose bumps down the back of his neck.

"I'm home," he said.

"Yes."

They held each other for a couple more minutes, and once again he put his hands on her shoulders and gently pushed her away from him and looked into her eyes. At that moment she was the only woman in the world, and he let his fingers glide across her forehead and he pushed her hair behind her ear.

"I can't believe it," she said.

"What?"

"That you're really here. That it's really you."

She took his hand in her own. Her hand was small and slender and soft, and he stroked the back of it with his thumb, then lifted it to his lips and kissed it. Her eyes were magnificent.

"Come on," she said as she pulled his hand and led him out of the room. "There's someone else who needs to see you."

They walked down the short hallway and entered a small

bedroom to the right. A single bed stood against one wall, a crib next to it, and a beautiful baby boy was standing up in the crib with his hands wrapped around the rail, looking up at them quietly with large, brown eyes. Larisa let go of Misha's hand and stood off to the side. She folded her arms in front of her and looked at the baby.

Misha glanced at her. "May I?" he said, pointing at the crib.

"Of course." Then she addressed the baby. "Kolya, this is your daddy. He's come home."

Misha walked slowly toward the crib and kept his gaze fixed on those big brown eyes that stared back at him. He examined the fingers on the rail, the hands, the little shoulders, the round head and puffy cheeks and thin hair. "He's beautiful," he said.

As he reached the edge of the crib, Kolya let go of the rail and sat down, stuck his fingers in his mouth and looked up at Misha curiously. Misha rested his hands on the rail and watched him for a few seconds, then held out his arms. "Kolya," he said softly. "Do you want to come see your daddy?"

The little boy gnawed on his fingers, and Misha saw a couple of tiny front teeth. Kolya's eyes looked perplexed. He stared at Misha and seemed worried, then he looked over at Larisa several times. Then the round face wrinkled up. The eyelids squinted and the brown irises disappeared, the fingers came out of the mouth and the mouth opened wide, the little lungs drew in a deep breath of air, and suddenly a frightened wailing sound pierced the air and sliced into Misha's ears like a razor. Another deep little breath, and the crying intensified.

Misha's heart sank. His chest cavity felt like it was about to implode, and he pulled his hands back and let them rest again on the rail.

Larisa stepped up next to him and leaned over the rail down into the crib. Her hands grabbed the baby around his sides under his arms and lifted him up, up to safety, up away from that frightening stranger that made him cry. "Oh, Kolya, Kolya. Shhhh. It's all right, Kolya. It's okay." She held the baby against her body, one arm under him, the other supporting his little back, her hand on the back of his head, and she stroked his thin brown hair. She rocked him back and forth. “It’s all right, Kolya. Don’t be afraid. It’s only your daddy. Don’t you remember your daddy? Shhhh. It’s okay.” The cries turned into muffled whimpers, and Larisa’s eyes were full of apology. “Don’t worry, Misha,” she said. “He was only a month old when you left. He just needs a little time to get used to you.”

She turned away from him and walked out of the room, and he could hear her pacing slowly down the hallway, back and forth, while Kolya calmed down. A little time to get used to him. To get used to his own father. The father that should have been here. Misha reached down into the crib and picked up a stuffed toy monkey, who looked back at him with a smile on its face, its brown furry arms dangling behind it. Misha put the monkey’s head up to his nose and inhaled, filling his nostrils with the scent of the fur, but he couldn’t detect any hint of his baby.

Two years he had been gone. Two years that he should have been here to see his son’s first teeth, to guide him through his first steps, to watch him grow from day to day and week to week and to play with him and toss him into the air and tickle him and blow into his bare stomach and laugh with him. Two years that were wasted. Gone. Vanished. There was no bringing them back.

It was their fault. Them. The Party. Malkov who denounced him and Colonel Braginski who recruited him and Semerov who breathed down his neck and never let him go a single minute of a single day without feeling the paranoid fear of having someone lord over you and watch your every move—waiting for you to make some tiny little mistake so that he can justify himself in sending you back to this black hole, where the rest of the world has no idea what the government is doing to its own people, where they can interrogate you and torture you and send you to a camp and take away your humanity and put a bullet in your brain when they’re done with you and no one will ever know.

And there was nothing he could do about it.

Misha tossed the monkey back. Larisa calmed the baby down and came back into the bedroom and set him back down in the crib, and Misha watched him for several minutes as Kolya slept.

Larisa stood at Misha's side. "I almost didn't recognize you," she said. "It's been so long. Time passes and people change and you think you know what they look like, but memory dims and when you see them again, all of a sudden you realize just how much time really has passed, and they don't quite look the same as you remember them."

"And you realize how much you've missed." Misha put his arm around her and pressed her closer to him. "But I don't remember you ever looking as beautiful as you do right now."

She smiled that soft, timid smile and looked up into his eyes. Yes, she still loved him. He could tell by the way she looked at him, the way she looked into him. She hadn't forgotten. And that was all that mattered. "Kolya needs to sleep," she said. "Let's go into the living room."

TWENTY-TWO

They sat on the couch and neither one knew where to begin, and the soft light of the late winter sun was still shining through the thin white drapes that hung over the large windows. The room was quiet and still.

They started by talking about Sverdlovsk. They hadn't thought she would be here this long. Misha was surprised to learn that it was Comrade Vorlakov who had evacuated her from Moscow. Misha mentioned that he hadn't received letters for a long time.

"Letters are worthless," she said. She told him that all of his letters had been censored, that she hated writing in generalities but felt she had to out of fear of being suspected. "But I was glad to get your letters, all the same," she said. "At least I knew that you were still alive. Sometimes those letters were all that kept me going. And Kolya. I'd get out of bed day after day, and my heart would beat and I would breathe, and I forced myself to go on. Whenever I was on the brink of despair, I'd pull out your letters and read them to Kolya. If it weren't for Kolya and your letters, I would have killed myself."

"So maybe letters aren't so worthless."

She smiled. "You're right. I didn't mean what I said."

So many days he could have spent sitting next to her, looking into those brown eyes. So many lost opportunities. "But you've been well taken care of?"

"Yes. We've always had plenty to eat. We've always been safe." She looked down into her lap for a minute, then back to the soft white light coming through the windows. "I felt guilty, though. You can't even imagine what it was like. People were so hungry and the weather was getting worse back in 'forty-one. The hospitals were overwhelmed and had no supplies left, and the government stores were all empty. There was chaos on the streets for a while, especially when the Germans were about to take the city in the middle of October. Every day I would look out the window and see orphans and widows who were starving and homeless, and while they were wandering around the city begging for food and looking for a place to spend the night, I was living in a comfortable apartment and eating good meals, and I always had enough to take care of myself and Kolya.

"One day I learned that in one part of the city, members of the Party were eating meat and cheese and drinking fine wine while all those people in other parts of the city were starving, and it made me sick to my stomach. And then I thought of the food and clothing and shelter that I had, and I couldn't hold back the tears. So I ran home and put Kolya in his crib and threw myself on the bed and started to cry. I've never cried so hard in my life, and I've never hated myself as much as I hated myself on that day. And I couldn't understand why I hated myself so much when I had done nothing illegal, and all I was trying to do was take care of my baby and keep myself alive. I was only doing what the government had told me to do. But I felt dirty.

"For years we lived in constant fear, and I always hated the Party. Our families and friends are all dead, all because of the Party. And even when we joined the Party after you started working at the Institute of Foreign Trade, we still weren't really Party members, at least not of the Inner Party. When Ivan and Olga disappeared and I thought I was going to lose you, I almost went insane. And then, magically, you joined the NKVD and we became members of the Inner Party overnight and we had more food and more clothing and an even nicer apartment. We had more money and were allowed to shop in special stores and were told that our children would have the best education available, and for the first time in my life I felt that I might actually have a future. Of course I was still afraid, but I knew that you were smart and wouldn't get us in trouble, and that as long as we were good Party members and always did what we were told, we would continue to receive all those advantages that had been out of reach for us for so long.

"I never felt truly free, but life was looking better, and when Kolya came along I began to think that maybe life did have some meaning and that maybe there was a reason that you were spared and that we had all these advantages. And I guess I just got used to it. I wanted a home and a family and a real life so badly that I pushed out all the bad memories of the Party and everything that had happened, and I convinced myself that I deserved the advantages that the Party gave us, and I wanted you to move up the ranks in your new career so that we could always keep these advantages and never go back to the life we used to have. But I never truly felt happy, because I always knew that at any moment either one of us could be denounced again, and everything we had would vanish away, and we'd be back to where we started, and then our lives would be over and we would be forgotten.

"Anyway, that night that I was hating myself—I think it was in September—I couldn't even sleep because of the guilt that I felt. And then it hit me that the reason I hated myself so much was that in spite of all the lying to myself that I did, I still hated the Party more than anything else in life, and now I had become one of the Party. Does that make sense? I had become the very thing that I hated most."

Misha nodded. "I know exactly what you mean."

"Well, I couldn't sleep and I couldn't get these thoughts out of my head, so I started rummaging through our things, and I came across that old wooden box that your uncle left you. I opened it up and pulled out the black book and started reading through parts of it to get my mind off of things. I skipped around and read several pages and didn't understand anything, but then I read a little story of a man who wanted a better life, and another man told him that he only lacked one thing and that all he needed to do was to sell what he had and give to the poor. But the man didn't want to do it, so hearing this made him very sad. I don't know why, but when I read that little story I felt my heart swell up within me, and all that emptiness and guilt that I had felt was replaced by this warm feeling that came over my whole body and calmed me down, and I knew what I had to do.

"The next day I looked out the window of our apartment and saw a young woman huddled at the corner of our building, and I knew—I don't know how I knew, but intuitively I just *knew*—that I needed to help her. I invited her into our apartment and made her some dinner, and we talked. She told me that her name was Elya. Her father and brother were in the army, her mother was dead, and she had no food at home. She stayed with me some nights and helped me take care of Kolya, and I made sure she had enough to eat. I knew that I couldn't take my food outside and give it away, because then everyone would know that I had food, and they would steal it and maybe kill me and I couldn't let that happen because of Kolya. But I could help Elya. I know it was a small thing, and I still felt guilty about having so much food compared to everyone else, but at least I was doing something."

"What happened to her?" Misha asked.

"During the crisis in October, when everyone was in a panic and trying to get out of the city, she decided to make a run for it and go to her aunt's home in Perm. I gave her some food, and she gave me a little bundle of cloth with a silver cross inside of it. Elya was always telling me about religion and prayer and how the Communists should never have destroyed all those churches. I've been doing a lot of thinking since she left, Misha."

"About what?"

"About life and the war and the Soviet Union. About us and Kolya and what's going to happen to us. I've also been thinking a lot about your uncle lately for some reason. Most of all I've been thinking about God. Do you believe in God, Misha?"

He pulled his hand away from her knee and propped it up under his chin. This was a question that he hadn't expected, especially not from her. He stared at his shoes. "I don't know," he said.

"Wasn't your uncle a priest? Didn't he ever teach you about God?"

"I never paid much attention to what he taught me. I was

young. It's been so long that I don't even remember any more. He gave me that little black book and told me to read it."

"I've been reading that black book that your uncle gave you."

"And?"

"It's interesting. I've read things in there that I've never even thought about before. When I first started reading it, I couldn't understand anything. It seemed like a bunch of fairy tales. But I've been reading it almost every day for the past year an a half, and the more I read it, the more I understand. Did you ever read it?"

"No." He felt guilty. All he had to do to fulfill the last wish of his uncle just before his uncle's death was to read a little black book. He'd had eleven years, and he hadn't done it.

"Why not?" she asked.

"I don't know," he said, and the guilt felt worse. "I looked at it once a few years ago when we thought that I was going to be repressed, but I haven't touched it since."

All this time she hadn't even been looking at him. She had been staring over at the white light coming through the window. Now she turned to him and put her hand on his arm. "What's America like, Misha?"

He reclined against the back of the sofa and put his arm around her. "America is an amazing place," he said. "I don't even know how to begin to describe it to you. It's nothing like the Soviet Union."

"Is it like the Party says it is?"

"You mean a place where a few rich people exploit the poor and control everything?"

"Yes."

He scratched his head. "I can't even consider it in those terms. The communists put everything in terms of political ideology, and I just can't think that way."

"Then what's it like?"

"It's a peaceful place. Most people there just want to be left alone. They never wanted any part of this war. It's also a very busy place. People are always running around going places. They are always on the move. I've never seen so much activity in my life."

"Are they happy?"

"Well, some of them are. The war has drained the happiness out of many people, and their economy has been suffering for over a decade, but I'd say in general that people are happier there than they are here."

"Are they rich?"

"Some of them. Actually, even the poor Americans have more than most Russians do. And even if you're poor as an individual over there, you live in a society that is rich as a whole. Their society is so complex and diverse. There are people there from all over the world."

"Is it better over there?"

He knew what she was getting at. This question made his stomach tense up, as if something were gnawing at his conscience that he was going to have to get off his chest sooner or later. He looked into her brown eyes and ran his hand across her hair. "Do you want the honest truth?" he asked.

"Of course."

"Everything is better," he said. "I can't figure it out exactly, but I think the main reason is that the government doesn't control everything over there, so people can do what they want and live their own lives. The people are free. Did they tell you that you're coming back to the United States with me?"

Her eyes were wide open now, and she gripped his arm tighter. "No."

"We only have a few days together here in Sverdlovsk. Then I'm going back to the United States by military cargo plane, the same way I got here. You and Kolya can't come with me on the plane, but you'll be taken to New York soon, probably by boat."

There were tears in her eyes again, and she threw her arms around him. "Oh, Misha, this is the best news you could have given me. I'm so happy that I don't even know what to say."

His heart was sinking. He had to tell her. "Larisa," he said, and he gently pulled her arms off of him and held them to get her attention. "There are some things you need to know."

"What's wrong?"

He put her arms down. "Larisa, it's not all good news."

"What are you talking about?"

He was about to speak, but then he stopped himself. She hadn't seen him in almost two years, and now, having just barely gotten her hopes up, he was going to dash them all to pieces by informing her they were in serious danger. How was he going to put this? "Larisa," he started, and he couldn't look her in the eye. He took her hands in his own again. "Larisa, when I was in New York, I did a terrible thing."

"What? What was it?"

"I did it because I thought that I had to."

"What? What did you do?"

"I spied on one of my coworkers and reported him to Comrade Semerov, my boss. The NKGB *rezident*."

Her hands were tense. She squeezed his fingers. "I don't understand."

"I was ordered to do it. I had no choice. Now Nikolai is under suspicion—"

"Who's Nikolai?"

"The man I spied on. Now he's under suspicion, and if the NKGB believes that he was betraying the Soviet Union, he'll be shot or imprisoned. All because of me. When we were on the plane between Montana and Alaska, we decided that we had to do something to try to save him, so we talked to the pilot and asked him to call the American intelligence services for us. Nikolai has contacts with the FBI who might be able to convince Semerov that he was not a traitor, that he was only trying to make a purchase of war materials for the Soviet Union when he met with some FBI agents. The problem is that if anyone in the Soviet government finds out that we talked to that American pilot, we're both dead."

"Where is Nikolai right now?"

"I don't know. Probably in Moscow. I was sent to Sverdlovsk, and he was taken somewhere else."

"To be interrogated?"

"I don't know. Maybe."

Her skin had been a healthy white a moment before; now it was a sickly pale. The sparkle in her eyes was gone. "What if they torture him? What if he talks, Misha?"

He didn't know how to answer her.

She stood up and walked over to the window. "Didn't you think about the possible consequences of your actions before you talked to that pilot?"

"Nikolai won't talk."

"How do you know?"

"I had to do the right thing, Larisa."

She covered her face with her hands, and after a few seconds of silence, she started crying again. He stood up and walked over to her and put his hands on her shoulders. She leaned back against him and put her hand on one of his hands. "I'm not angry at you, Misha," she said through her tears. "It's just that I've been suffering here for two years now without you, and every time I think that we finally might be able to be together, something comes along and threatens to take you away from me again."

"I'm sorry, Larisa. I didn't intend for things to happen this way, but I could never live with myself knowing that I had killed an innocent man."

"I just can't live like this any more, Misha. The fear and the worrying and the loneliness. It's too much. And now it's more than just you and me. Kolya's a little boy. He has his entire life ahead of him. We have to be thinking of him, too."

He turned her around and embraced her. "There's another thing that I have to tell you, Larisa."

"I can't take any more bad news."

"No. This is different. America has changed me, Larisa. Forever. I can never go back to the way I was before, knowing the things I do, having seen the things I've seen. There's no place for us here in the Soviet Union."

"What are you talking about?"

"Once you and the baby and I are all back in the United States, we're never going to return to the Soviet Union again."

She looked up at him and had a frightened, desperate look on her face. "Misha, what are you saying?"

"Do you remember that day when I told you that if I could find a way, I would get us out of here?"

"Yes."

"An idea occurred to me when Nikolai and I were talking to that American pilot. I've found a way."

"How?"

"I'm not exactly sure yet," he said. "But I think I'll start by making contact with that American FBI woman whom Nikolai was working with."

☆

As Misha slept that night, the dream came to him for the last time. He lay on the ground and stared up into a gray, cloudy sky. His arms were stretched out to his sides, and the hard dirt beneath his back was cold. Several small pebbles poked him through his shirt. He propped himself up on his elbows and shook his head to regain his senses. A large iron spear lay to his right, and it all came back to him. He felt his chest with his hand. The wound was gone. He was whole.

The church loomed large in front of him, white walls and a brown roof. His uncle still stood in the tower window and was pointing down at something next to him. "The key," his uncle said. "Take the key and enter."

Misha stood up and brushed the dust off of his pants and shirt. The old brown box lay on the ground off to his left, and he picked it up and opened it. The black book and the key were together inside of it. He pulled the key out and felt its cold, heavy weight in the palm of his hand. He walked over to the door, inserted it into the keyhole, and turned. There was a brief metal clink, and the enormous wooden door was ajar.

He pushed it open and stepped inside. The room was dark and smelled of wet mildew. He stood on a hard stone floor and heard a distant dripping noise, but when he looked around, he couldn't locate its source. With what little light came through the open door and a single small window, he could see that the walls and the floor were utterly bare. There was nothing here.

His uncle descended a narrow flight of steps in the corner and walked over to him. He stood before him, and Misha looked searchingly into his uncle's eyes. His uncle had a large head and rough skin, weathered by years of poverty and war and oppression. Creases outlined the eyes and forehead, and the long scraggly beard, once thick and jet black, was now thin and gray. But the eyes were still warm.

"Misha," his uncle whispered.

They embraced. "Uncle Konstantin," he said, and he could feel tears running down his cheeks, "I've missed you so much. Why weren't you with me all these years? You don't know how much I've needed you."

His uncle patted him gently on his back. "I never left you, Misha. All this time I have been watching over you." His uncle put his hands on Misha's shoulders. "Look around you, Misha. What do you see?"

Misha again swept the room with his eyes. All the walls were bare. The ceiling was bare. The floor was bare. Cracks lined the walls in several places, and he could still hear the distant sound of dripping water. The air smelled dank and stale. "Your church is empty, Uncle. Why is your church so empty?"

"You no longer belong here, Misha. You must find what you are searching for elsewhere."

"But where? What is it that I am searching for?"

"I must leave you now, Misha. I have called you to this place to show you what is here and to leave you this message, but I can show you no more and can call you no further. From now on you must make your way alone."

"But how? I don't even know what I'm looking for."

His uncle looked up to the ceiling for a few seconds, then back into Misha's eyes. "You will know it when you find it."

"Don't leave me, uncle. Tell me what it is."

"I'll be waiting for you, Misha."

"Uncle Konstantin! Don't leave me!"

His uncle vanished, as did the church around him, and once again he found himself standing alone in the middle of a vast field of grain.

TWENTY-THREE

Malkov listened eagerly to the sweet sounds that percolated through the closed door. Shouting, screaming, slapping, the deep thud of Vorlakov's massive fist plowing into the man's abdomen. Then a brief moment of intense silence while the man struggled against the initial shock of having the wind knocked out of him so completely. Right now the man's body was probably all buckled over and crumpled into the fetal position. Was he still sitting on the chair, or did Vorlakov's blow knock him to the floor? The silence was more drawn out than usual. The gasp, the gasp, where was the gasp?

The suspense was killing him as he stood outside the room in a basement corridor of the Lubyanka. He was holding his own breath as he waited to hear that climactic gasp that always came after one of Vorlakov's powerful blows. Malkov's forehead broke a slight sweat, and he couldn't hold his breath any longer. He released it and started breathing in short, excited spurts through his nose, which he tried to suppress even though no one else was around him to notice it, but the ecstacy that swelled within him was too great to contain. He pulled a handkerchief out of his coat pocket and put it up to his upper lip to dab the beads of sweat that accumulated there, then up to his forehead.

Was it? Yes. Yes! There it was. There it was! That ghoulish sound of air as it whined through the windpipe of a man whose lungs were yearning for relief, yet were being clamped and pressed and crushed by the man's own diaphragm as he reeled from the blow. Malkov took a deep breath through his nostrils and slipped the handkerchief back into his pocket. The adrenaline rush engulfed him. Nothing in the world could be more stimulating than this.

The door opened and Vorlakov stood before him, tall and massive and powerful, his eyes black and fiery and seething with the intensity of a maniacal serial killer, his shirt wrinkled, his sleeves rolled up. Finally it was time. "We're ready for you," Vorlakov said, still panting from his work.

Malkov stepped into the room and took another deep breath to calm himself. The floor was bare concrete. A single chair stood in the middle of the room under a bright lamp. A tall, slender man with light hair sat on the chair with his arms crossed in front of him, gripping his stomach and his sides. He was hunched over but was trying to right himself. His nose was disjointed now, definitely broken, with thick lumps of half-coagulated blood still oozing out of it. His eyes were black and puffy and swollen, and his lips were mashed so badly and were so puffy and had so much blood all over them that Malkov couldn't tell where they were bleeding from. The man tipped his head back and looked at Malkov out of the little slit that not long before had been a normal, healthy eye.

"Well, Comrade?" Malkov asked in a calm, soothing voice.

It took all the strength the man had just to shake his head slowly back and forth. The man whimpered. Tears emerged from the two little slits in the puffy blotches of purple and black and slithered down the sides of the now-unrecognizable face, over the prominent cheekbones, down to the jaw. Pathetic.

"I don't think you're being totally honest with us, Comrade," Malkov said. He kept his voice as calm and smooth and gentle as he could.

The man's head hung down again, dangling at the top of the neck, and the torso shook as the quiet whimpering continued.

Malkov walked slowly around to the back of the man's chair, letting his shoes make a crisp, clear clopping noise with each little step. Malkov stood behind the man. He put his hands on the man's trembling shoulders. Touch him. Yes. Touch him. He always touched them. He could feel the man's fear and pain and regret and terror churning within him like a ball of energy, and as Malkov rested his hands on the man's shoulders, he could feel that ball of energy rise up and flow into his own fingers, through his arms and into his own chest, and he had to take another deep breath through his nose to keep himself from losing all control. Except the energy was different now. It had changed. What had been terror and dread and panic inside of the man had now become pure power inside of Malkov, and it flowed through Malkov's body and pulsed within his soul. It was soothing, comforting. No pleasure in the world was greater than this.

"I know," Malkov said in a voice that was almost a whisper. "It's all right. It happens to everybody." He took his hands off of the man's shoulders and walked back around to the front of the chair. "It isn't hard, Comrade," he said, his voice now normal again. "It's the easiest thing there could possibly be. You met with the American woman and handed her the diplomatic folder, and she promised to help you escape. You've told us that much. And wasn't it easy to tell us that? Now we just want you to finish your story. Who else was in on it with you?"

The man shook his head. "No one, Comrade."

"We know you didn't act alone. You couldn't have. Who else is there?"

The man was still crying. "I swear it, Comrade. There was no one else. I was the only one."

Malkov stepped forward and crouched down in front of the man. He reached out a hand and lightly touched the man's knee. He spoke slowly, calmly, gently, pausing between each sentence. "Comrade, we want to help you. We know you didn't mean to betray your country. We understand the pressures of your job, the lures of the imperialists. And we want to help you. We believe in you, Comrade. We know you can be rehabilitated." He pulled his hand back and stood up. "But only if you tell us who else is a traitor."

The man's sobbing fell silent, and Malkov couldn't tell if the man was crying again or if he had stopped. Malkov could see the back of the man's head, which rocked back and forth. "I swear it, Comrade. I was alone. There was no one else."

Malkov turned to Vorlakov. "Well," he said. "What do you think?"

Vorlakov's face was void of expression. He looked like a

bronze statue. “I think we’re through with him,” he said. His voice was chilling. “He’s broken. I think he’s telling the truth.”

Malkov turned back to the whimpering, disgusting, worthless little man writhing on the chair before him. “I agree.” Malkov turned away from them both and exited out the door. He never liked to watch the final part, but he always made sure that he listened to it from the hallway. There was something about it that made him feel lighter inside, more pleased with himself. It gave him that final jolt of euphoria that would last him for days, weeks, even months, until the next one was brought in. As he walked down the corridor, the explosive blast of the revolver reverberated off the walls, and then came the thud as the body hit the floor.

TWENTY-FOUR

"Karen, I've got a bad feeling about this whole thing," the Chief said. "Those two guys from Amtorg disappear, and then I get a strange phone call from an American guy named John who just happens to know my name, my phone number, and all of Alfred's code words. And now, after a couple of years of keeping yourself hidden, you stroll into Semerov's office and chat with the big man himself, face to face." He drummed his fingers on the desk and stared at her. "I don't like it, Karen. This is not how we planned things. This is not a good way to conduct surveillance."

She sat on the chair in front of his desk, her legs crossed. She felt calm. "I know, Chief."

He shook his head and let out a sigh, but she could tell by the way he peered over the top of his glasses at her that he wasn't angry and she wasn't in trouble. At least not yet. "So how did it go?" he asked.

"It went well," she said.

"Was he convinced that you're a nickel dealer?"

"No. He's still suspicious. But we've bought ourselves some time. He doesn't know what to think."

"Did he make the phone call to the Soviet Union?"

"Yes."

"And?"

"I don't know."

"You don't know." He stopped drumming his fingers and took his glasses off so that he could look at her straight. "So in other words, we have no idea what's going on with Alfred right now, correct?"

"That's correct."

"And the other guy that you've been watching? The one that Alfred told you about?"

"Boris?"

"Yes."

"Same story, Chief. Boris and Alfred left on that plane together. We haven't seen either one since."

"What about John? Have you figured out who that is yet?"

"Yes, I have. His real name is Mark Daniels. He's a captain with the Army Air Corps, stationed at Gore Field near Great Falls, Montana. He was the pilot of the plane that flew Alfred and Boris to Alaska."

The Chief's bald head nodded slowly, and his eyes twinkled. "That explains it."

"Alfred would have called sooner if he thought he was in trouble, so that makes me think that he didn't realize he was in danger until after he was on that plane. By that time it was too late for him to escape—"

"So he panicked and talked to the pilot."

"Exactly."

"What about Boris? Do you think he's in on this, too? Or was he just along for the ride?"

She leaned her head back a little and looked up at nothing and thought for a moment, then looked back at the Chief. "I've never been able to figure Boris out," she said.

"What do you mean?"

"Well, from observing him in his work, you'd think he was one of their best agents. He has a talent for making contacts and winning people's trust, and he never talks. He's very cautious, and he's very thorough, and he has excellent judgment. But Alfred has worked with him for almost two years now, and Alfred thinks that the only thing that keeps him going is the fact that he has a wife and son back in the Soviet Union."

"Have you ever had any contact with Boris?"

"Are you kidding? He's untouchable."

"Well, maybe it's time to change that. Alfred said that Semerov is on to us. That means Alfred is in real danger, and so are you. And if Alfred told us about Boris——"

"Then Boris might come under suspicion soon, too."

The Chief stood up and walked around his desk, and Karen stood up as well. "We'll have to put Boris on the back burner for now, see if he shows up again," the Chief said. "I've got a feeling that he will, and I'd bet a million dollars that he'll come back via the Alsib Pipeline. As for Alfred, we can only hope and pray that he'll show up again, too. I'll send Agent Howard up to Alaska to keep an eye out for them. In the meantime, the next step for you is to have a little chat with that captain."

☆

Back at Gore Field, Mark closed the door behind them and led the woman over to a solitary chair in front of a metal desk. "Have a seat," he said. "I apologize for the arrangement here. I know it's not much of an office." He brought another chair around and put it a few feet in front of her, next to the desk so that he could rest his arm on it.

She sat down and crossed her legs. She was dressed sharply in a lady's business suit, dark gray. Her jacket was buttoned, her skirt almost covered her knees even when she was sitting, and she wore a gray hat with a small black veil in front of it that covered her eyes. He took off his cap and set it on the desk. In spite of the hat and the veil, he had a clear view of her face, and he was struck by how beautiful she was. She had long, straight blond hair and icy blue eyes. Her skin was smooth and healthy, and she had the same full, pouty lips that he had seen only on the faces of Hollywood actresses in the movies. Her make-up was modest and highlighted her features well without drawing attention to itself, and for some reason this one quality all by itself made him feel that she was a woman to be respected.

"How can I help you, ma'am?" he asked.

"Captain Daniels, my name is Karen Jones." She whipped out a badge. "I'm an agent with the FBI. Should I call you Mark, or would you feel more comfortable if I just call you John?"

His stomach was churning. She paused to put her badge away, then looked at him with a smug twinkle in her eye. Never had he seen a woman like this. The last time he had felt so intimidated by a woman was when he had taken Mary Parker to the high school graduation dance. "You're Rose Petersen, aren't you."

"Touché," she said.

This pleased him, that she wasn't the only one who knew the other's alias. He wanted to see her blush, but she didn't. She raised her eyebrows and tipped her head in a gentle nod to answer in the affirmative, but said nothing. She had aplomb. She had real style.

"You found me pretty fast," he said.

"Two plus two makes four, Captain Daniels. All it took was a couple of phone calls."

Straightforward and intelligent. Nice to work with people like that, but she still intimidated him. "You want to know about those two Russians, don't you."

She asked him a million questions, and he answered them all. He told her about the black suitcases and the wooden crates and the Soviet operations in Alaska and Montana. He told her how he first met Misha and Nikolai, how they were definitely in on this together, how genuine and sincere and thankful they seemed—and how terrified. The conversation went on for over an hour.

"You've been very helpful, Captain Daniels," she said when she had finished grilling him. "I have one more request to ask of you."

"Go ahead."

"We believe that Boris will be coming back to the United States soon along the Alsib Pipeline."

"That's Misha, right?"

"Yes."

"What about Nikolai?"

"We don't know about Alfred yet. We're hoping he'll show up, too, but right now we're focusing on Boris. We have an agent in Alaska watching for him, and if he shows up, that agent will make sure that he flies from Alaska to Montana on your plane, and that he will be the sole Soviet courier."

"How is your agent going to arrange that?"

She smiled a coy, condescending smile, as if to say, my dear little boy, don't you know who you're talking to? He felt himself blushing. "You needn't worry about that," she said. "We'll take care of it. But when Boris comes, we need you to make contact with him while he's on the plane."

Man this lady was intimidating, but Mark composed himself quickly. "You mean, talk to him as I did before?"

"Yes."

"About what?"

"Well, about anything, really. The first thing you want to do is establish a rapport with him. Get a feel for what he's thinking. We think he might be willing to give us some information soon, but we're not sure yet. So just talk to him. He probably trusts you already."

"I suppose so."

"Then, when you feel the time is right, tell him that the government is willing to offer him political asylum here in the Unites States in exchange for his cooperation. We'll provide protection for him. Can you do that?"

"Sure. But what should I tell Colonel Griggs?"

"Don't tell him anything."

TWENTY-FIVE

It had taken much longer than Malkov ever had expected, but finally his transfer was approved and he was standing on American soil. Alaska wasn't New York City, but it wasn't the Soviet Union, either. He had made a mistake with Comrade Kostrina when he had threatened her a year and a half before; that much he finally admitted to himself. That one little incident in Sverdlovsk had cost him his original assignment to work in overseas intelligence, and he had ended up stuck in Moscow at the Lubyanka for an extra year until he regained Vorlakov's trust. But in the long run, it had actually worked out to his benefit, because it gave him valuable experience in torture and interrogation.

His patience had now paid off. Vorlakov trusted him again, and Braginski had approved the reassignment, thanks in large part to the New York *rezident* request for a man who could weed out enemies of the people. He knew that he was perfect for the job. There was no man better qualified than him. He already suspected who the traitors at Amtorg were—or rather, he already knew whom he would denounce. He was eager to finally get rid of Comrade Kostrin, and if he couldn't have Kostrin's wife, then he would find a way to get rid of her, too. And what better way to begin his new role in the United States than by meeting with an American insider who could potentially make it all possible?

Malkov waited inside of an empty airplane hanger. It was a warm, sunny day, and the sunshine seemed particularly bright. The wind was pleasant and cool, and a soft breeze blew in front of the building. A beautiful day for flying.

He waited for about twenty minutes, and when the American finally showed up, Malkov was astonished at how large the man was. He stood over two meters tall and must have weighed over a hundred kilograms at least. He wore a dark brown suit with a matching fedora on his head, and a pair of thin spectacles sat upon the crest of his nose. His neck was thick. His face was stern and serious. He reminded Malkov of Comrade Vorlakov, except that this man's eyes were much more dull than Vorlakov's. Vorlakov was an excellent actor, but his eyes had a wild glint in them that Vorlakov couldn't hide. This American was much less intriguing. He looked like he didn't care about anything and hadn't smiled once in his entire life.

Malkov approached the man and extended a hand.

The American looked at the outstretched hand with disdain. He didn't shake it. "You're Malkov?" the man asked. "The guy I talked to over the phone regarding our last deal?"

Malkov put his hand to his side. He didn't care how rude this American was. He only cared about what the American could offer him. "Yes. And you must be—"

"Agent Howard. How about we cut the formalities and get right to the point."

"Of course."

"I have some information for you concerning a couple of your agents in New York City. The FBI has been watching them for a long time, and they're just about ready to crack. Would you be interested?"

The similarity to Vorlakov was striking. No facial expression at all. "It depends on who we're talking about."

"They're big fish. I know that much."

"How can you be so sure? We have many people working for us in New York. Most of them are nobodies. Just regular personnel."

"Don't try to pull a fast one on me. I've been watching you Russians operate for years, and I know what you're up to. I'd be surprised if there's a single Soviet in the United States who isn't a spy. These two are big fish. What I'm offering you is information about one of the biggest double-crosses your organization has ever had. Now what's that worth to you?"

Still no facial expression. Just cold, calculated words. Vorlakov should meet this man. "How about a thousand dollars?"

A massive hand grabbed Malkov by the shirt at his chest and pulled him closer. Malkov's heart jumped up into his throat, and he almost lost his balance. The power in that arm sent an involuntary tremor through Malkov's body. Howard's face was inches from his own. "I've never liked Russians," Howard said calmly. "You're getting on my nerves. If you offered me ten times that much, I wouldn't take it."

Howard let go and backed off. Malkov brushed his shirt off and adjusted his glasses, then smiled at Howard, trying to appear collected. "In that case, what would be a more acceptable offer?"

"If you can give me twenty thousand dollars and guarantee me safe passage on one of your ships to South America, then I'll deliver the goods to you. Otherwise no deal."

Malkov nodded. "All right," he said without looking at Howard. "I'm listening. But I am curious. You're an FBI agent with over eight years on the job, and now you decide to sell out to us for no apparent reason other than greed. Don't get me wrong. I want your information. But I have to be careful about these kinds of things. You understand, don't you? How do I know you're not setting me up? How do I know this isn't some scheme that you've dreamed up to trap me and compromise my government's affairs with your country?"

"Fair enough," Howard said. "I delivered the other guy, didn't I?"

"That's no guarantee that you're legitimate."

"Think of it this way. If you say no, what do you have to lose?"

"Nothing. Except for your information, assuming you have it."

"And if you say yes, you still have nothing to lose. I either tell you about your turncoats or I don't. The worst that can happen is that I take your money and skip town, but I'm sure you won't give me a penny until I've given you something first, right?"

"Absolutely."

"So you're still in control. I give you something, you verify it and give me a down payment. Then I give you the rest, and you give me the rest. And to guarantee that you don't double-cross me on the second part of the bargain, I'll have a special friend wait for me to call him from South America after the deal has gone through. There's a safe deposit box at a certain bank that contains a whole bunch of dirt on you reds, and my friend has a key to that box. If my friend doesn't hear from me, he'll mail all that stuff anonymously to several big-time American newspapers. You think the American public would continue all these Lend-Lease shipments if they knew what you were up to? Don't count on it. See how that works? You get what you want, I get what I want, and we're both protected from the double-cross. What do you say?"

Malkov acknowledged him with a slow nod. This man was brusque, but business-like. "What do you have in mind?"

"I want a five-thousand-dollar down payment. I'll give you the scoop on one of our agents who's been running surveillance on you. Just enough detail so that you can verify what I tell you. Even if you break off the deal then, you'll have enough information about the FBI that you'll be able to do some real counter-intelligence damage. Then, once my down payment is sitting in a South American bank, I'll give you the scoop on a couple of your agents who are about to sell out. For the second part of the deal, I want five thousand in cash on the spot, and the rest transferred to the same bank account. You can plug the hole in your secrecy, and I'll disappear."

"All right," Malkov said. "I'll deal."

TWENTY-SIX

Mark stared at the silver C-47 for a moment as it sat near the runway in Alaska. He felt strange as he looked at it and thought of who was waiting for him inside. There was an FBI man at the airfield now, Rose Petersen's partner, and just a couple of hours earlier, this FBI man had informed him that Boris was at the airfield and would be on the next flight out. On the one hand, he was relieved to hear it. On the other hand, he wondered why Boris was alone.

He walked over to the aircraft and climbed the stairs that led up into the cargo area, but when he looked around, he saw no one. He took his seat in the cockpit and started going over his pre-flight checklist, and a few minutes later he heard people in the back of the plane. He recognized Misha's voice, and then Paulsen and Burns entered the cockpit and joined him.

After they were airborne, Mark headed back to the cargo area and sat next to Misha.

"Hey," Mark said as he sat next to him. "You made it."

Misha nodded. "Yes."

"Where's your friend Nikolai?"

"I don't know."

Neither had to say anything more about the matter. They were both thinking the same thing, and neither wanted to discuss the possibility that Nikolai might not be coming back, so Mark changed the subject. "I talked to that FBI agent that Nikolai had been meeting with. That Rose Petersen lady. She went to Semerov's office just as you guys asked her to, and he made the phone call to Moscow."

"That's good to hear," Misha said. He looked depressed.

"Did you see your wife?"

Now Misha smiled. "Yes," he said. "She was more beautiful than I remembered."

"And your son?"

The smile faded a little, and the eyes looked down. "He's a beautiful little boy." Misha rubbed his nose with the back of his hand. "But he doesn't remember me." The smile brightened a little. The eyes relaxed. "They're coming to New York this summer."

Both men were sitting with their elbows resting on their knees, their bodies slouching forward, their heads hanging down. "You look tired," Mark said.

Misha put his hands on his knees and sat up straight. He took a deep breath and let out a long sigh. "I'm worried about Nikolai. And I miss my family."

Mark leaned back, turned toward Misha, and rested his elbow on the back of the seat cushion. "What are you going to do?"

"There's really only one thing that I can do. If I stay in the Soviet Union, I'm a dead man, and my wife and son, too. We have to get out."

Mark couldn't have asked for a better segue. He told Misha about Rose Petersen's offer of political asylum.

Misha was listening, but he didn't really seem to care. "I feel empty," he said.

The statement struck Mark as odd. "In what way?"

"I don't know how to describe it," Misha said. "It feels like there's a hole inside of my chest, and I am searching for something to fill it, but I don't know exactly what it is." Misha looked into Mark's eyes. "Are you a religious man?" he asked.

"Yes," Mark said.

"Do you pray?"

"Every day."

"And you really believe that there is a God who listens to you and watches over you?"

"I know there's a God. And I know He answers prayers."

Misha stared at the floor again and clasped his hands in his lap. "My uncle was a priest. He had his own church in our village when I was a boy. He was taken away and put to death as an enemy of the people because he wouldn't deny his faith. He was a good man. I've missed him very much."

Mark thought of the two frightened men who stood in his cargo hold just last week, how irritated he had been at them and how much he had disliked every Russian that he saw. Now there was only one of them in his cargo hold, not as frightened as before, but still exhausted and depressed and void of hope. Mark's stereotypical impression of the USSR's faceless masses had been replaced forever by the melancholy countenance and drooping shoulders of this one Russian accountant from Moscow. "What's it like in the Soviet Union?" Mark asked.

Misha put his hands together and brought them up to his lips for a moment, pausing as if to gather his thoughts. "It's a dark and evil place," he said slowly in a sorrowful voice. "The people who have all the power have no conscience. The government controls everything, and people are taken away and shot for no reason at all. It's been this way ever since I was a little boy, and I've never been able to understand why. I have no family left except for my wife and son, and no friends except for Nikolai, and I don't even know if he's still alive. Every day I live in fear, not knowing if I will be denounced and never see my wife and son again. I didn't understand how evil the Soviet Union is until I came to America. When I first saw your country, I couldn't believe that such a place existed. I thought that it was some kind of deception at first, or a strange fantasy that I would awake out of, but the more I saw of it, the more I realized just what kind of a country I came from."

Misha's words came out slow and heavy and settled on Mark's soul like a dead weight of iron. "Do you want to stay in the United States?" Mark asked.

"Yes," Misha answered without hesitation. "When I was an accountant back in Moscow working at the Institute of Foreign Trade, I used to tell my wife that all I wanted was a quiet home in the country, where I could raise a family and be left alone, where I could take my children to a local church every Sunday to make sure they had good principles, where I knew my neighbors and they knew me and we all lived in peace. That's how things were in my village for a short time when I was very young." Misha looked at Mark. "Are you from the country?"

Mark reached up and took his cap off. "Yes, actually. My family lives in southern California, not far from San Diego. My father grows oranges on a large orchard. We have some other fruit trees, too. Tangerines, lemons. But mostly oranges."

"Is it quiet there? Does the government leave you alone?"

Such odd questions. If Mark were asking another man about his home, the last thing he would think of would be to ask the other guy if the government left him alone. "For the most part, yes," Mark answered. "It's always warm there, all year long, and there's a lot of space to run around. It was a great place to grow up."

"And your whole family is religious?"

"Yes."

"It seems that all Americans are religious. Is it true that Christianity played a major role in your culture and history?"

More strange questions. "Yes, I'd say that's true. Not everyone is religious, though, and some people say they're religious, but they don't act very religious."

"What is your religion?"

Mark looked up into Misha's dark eyes and felt his heart soften toward this Russian even more. Misha's face was tired and despondent, but his eyes shimmered with curiosity and his voice was sincere. "Have you ever heard of Mormons?" Mark asked him.

Misha shook his head. "No."

"Well, that's what I am." Mark nodded toward the cockpit. "My co-pilot up there is a Methodist, but he's not a very religious guy; and my radio man, Burns, he's a devout Catholic. My commander, Colonel Griggs, is Episcopalian. Come to think about it, I've never known a true atheist. Just about everyone I've known in my life has had some kind of religious affiliation. Usually Christian, sometimes Jewish. So I guess America is a pretty religious place. How about yourself?"

"I don't know," Misha said, and he stared ahead into the empty cargo hold as if something were weighing him down. "I've always tried to be a good person, because that's what my uncle taught me. I was baptized into the Russian Orthodox faith, but I've never really felt that I belonged to any particular religion. The communists don't believe in God, and they've tried to destroy religion as much as possible in my homeland. Nikolai thinks that's one of the things that went wrong in the Soviet Union. We've forgotten God, and now He has forgotten us."

"Have you ever read the Bible?" Mark asked.

"No. My uncle left me a little black book, but he had erased the title of the book so that the communists wouldn't recognize it unless they opened it, so I don't know exactly what book it is. I don't think it's a Bible, though. It's too small to be a full Bible. I think it might be part of the Bible."

"Why are you so interested in religion?"

"It's as I said. I feel empty, and I'm trying to figure out why. I think that religion has something to do with it. And I'm trying to understand what went wrong in my country, why so many people suffer all the time. Nikolai thinks America is great because it is religious, and because her people are free. I've thought about what he told me when I talked to him last, and I think he might be right. What do you think?"

Mark adjusted himself in his seat as he tried to come up with something to say. "Well, I haven't really thought much on the subject. I know what my father has always said about it."

Misha listened attentively. "What does your father say?"

"My father always taught me that America is a chosen land, blessed above all other lands. He says that God raised up this nation and blessed it with freedom and prosperity for His own purposes, and that through this nation God intends to bless all the nations of the earth."

"Including the Soviet Union?"

At first Mark thought Misha's question was an expression of skepticism, but when he looked at Misha's face, he realized the question was sincere. "Sure," Mark said. "I mean, look at us, for example. You and me, sitting on this plane. We're giving your people trucks and food and ammunition and airplanes and all sorts of weapons to help you fight the Germans. And we're helping England and China and other countries, too."

"Do you think we'll win this war?"

"Absolutely. Things are already turning around for us. It's just a matter of time."

"And after the war? What do you think will happen then?"

He knew what Misha was thinking. Misha was thinking about the Soviet Union and what kind of life the Russians would have once the war was over, and whether the US and the USSR would get along, and they both knew that there wasn't a chance as long as the communists were in power. He didn't know what to say.

"You seem like a good man, Captain Daniels. There is goodness in your eyes. Your eyes are like my uncle's."

Mark smiled. "Thank you for the compliment," he said.

Misha rested his head back against the wall. "If things work out for me and I am allowed to stay here in America with my wife and son, could we live where you live?"

Mark patted Misha on the shoulder. "Sure. You seem like a pretty good guy yourself. I'd love to have you as a neighbor."

Misha blinked several times, slowly, ponderously. "Good," he said. "If I can escape from the Soviets, and if the FBI can protect me and my family, then I will come and live in your town. I will spend the rest of my life there and raise my children there, and maybe I will grow oranges as your father does. And if the government lets me, I will become an American."

Mark unzipped his flight jacket halfway and reached into his breast pocket. He pulled out a small brown book and handed it to Misha. "Here," he said. "Take this. I want you to have it."

"What is it?"

"This is what I believe in. I carry it with me everywhere I go. It's like a good luck charm, only it goes deeper than luck."

"I cannot accept this from you."

"No, take it. That's just a serviceman's copy; I can get

another one. I want you to have it to remember me by. I don't know if it has what you're looking for, but maybe it will help you out, give you something to think about."

Misha held the little brown book in his hands and rubbed its cover with his thumbs. "Thank you," he said quietly.

"Whenever I feel empty, this is what I turn to," Mark said. "And then I pray."

"My uncle had a book of prayers," Misha said. "I read some of them once, but I don't think they did me any good."

"What about praying without a book? Have you ever tried talking to God the way you're talking to me?"

Misha let out a brief laugh. "No."

Mark looked at Misha carefully. "Maybe you should try it sometime," he said. "You'd be amazed what it can do for you when your heart is in the right place."

Misha's smile faded. Misha stared at the little book for a few more seconds, still rubbing its cover with his thumbs, then he put it away into his own pocket and looked at Mark. "I will always remember you, Captain Daniels. Thank you for helping me and my friend. You've given me a lot to think about."

Mark's heart swelled inside of him, and he felt a tightness in his throat. Misha's face looked gaunt and pale and tired. His eyes were despondent, yet they were softer now, less fraught with fear and anxiety. I'm not going to let them destroy this man, Mark thought. Not if I can help it. If there's anything I can do to help him out, I'm going to do it.

Mark patted Misha on the knee and stood up, then headed back to the cockpit.

TWENTY-SEVEN

Semerov looked smaller for some reason. Shorter, skinnier, more gaunt, even less color in his skin than usual. Several gray hairs had appeared around the sides of his head. But the pupils had remained exactly the same. Black and cold and penetrating, like two shiny pieces of coal, surrounded by white, with large black circles enveloping the eyes.

"It's good to have you back, Kostrin."

"Thank you, Comrade Semerov."

"How is your wife?"

As if Semerov even cared. "Very well."

"And your son?"

"Also."

"Good." Semerov paced slowly over to the window, his hands clasped behind his back, his head tilted slightly forward, his eyes fixed on nothing in particular. He stood at the window and looked through the blinds at the street below. "The war seems to be going better now," he said. "The Red Army is driving the Germans back toward the west, and the Americans and British are still pounding them from the air. Italy is weak. It's only a matter of time before the fascists are defeated." Semerov turned his head to the left, but not enough to look directly at Misha. "What do you think of all this, Comrade?"

"It is good news indeed."

Semerov turned around and stood with his back to the window, his hands still clasped behind him, and he looked at Misha for a moment as if studying him. "I have another assignment for you, Kostrin. Shipman has once again proven to be more resourceful than we earlier gave him credit for. The Stanton Chemical Company has recently decided to get into the radioactive element business, and Shipman has told me that he can probably get more uranium chemicals for us. The beautiful thing is that we won't even have to steal them. Approval of the shipment will likely pass through the War Production Board without any problems, just as our last shipment did. Lend Lease will give its stamp of approval—that is certain—and the uranium could be on its way to Montana sometime in June. I'll give you a list of exactly what the Centre needs, and I want you to meet with Shipman in the next few days to have him place the order with the Stanton Chemical Company. Do you have any questions about this assignment?"

"No, Comrade Semerov."

Semerov strolled back to the desk, taking long, slow steps, placing his feet methodically in front of him, heel toe, heel toe, his hands still clasped behind his back, his head still tilted forward. He stared at the floor in front of him as he walked. When he reached the desk, he lifted up his head, then pulled his hands out from behind his back and stretched one of them out toward Misha. "You're still standing, Comrade. Don't you want to sit down?"

Misha stood with his hands at his sides. "You didn't invite me to sit down, so I remained standing."

Semerov smiled with his lips, but his eyes were colder than ever and seemed to penetrate Misha to the soul. "Always obedient and deferential, aren't you, Kostrin."

Misha did not respond.

"Please," Semerov said, motioning with his hand toward the chair. "Sit down."

Misha stepped around the front of the chair and slowly lowered himself onto it, holding the arm rests with his hands. It was a wooden chair, a new one, light brown in color, hard and smooth to the touch. Misha kept his eyes on Semerov and leaned back until he felt his spine rest gently against the back of the chair. Semerov remained standing.

"When did you last see Comrade Ryzanov?" Semerov asked.

"In Kuybishev, when we got off the cargo plane. I was taken to Sverdlovsk, and he was driven to another location."

"Do you know where?"

"No."

"He was taken to Moscow—to the Lubyanka—to be questioned." Semerov watched Misha intently, so much that Misha could feel the cold weight of that diabolical stare settling in around his head, moving down to his shoulders, pushing him into the hard wooden chair. Semerov sat down in his cushioned armchair and leaned back, still scrutinizing Misha. "Nothing strange about that, now, is there?"

Of course not. You slip up once, they torture you and shoot you and drop your body off in some mass grave in the middle of the forest. "No, Comrade Semerov."

"But there was one strange thing that happened here after you and Ryzanov left. Would you like to hear about it?"

The little black eyes weren't moving. They were fixated on him, dissecting him, analyzing his every twitch, his every cough, his every blink. Was he on to him? "Do I need to hear about it?" Misha asked. That was good. Very good. His voice sounded bland, disinterested.

Semerov's eyes twinkled and opened wider, then squinted a little. "I suppose not, but I know that it interests you. Do you remember that American woman we talked about before you left for the Soviet Union, the one in the photograph?"

Rose Petersen. Karen Jones. Don't mix the names up, Misha, whatever you do. Keep them straight. Better yet, don't mention names at all. "I think so," he said. Another good response. Uncertainty is good. A fuzzy memory means that it isn't important to you. "You have in mind the lady who might be an American agent, correct?"

Those unrelenting little black eyes were staring, examining, studying, piercing to the very center of the universe. "That's right, Comrade Kostrin. She came to visit me in my office the morning after you and Ryzanov flew out of Montana."

Misha raised an eyebrow and made sure that Semerov noticed it. "Really?" he asked in a disbelieving tone. "What did she want?"

"She wanted to speak with Ryzanov. She said that her name

was Rose Petersen, that she was a dealer in nickel who had connections with the Communist Party here in America, and that she could get around the export restrictions on nickel and supply us with whatever we needed. She said she had met with Ryzanov several times and was ready to close the deal, but for some reason he had disappeared. She didn't want to lose this deal because she was short on money, and all she needed from Ryzanov was to work out the final details. Interesting, is it not?"

Misha nodded deliberately, genuinely. "Do you think that this is what was going on when I watched Nikolai that night?"

Semerov's stare softened, and he seemed to relax. "I don't know. But I played along and worked out the final details of the transaction with her, and by the end of the week there was a boat loaded with nickel heading east across the Atlantic."

"Do you think she's legitimate?"

"Why don't you tell me what you think first."

Misha cleared his throat. "I don't know, Comrade Semerov. Didn't you say she's been observed in several other places where our agents have made contacts?"

"Yes."

Misha wrinkled his lips and shook his head slightly, staring at the corner of the desk as if truly pondering the matter over. "Sounds suspicious to me, Comrade Semerov. Maybe she's an agent posing as a dealer in nickel."

Semerov tilted his head back slightly and put a hand up to his chin, covering his lips with a single finger, and his eyes were fixated on Misha again, studying him, examining him, cutting him to pieces. "You have excellent judgment, Comrade Kostrin," he said, then put his hand down. "Those are my thoughts exactly." Semerov stood up again and looked across the room at the window. "The question now, however, is what to do about Comrade Ryzanov. The alibi makes sense. I assigned him to obtain nickel for the Soviet Union, but the United States put an export ban on nickel. So, to fulfill his assignment, he went through unofficial channels, even though that meant entering a part of town that he knew was forbidden. The problem with this alibi, however, is that he never told me about it. All he had to do was inform me of the problem and ask my permission to meet with this woman there, this Rose Petersen person, but he didn't do it. He just met with her on his own initiative, knowing that he should not be there without my knowledge. Yet he did it anyway. This is what's bothering me."

The bloodhound at work. "Where is Nikolai now?"

"Petersen told me that she would only meet with Ryzanov in the future, that she knew him and trusted him and felt uncomfortable with anyone else. I realized that we might have been a little hasty in our suspicions about Ryzanov, so I immediately called Moscow, right in Petersen's presence, and told them to take no action. I didn't speak in specific terms, of course. I spoke in generalities and used a few code words to get my message across. The strange thing about that phone call is that she seemed to be paying close attention to what I was saying, as if she understood Russian." Semerov faced Misha. "What do you make of that, Comrade Kostrin?"

"Are you sure?" Misha asked.

Semerov rubbed his chin. "I'm positive," he said. "I think that woman is up to something."

"Perhaps she's probing us, trying to find a weak link. Maybe she posed as a nickel dealer just to make contact with Nikolai. Maybe she's trying to take advantage of him and he doesn't even know it."

Semerov was thinking. "But how did she know to pose as a nickel dealer in the first place?"

"Maybe Nikolai was asking around about nickel, and she picked up on it. Or maybe she really is a nickel dealer. She did deliver the goods, didn't she?"

"Yes, she did." Semerov put his hands on the desk and hung his head down. "I don't like it. Something still feels wrong."

It was good to see Semerov perplexed. "What should we do?"

Semerov lifted his head. "We'll just have to keep an eye on that woman—see what she's up to."

"Should I follow her?" Misha asked. This was the question he most needed an answer to. That would give him a pretense to make contact with her.

"If you think you can figure out what she's up to, then yes," Semerov said. "Perhaps you could meet with her. You could tell her that Comrade Ryzanov has been reassigned and that she should contact you from now on instead. You seem to have a way with people, anyway. Maybe she'll trust you. Everyone else seems to."

Misha could not have asked for a better response. "And Nikolai?"

"Comrade Ryzanov will likely be reassigned to the Soviet Purchasing Commission in Washington, so we need not worry about him for now. His replacement will arrive tomorrow."

So Nikolai was most likely still alive. Misha felt as though a boulder had been lifted off of his shoulders. But the thought of someone coming in to take Nikolai's place was disturbing. "Replacement?"

"Yes. I think you knew him when you worked at the Institute of Foreign Trade in Moscow."

Misha felt hollow inside. There was only one possibility. His stomach became ill. "Oh? Who is it?" he asked, even though he didn't want to hear the answer.

"His name is Malkov. He was deputy director of the Institute of Foreign Trade when he was recruited into the NKVD. He was supposed to come to New York over a year and a half ago, but the Centre reassigned him to the Lubyanka. They put him to work interrogating suspected enemies of the people, and word has it that he's very effective at weeding out disloyal elements. I specifically requested him. Maybe he can help us get to the bottom of this matter with Comrade Ryzanov."

Misha thought of Ivan and Olga at Ivan's birthday party, then of Larisa and Kolya on some passenger ship in the North Atlantic, thinking they were escaping the nightmare when in fact they were headed right back into the lion's den. "Is there anything else, Comrade Semerov?"

"Yes. You said Ryzanov was with two people, right? That

there was a man with Petersen on the night you followed Ryzanov."

"That's right."

"Comrade Malkov is in Alaska right now, and he just met with an American agent who fits the description you gave of the man who was with Petersen on the night that Ryzanov met with her. He's offered Malkov information about traitors within our organization here, and I believe it's the same man. We haven't figured him out yet, though. Either he's some kind of double agent who's serious about selling out the FBI, or else he's trying to bait us. We're not sure."

Misha's stomach was churning. "And this man was working with this Petersen lady?"

"I believe so."

It didn't take Misha long to put the pieces together. Petersen knew all about him and Nikolai, which meant that anyone in the FBI who worked closely with her probably knew about them, too. If what Semerov was saying was true, then he and Nikolai were in greater danger than he had realized. "Is there anything else I should know, Comrade Semerov?" he asked.

Semerov leaned forward and looked directly at him with those eery, devilish eyes of his that seemed to see right through him. "Be vigilant, Comrade Kostrin. It's always when things seem to be going well that problems creep in on you unexpectedly. Stay focused. Be diligent. You've been doing excellent work so far, but you never know when you might be caught off guard. As I told you before, don't let anything distract you."

Misha's knees felt weak. Don't let him see you trembling. Just take it easy. Relax. He doesn't know anything. "Yes, Comrade Semerov."

TWENTY-EIGHT

Misha's fear of the Party usually made him cower, but there was one exception where his fear engendered anger, and his anger gave rise to a defiant, almost absolute, confidence.

As Misha sat at his desk in the Amtorg building, he caught sight of Comrade Malkov out of the corner of his eye. Misha had spent the past two hours looking over the paperwork and financial records associated with the upcoming uranium shipment scheduled for June, although for the first time since he had come to work in New York City, he had found it hard to concentrate. All morning images of Larisa and Kolya and Rose Petersen and Nikolai and Captain Daniels and Comrade Semerov had flashed through his mind, each one with a different facial expression, each one speaking different words in a different tone of voice, each one producing a different emotional reaction within him. And now came the most unpleasant image of them all, except that this image was real.

Malkov was fat. Millions of Russians had bled and frozen and starved to death during the past two years, but Comrade Malkov was fat. Huge fleshy jowls hung from the sides of his face, and a puffy double chin cushioned his neck against the collar of his shirt. Even his nose looked larger. His forehead was wide, his black hair parted now by a massive bald spot in the middle of his head, and a thin pair of perfectly round spectacles lay upon the bridge of his nose, which reminded Misha more of a beak. Malkov's skin was rougher than it had been four years ago. There were more moles and bumps and creases, and the eyes were darker; not that they had changed color in any physical sense, but morally, spiritually, they were—darker. They reminded him of other eyes that he had seen before. They were the same eyes that he had seen in Comrade Vorlakov. They were the eyes of Comrade Semerov.

Malkov walked casually over to Misha's desk, and he looked pleased. "Well, Comrade Kostrin, we meet again. It has been a very long time, has it not?"

Misha's stomach felt hollow. "Not long enough," he said, staring into that fat face with the evil eyes glistening behind the fiendish little lenses.

"Why so hostile, Comrade? You and I are going to be working together." Malkov's lips curled upward slightly, almost unnoticeably. A smile?

Misha set down on the desk the papers he had been holding in his hand and held his eye contact steady. "Did you want something?"

Yes, it was a smile. A thin, transparent smile that veiled nothing. Malkov's eyes sparkled, and the skin around his mouth and nose creased into a haughty sneer. "I met your wife for the second time while I was in Sverdlovsk a year and a half ago. You were fortunate. She is a very beautiful woman. She was heartbroken by your neglect, I must confess, but fortunately I was there to satisfy her needs."

Misha slowly stood up, keeping his eye contact steady. Malkov's hint was far from subtle. Misha thought of Larisa in an isolated apartment on the outskirts of Sverdlovsk, alone and afraid, Kolya sleeping in a back bedroom, with this murderous swine prowling around her, intimidating her, preying upon her. Misha couldn't even imagine what kinds of sick and twisted thoughts must have passed through that warped, massive head behind the little spectacles, nor did Misha want to think about it.

Met his wife for the second time. Misha remembered the first time, Ivan's birthday party at the end of thirty-eight, Ivan and Olga together, talking and smiling, almost happy, real living people with a past and a future, with hopes and dreams and aspirations; and Comrade Malkov with them, smiling with them, joking with them, speaking so properly and softly that even Larisa had been fooled into thinking that he was a decent person.

The white tree in the forest came to mind, leaning, tipping, falling, the roots beginning to pop and tear and break and jut out of the ground, the massive trunk moving through the air, slowly at first, then gaining speed, slicing through the black vortex that threatened to swallow Misha whole, crashing into the ground with such a tremendous boom as to send shockwaves throughout the earth. Then blackening, rotting, vanishing away, another meaningless existence now terminated and seeping into the cold dirt of oblivion, silenced forever, lifeless. He imagined how Olga must have appeared when she was found in her bathroom, her wrists slit open, her expression vacuous and apathetic. Two innocent people. Two innocent lives. Vanished. Gone. Mere stepping stones on Malkov's career ladder.

As Misha watched his nemesis before him, time stood still.

Malkov's face was still smug, the dark, empty eyes implanted deep into the sockets, the fake, shallow smile still dripping with deceit. The hollowness in Misha's stomach was now churning, and a strange sensation of warmth began to flow throughout his body. It started in his stomach and rose into his chest, where it paused to fill and pulsate and thrive and intensify, then moved up to his throat so that he had to swallow to cap it off and push it down, but it went from there into the tops of his shoulders and through his arms to his very fingertips; and from the depths of his belly it flowed downward as well, down into his thighs, down into his calves, down into his feet and out to the tips of his toes; and finally it surmounted the pressure he exerted upon it in his throat, and it moved up the sides of his neck, up into his ears, up across his scalp and into his forehead and throughout all the skin beneath his hair so that his ears felt hot and his forehead felt hot and the skin was tense all over and it was as though his entire body had become a radiator and was gearing up for an explosion that he knew he would be unable to control.

Misha was invincible now, almighty. The fear was gone. Now there was only anger, and a supreme feeling of power. Fear had become power. And a curious feeling of joyful anticipation singed the edges of that power. Pleasure. Satisfaction. He had become something. And Malkov was nothing.

Without any thought or hesitation, Misha reached out with his right hand and extended it forward, and he could feel flowing through his arm the warmth of that strange power that filled his body, and he knew that his arm was now like a hydraulic jack and that it could crush anything that it grabbed. His hand shot forward and managed to get under the fat cushion under the chin, and although the neck was large, Misha got a good hold. His fingers gripped solidly, tightly, so that Malkov's larynx was in Misha's palm, and with his thumb Misha pressed up and inward beneath the fat layer until Misha could feel the wall of the windpipe quiver within his fingers.

Pleasure. Satisfaction. The greatest feeling in the world. But in the back of his mind, some quiet voice warned him not to yield to it. The power of his anger produced ecstasy, but the ecstacy was dark.

Malkov's sneer dissipated into an expression of shock and surprise. The smile vanished. The black, empty eyes were wide and frightened. Malkov choked and struggled to breathe, but it was futile. Instinctively he put both of his fat hands up to Misha's forearm and grabbed it, trying to pull it away, but there was a strength and a power and an invincibility now in Misha's arm that Misha knew Malkov could not overcome.

Misha kept his grip but retracted his arm, pulling Malkov toward him so that Malkov's upper thighs pressed into the edge of the desk and set his weight off balance, and Misha could feel Malkov's enormous weight shift from the feet to the front of the thighs. And the neck. But Misha's grip was solid and his arm was like the arm of a crane and he easily held Malkov off balance, and there was a sick, evil, dark pleasure that welled up inside of Misha's soul as he stared into Malkov's empty black eyes and felt Malkov sprawling across the desk, his disgusting fat throat quivering in Misha's hand.

Malkov took his right hand off of Misha's arm and arched it back behind him, then brought it forward with as much force as he could in an attempt to strike a blow to Misha's face, but the strange powerful warmth made Misha's reflexes quick and accurate, and with his left hand he caught Malkov's arm by the wrist, then flung it back. Malkov's body twitched, then he again held on to Misha's right forearm with both hands and struggled desperately to breathe. Misha let up with his thumb slightly, and a faint gasp of air was sucked into Malkov's windpipe, just enough to keep him from losing consciousness, and Misha could feel Malkov's throat quivering against his finger as the air flowed through.

But the dark pleasure was waning. The quiet voice of conscience deep in the back of his mind was calling to him. Misha was beginning to regain control of this strange insanity that had gripped him.

Misha leaned forward so that their faces were just inches apart, and he made sure that he didn't flinch at all while he stared into Malkov's eyes, which stared back in an ocean of fear and desperation and uncertainty. With a slight rotation of his hand, Misha turned Malkov's head a few degrees to Misha's right, just enough so that Malkov's right ear was exposed, but not enough to prevent Malkov's eyes from maintaining a strained contact with Misha's.

Misha spoke quietly, calmly, almost in a whisper. "I'm not afraid of you, Comrade Malkov," he said. "I'm not afraid of Semerov, I'm not afraid of the Party or the NKGB, I'm not afraid of Stalin himself. I'm not afraid of anything. Not even death. Not even torture. And I'm going to be watching you from now on, you understand? Everywhere you go. All the time. And you're going to stay out of my way, and you're going to leave me and my family alone, and if you do anything to harm my wife or son, I'm going to kill you. And I won't think twice about it. Do you understand that?"

Malkov's eyes were terrified, and with what little mobility he had, he made a nodding gesture.

The pleasure was gone, the warm flowing power inside of Misha was fading, darkness was creeping in all around him. He shoved Malkov backward and let go. Malkov gasped and coughed and held his hands up to his throat and could barely stay standing. A few other accountants, who had been standing several meters away down the row of desks, now took notice of what was going on. They stopped talking to each other and looked at Malkov, then at Misha. Misha ignored them and turned his back on Malkov, walked away from his desk in the opposite direction of the staring workers, and made his way outside of the Amtorg building.

He immediately went to the new apartment that he was living in, threw himself on his bed, and buried his face into a pillow. I didn't want to do that, he told himself. I didn't mean to do that. Everything is worse now. Why did Malkov make me do that? He dared not think of what consequences would follow from this, what Semerov might do, what might happen to Larisa and Kolya now. His body trembled and shook from head to toe, and he sobbed uncontrollably into the pillow for what seemed like hours, until he finally fell asleep.

TWENTY-NINE

It was a warm day and Karen Jones wore a modest business outfit: long brown skirt, button-up blouse, snug-fitting jacket. The sky was a beautiful blue, and several puffy white clouds sailed gently overhead while a slow-moving breeze wisped through the treetops, making a soothing rustle as it passed over the lush green leaves that shaded the walkway. She walked through the doorway and sized the place up: empty tables and chairs almost everywhere, two men at the lunch counter. The owner of the place wore a white apron and held a broom in his hands, and was making his way in and out of the tables and chairs, sweeping the floor. He looked to be in his forties, and he gave her a big friendly smile. "Good afternoon, miss," he said. "Can I get you something?"

"Not now, thanks," she said. "I'm waiting for a friend."

"Suit yourself," the man said as he went back to his sweeping. "Just let me know when you're ready."

She walked to a table against the wall and sat down, setting her purse beside her, and pulled out a small book and pretended to read. Boris showed up five minutes later, and he looked like a nervous wreck. His dark hair was uncombed, his eyes had circles under them, his tie was crooked, and his shirt and jacket were both wrinkled. What did he do, sleep in his clothes? He looked around nervously once he came through the door, spotted her immediately, then hurried to her table and sat down. He hardly even looked at her. He just sat there for a minute in silence, running his fingers through his hair.

"Should I call you Boris or Misha?" she asked in a casual way, hoping to put him at ease.

"Misha," he said, but he didn't look at her when he answered, and his mind seemed to be somewhere else.

"Are you all right?" she asked.

"Terrible," he said.

She noticed that he hadn't shaved. "Is something wrong?"

"I'm a dead man."

She looked around. One of the men at the lunch counter stood up and left some money next to his empty plate, then thanked the owner on his way out. "Are you being followed?" she asked.

"I don't know. I don't think so."

She watched him for a few seconds. His nervousness wasn't the panicky, urgent kind; it was the generalized, chronic type. "Are you going to be okay?"

He shook his head several times, which made her wonder if he had a grip on things, but then he took a deep breath and seemed to relax. "It's getting too dangerous," he said. "I can't do this any more."

"What's too dangerous?"

"I'm going insane. They're driving me insane."

"Who? What are you talking about?"

"Semerov is suspicious of me. Of you, too. He wants me to report to him about you so that he can figure out whether or not you're a legitimate dealer."

"What does he think right now?"

"He thinks you're working for the FBI."

She put her book back into her purse. "What about Alfred?"

"Nikolai's disappeared and I don't know where he is."

"Is he still alive?"

"I think so. But I can't be sure. If he is, then he's probably at the Soviet Purchasing Commission in Washington. We're preparing another uranium shipment for later this month. Same route as last time."

"What about your wife and son? Where are they right now?"

His ran his hand through his hair again and stared down at the table. "They'll be here soon. They're on their way right now. I thought they'd be here already, but there have been some delays. I think they'll arrive next week."

"Are you going to accompany the next shipment?"

"Yes."

A perfect time to repress him. It bothered her that she didn't know where Alfred was.

"There's another thing, too," he said. "One of your agents is going to sell you out."

She raised her eyebrows and cocked her head back. "I seriously doubt that."

He shook his head. "It's true. The agent that you've been working with, the one who went to Alaska. He recently approached one of Semerov's people with an offer to exchange information for money and safe passage to South America."

"Agent Howard? Not possible. He's been with the bureau for years. He's one of the most serious agents we have. Not much of a socialite, but well respected and highly trusted. He would never sell out, especially not for money, and definitely not to the Soviets. He hates all of you people."

"I heard it from Semerov himself. I can't be absolutely positive, but I think this agent of yours wants to exchange information about me and Nikolai. I'm worried sick about it."

Karen shook her head. "Howard is solid," she said. "You have to trust me on this one. If he did approach one of your men—"

"He did."

"Then it's probably because he's baiting your organization. He's probably trying to pry open an even wider crack in Semerov's circle of agents."

Misha looked up at her, and she could see the worry in his eyes. "Are you absolutely sure?" he asked.

"Yes," she said.

"All right." He slowly let out a deep breath. He was calmer.

"Once your wife and son arrive, I'll keep an eye on them. With Nikolai we were planning to stage an accident or something like that to make him disappear; maybe we can do the same for you. But we can't put a plan into effect until after your wife and son are here. If they're not here in the next week or two, you'll have to accompany the next shipment of uranium.

Otherwise we'll arouse too much suspicion. In that case I'll try to arrange for you to escape in Montana, but I can't guarantee anything."

He nodded. "I understand."

"Hey," she said, and she squeezed his hand. "Take it easy, all right? You're almost there. Just hang in there a little longer, and this will all be over."

Two weeks later, Misha sat on a park bench and threw bread crumbs at the pigeons. Larisa still hadn't arrived, and he knew that in a few days he would again be on a transport plane to the Soviet Union with the next shipment of uranium chemicals. That was the bad news. The good news was that nothing had happened at Amtorg in regard to his last encounter with Malkov. The other workers who had been in the room that day apparently hadn't paid attention to what was going on until it was all over. All they saw was Malkov gasping for air and Misha leaving. They probably assumed Malkov had been choking on his own spittle or something like that. And Semerov hadn't said anything when Misha talked to him the week before. Maybe Malkov hadn't told the old demon after all. Maybe Malkov was too much of a coward. In fact, Misha had seen Malkov a few times during the past couple of weeks, but hadn't talked to him. He and Malkov were avoiding each other like the plague, and that was just fine with him. Too bad life hadn't been this way back in his old days at the Institute of Foreign Trade. But then he thought better of it. No, Malkov is definitely up to something. Right now he's just biding his time, waiting for an opportunity. It's all just a game, just a matter of time.

Shipman sat down next to him and handed him a package without making any attempt at all to ensure they were unnoticed. Good old Shipman. Clumsy, awkward, conspicuous as black dirt on fresh snow. But effective. And reliable.

"How's Wheeler?" Misha asked.

"Oh, Wheeler. What a whiner. He got offended again and

says he won't help us any more. We've heard it before. But I don't care because I've got another contact now who has access."

"You always come through for us, Sam. Semerov says you're going to be named Hero of the Soviet Union for your work."

Shipman's eyes sparkled. The yellow grin was wider than ever. "Marvelous," he said.

"It's all here?" Misha asked, patting the brown package.

"All of it. Good stuff this time, too. Specs for gaseous and thermal diffusion plants, whatever those are. I assume it has something to do with all those uranium compounds you've been asking for."

"Don't get too curious, Sam. And don't ask questions about this stuff."

The smile disappeared instantly. "Of course not, of course not," he said. "I would never even dream—"

"This might be our last meeting, Sam."

"Oh? Why is that?"

"I'm going back to the Soviet Union with the next shipment. And Semerov believes the FBI is on to us. He wants us to keep a low profile for at least a few months, until things cool off a little. Besides, most of the stuff you're giving us right now we can obtain ourselves through the Lend-Lease program."

"That's too bad, Boris. I will miss this work."

"It's not over for you yet, Sam. Semerov wants to see you. He'll keep in touch with you and find something for you to do, if you're still interested."

"Oh, yes. Yes. Of course."

Misha stood up and looked at Shipman's face. Bulbous nose, ruddy complexion, yellow teeth, mischievous eyes.

What a fool.

Misha extended his hand, and Shipman shook it. "Take care of yourself, Sam."

"Good luck to you, Boris."

THIRTY

The door opened and Comrade Malkov walked inside, and Semerov raised his head from the paperwork he had piled on the top of his desk. The fat head and paunchy figure rotated a half circle to close the door behind it, then it turned back around to face Semerov. Malkov's face had that zealous, self-righteous look on it that only religious fanatics and devout, self-justifying, hypocritical communists could make. The jaw was set, the lips tight, the brow wrinkled slightly. The eyes were steady and determined, the sure indication that whatever it was that the person behind those eyes was thinking was of the utmost gravity in that person's mind. But Semerov knew that it probably wasn't nearly as important as the person thought. It never was.

If there was one thing that Semerov hated, it was self-righteous, self-serving careerists.

"You could have knocked, Comrade Malkov."

The ugly face came closer, right up to the desk. "I had an appointment to speak with you, Comrade Semerov."

Semerov casually lifted his left wrist and looked at his watch for several seconds, dragging it out to make sure the hint was not overlooked. "So you did," he said. "Five minutes ago."

"I apologize for the delay, Comrade Semerov. But I assure you that what I have to say is of the utmost importance."

Semerov calmly stood up and looked into Malkov's face. "If it's so important, Comrade, then why are you late?"

Malkov seemed taken aback. He said nothing.

"Sit down, Comrade Malkov."

Both men took a seat.

"Now, what great piece of news are you going to reveal to me today?" Semerov asked. Semerov's high hopes and expectations of his newest employee had all been shattered, and that's why he deliberately made his tone condescending. Pieces of scum like

Malkov had to be kept in their places.

Malkov cleared his throat and sat up straight. That's right, Comrade Malkov. Get yourself prepped. Make your big announcement. "Comrade Semerov, I have reason to believe that Comrade Kostrin is an enemy of the people."

Malkov went silent for several moments, and Semerov could tell by looking into that sniveling, sneering face that Malkov was waiting for some kind of dramatic reaction from the NKGB resident. But Semerov was cool and calm. No reaction was forthcoming. "That's a very serious charge, Comrade Malkov. Comrade Kostrin is one of my most productive and reliable agents. Do you have any evidence to support your claim?" Malkov looked disappointed, and this pleased Semerov. Shallow egos are so easy to deflate.

"Of course, Comrade Semerov."

Semerov waited. No response. Only a blank stare from Malkov. "Well, Comrade Malkov? Are you going to tell me what your evidence is, or are we going to sit here all day staring at each other?"

Malkov straightened his tie and cleared his throat again. That's right, Comrade Malkov, prep yourself one more time. Give it another try. "Comrade Semerov, I've been distrustful of Comrade Kostrin since the moment I arrived here, and I've kept my eye on him. Yesterday I followed him to that Jewish part of town that you told us to stay away from, and I saw him meeting with that FBI woman that you warned us about."

Again there was a long pause as Malkov waited for the dramatic reaction, and again Semerov denied it to him. "Rose Petersen?" Semerov asked.

"Yes."

Semerov blinked slowly, deliberately. "I already know, Comrade Malkov."

Malkov's eyes were shifty. He examined Semerov's face. "You already know?" he asked. His tone of voice was surprised, uncertain.

Semerov nodded his head a couple times, just a little to

emphasize his disinterest, and he blinked another slow, apathetic blink. "I know everything, Comrade Malkov."

Malkov looked confused. "But . . ." He stuttered as he tried to find the words. "But shouldn't we do something about this? Comrade Kostrin represents a serious security threat."

"So what do you want me to do, Comrade? Denounce him? Ship him back to the USSR and have you put a bullet in the back of his brain so that you can take his place?"

Malkov looked stunned.

"Comrade Malkov, I personally asked Comrade Kostrin to meet with Rose Petersen. Thanks to the reports he's been giving me the past couple of weeks, I now know for certain that she's an agent with the FBI and that she's specifically targeting our operations. If it weren't for him, I'd still be guessing. And now you come in here acting like you see the big picture and know what's going on, when in reality you don't know anything."

Malkov's skin was losing its color.

Semerov rose from his chair and sarcastically clapped his hands several times as he strolled around the back of Malkov. "Bravo, Comrade Malkov. I applaud you. What do want now, a medal? Or do you just want Comrade Kostrin's job? Or is it something else? Jealousy maybe? Envy? Did Comrade Kostrin spite you long ago? Is that what this is all about? Revenge? Just because he's always been better than you whenever you've competed with him?" Semerov walked around to Malkov's left side and stopped. He looked down at Malkov sitting in the chair, but Malkov didn't look back up at him. "There's only one assignment that I've given you that I need you to report to me about, and that's your contact with Agent Howard. Nothing else concerns me. Now, have you met with him yet or not?"

"I'll meet with him at the end of the week, Comrade Semerov."

"The end of the week. Good. And you'll bring me a full report?"

"Of course, Comrade Semerov."

"Excellent." Semerov strolled back to his chair, but didn't sit down. "Comrade Malkov, how long have you known Comrade Kostrin?"

"About five years."

Semerov opened a drawer, pulled out a folder, and dropped it on top of the desk, making a gentle slapping noise. "This folder has some information that I've gathered about you, Comrade Malkov. You denounced one of your instructors at the Institute of Foreign Trade, as well as Comrade Kostrin's best friend, who were both promptly repressed. Then, seeing that Comrade Kostrin was the only accountant ranked higher than you, you denounced him as well. What a shock it must have been to you when the NKVD not only didn't repress him, but recruited him." Semerov paused for a second to enjoy watching Malkov's face continue to grow pale. "I must say that you've disappointed me. I requested that you be sent here because I was told that you're an excellent agent with a knack for rooting out enemies of the people. Now that I've actually had to work with you, however, I've learned the bitter truth that you're just another murderous careerist."

"That's not true, Comrade Semerov."

Semerov placed his hands on the desk and leaned forward eagerly. "Oh, but it is true, Comrade Malkov. You've underestimated me. Don't you remember that little conversation we had when you first arrived, when I told you that I have a special talent, that I can see through people, that I know you better than you know yourself?"

"Of course I remember, Comrade Semerov."

Semerov smiled. "The Party is full of murderous little pigs like you, Malkov. You are a tiny little man, like an insect on the wall. You're petty and you're weak, and I don't trust you. Do you know why? Because I've dealt with swine like you before, and I know that if I let you stay here, you'll be after my job, and you'll be denouncing me just as you're denouncing Comrade Kostrin right now. But it won't work, Comrade Malkov. You've already made the one mistake that no agent of mine can afford to make. You've underestimated me."

Malkov was white as a sheet and sat in absolute silence.

"Just so you know, Comrade Malkov, you will have no more assignments under my direction after tomorrow. I've already sent my recommendation back to the Centre that you are unfit for overseas assignment. You're much better suited to the internal purges of Moscow and the torture chambers of the Lubyanka. So this is what you're going to do. You're going to meet with Agent Howard this week and find out who the leaks are in our organization. Then you're going to report back to me."

Malkov looked up and scowled viciously. "And if it turns out that the traitors are Ryzanov and Kostrin?"

Semerov laughed. "Then when you give your report, you can stand here and laugh in my face all you want. But I still can't work with you. And it won't change anything, because when Kostrin and Ryzanov accompany the next uranium shipment, you'll be on the cargo plane with them. Do you have any other questions?"

"No, Comrade Semerov."

"Cheer up, Comrade Malkov. Don't take this personally. And don't be sore at me. I'll tell you what. If it turns out that you're right about Comrade Kostrin, then I'll send a special recommendation for you back to Moscow Centre and let them know that you deserve a promotion. Our soldiers are already making their way toward Europe, and I'm sure we'll need a man like you to process them once they return home with their new knowledge of how much better life is outside of the Soviet Union. Trust me, Comrade Malkov, you'll have plenty of work to do back home. But I've already seen to it that you won't have a career in foreign intelligence gathering. So get in touch with your buddies back in Moscow. Shore up some support for yourself. Make sure your connections there are intact, because that's where you're heading. Now get out of my office."

Malkov arose slowly from his chair, defeated, angry, crushed, hateful. For once the little sycophant had nothing to say, which suited Semerov. Semerov waited until Malkov reached the door and had his hand on the handle before addressing him again.

"One more thing, Comrade Malkov," he said. Malkov stopped at the door but didn't turn around. "It's a shame that you're not more like Comrade Kostrin. He's the kind of man that I was hoping you would be when I requested you."

The door opened, the fat ugly wretch slipped out, and the door closed gently behind him.

Once Malkov had left out the front door of the office, Semerov walked over to another wall and opened a door that led into a small adjacent room. A special courier from the Soviet consulate in New York stepped out and closed the door behind him.

"You were awfully harsh with him," the courier said.

"I had to be. He's ruining my entire organization here. Everyone has caught on to him, and now my agents are so paranoid about getting denounced themselves that it's distracting them from their work. His credentials looked so good on paper, and the bureaucracy at the Lubyanka loves him, but having him in this office has been a nightmare. Bringing him here was the worst mistake I've ever made."

"Don't you think you should have waited until after he met with Agent Howard?"

"It doesn't matter. You'll eavesdrop on their meeting at the end of the week, so even if he doesn't report back to me, I'll still get the information. But knowing Malkov, he'll be eager to make that report, especially since I insulted him."

The courier nodded. "What about Kostrin and Ryzanov? Do you think they're the ones?"

Semerov stared at the floor. "I'm pretty sure Ryzanov is guilty. But as for Kostrin, I need Howard's information to be sure about it. My instincts tell me something is going on with Kostrin, but I'm not sure what it is."

"What about Kostrin's wife?"

"She'll be here any day now. When I had the Centre put her on that boat, I had no idea we'd be suspicious of Kostrin, too. Kostrin needed a morale boost, and since he was one of my best agents, I decided to give it to him. I thought he just missed his wife. I didn't realize that other things might be distracting him as well. But it's no big deal. If Kostrin turns out to be guilty, we'll bring his wife in, too. We'll get Agent Howard to do it so that we don't have to waste the manpower. All of this suspicion about our people is hurting our efficiency."

THIRTY-ONE

Mark Daniels entered the makeshift office, closed the door behind him, turned around, and gave Old Eagle Eye a sharp salute.

The colonel arose from his chair and saluted back. “At ease, Daniels,” he said.

Mark removed his hat and approached the desk. “You wanted to see me, sir?”

“I just wanted to let you know that we’re expecting another special shipment in the next few days, and I want you to be the pilot for it.”

“More black suitcases?”

Griggs wrinkled his eyebrow as if to say, Daniels, we’ve talked about the suitcases already and I don’t want to go over it again with you. “Probably,” he said. “We’re going to ship it out on that same bird that you flew the last time we had a special shipment—the silver plane that we still haven’t painted green yet.”

“I know the one.”

“Good. Now these Russians have been getting more and more pushy and secretive all the time, especially with regard to this particular shipment. I don’t know what it is they’re so touchy about, and I don’t care, but I want you to be careful and keep an eye on their people all the same. Leave the cargo alone, but watch the couriers.”

“Is there something wrong?”

“I’m not sure, Daniels. A few days ago some very unfriendly Russians showed up at the airfield. Very serious bunch. Very secretive.”

“I thought all Russians were unfriendly.”

The colonel smiled. “They are.” The smile vanished instantly. “But these guys are even worse. There’s something different about them, something in their eyes, something in the way they behave. There's a harder edge to them. Something dark and sinister about them. And they carry weapons."

"What do you think is going on?"

"I don't know. I'm not even sure that there is anything going on other than another shipment of highly classified chemicals. But they're particularly concerned about this next load, and a couple of them will probably escort the crates, so I want you and your crew to watch yourselves, just in case they pull anything. And I want you to be armed."

"What could they possibly pull?" Mark asked. "If they want their cargo to go through, then they won't interfere with us, don't you think?"

Griggs nodded. "I agree. I'm sure this mission will go just like every other flight out of this airfield, and I didn't intend to get you all worked up over it. But I still feel uneasy about this new bunch of Russians, and I want you to take extra precautions."

☆

Misha sat on the couch next to Larisa, staring at her with a sorrowful longing in his heart, admiring the shiny waves in her hair. Her eyes were melancholy today; the corners of her lips were tight and turned down. They had been together in New York barely three days now since she and Kolya had finally arrived, and he was preparing to leave for Montana the next day. It wasn't enough time.

The apartment was nice, though, and afforded them more autonomy from Amtorg. Being on the third floor, it didn't have much of a view, but the interior was better than anything he had ever lived in before. Spacious, comfortable, clean. By all outward appearances, he was doing very well. Semerov considered him one of the most valuable agents at Amtorg now and had recommended him for promotion and higher pay. And to have Larisa and Kolya here, who were allowed to travel across the Atlantic at the expense of the Soviet government in the middle of the war—

it was unbelievable. Unheard of. The fact that the Centre had allowed such extravagancies for him during such a desperate time meant that whatever he was doing here in New York must be extremely valuable to the Party apparatus back home. Only ambassadors and *rezidents* and high-profile diplomats received these kinds of perquisites. Something about uranium was very special, and his success in obtaining information about it through the contacts he had established had made him into one of the Centre's most favored agents.

He thought of the millions of his countrymen back home, fighting and dying as they battled against the Wehrmacht; and he thought of the millions of farmers and peasants and others who had died under the communists during the years leading up to this war, like Ivan and Olga and Lindenbaum; and he thought of himself, how close he had come to extermination only a few years before; and now he was in one of the most enviable positions a man could be in, living out the war in comfort and peace, far away from the bloody fields of combat and the constant threat of the secret police. Not bad for a destitute orphan from an unknown village whose parents and uncle had all been liquidated.

But there was no pleasure in it. Only anxiety. And fear. Semerov had been acting oddly the past couple of days. The demonic little black eyes had looked at him differently than they used to. There was an air of suspicion at the office. Everyone was under enormous pressure to finalize this latest shipment of uranium chemicals, and the thought of Semerov watching him the way he had watched Nikolai was agonizing.

"What are you thinking?" Larisa asked.

"Nothing," he said. He held her hand.

"You're worried about tomorrow, aren't you."

"Yes."

"Something is wrong, isn't it. You're worried about tomorrow because you're not sure you'll be coming back."

He turned his head toward her, surprised by her pessimism. "Why do you say that?" he asked.

Her eyes showed the weight of her concern. “Because the last time I saw you like this was when you had to go back to the Lubyanka when you were first recruited. You can’t hide these things from me, Misha. We may have been away from each other for a long time, but I’m still your wife, and I can tell when things are going badly.”

He hung his head down and stared at their interlocked hands. “I can’t put my finger on it exactly,” he said, “but I think Semerov is suspicious of me. He knows I’ve been meeting with this American FBI woman, and I thought I had him convinced that I was just doing surveillance work on her, but I’m beginning to think that he suspects I have an ulterior motive.”

“Has he said anything to you?”

“No. Not yet. But he’s assigned Malkov to accompany this shipment with me, and I think it’s because he wants Malkov to keep an eye on me. Malkov’s been working as an interrogator. He’s an insider at the Lubyanka. Semerov requested him in order to find out what was going on with Nikolai, and now I think the two of them are focusing their attention on me.”

“Do you think they’re sending you back to have you repressed?”

“I don’t know. But it would be a perfect opportunity for them.” He released her hand and fished through his pocket for a small notepad that he always carried with him, then he pulled out a short pencil and started writing. “There’s something I need to give you, just in case. I’ve told Rose Petersen about you and Kolya. She’s going to try to get me and Nikolai out of Montana, and she’ll come to the apartment to pick you up after I leave New York. Here’s a number where you can reach Rose Petersen. She speaks Russian, so you can talk to her in Russian or in English. If anyone other than she comes to the apartment, dial this number.” He ripped the paper out of the notebook and handed it to her. She stared at it for a few seconds, then put it in her purse on the stand at the side of the couch.

Next to the purse lay the small brown book that Captain Daniels had given to Misha on the flight from Alaska to

Montana, and it rested on top of the little black book that Misha had received so many years ago from his uncle. Misha noticed Larisa looking at the two books. She gently rubbed her finger over the top of the brown book. She rested her hand on it for a moment, then picked it up.

"What are you doing?" Misha asked.

She turned her head to him, and her brown eyes reflected the light of the lamp across the room. Her face looked exhausted, but placid. "The past couple of days I've been reading this book that the American pilot gave you," she said. "Have you read it?"

A twinge of guilt passed through him. "No," he said. "I've browsed through it a little, but I haven't read it yet. I've had my mind on other things."

She held the book in her hands and rotated it a couple of times, looking over its cover and edges and title as if it were some kind of jewel. "There's something special about this book, Misha. It's similar to the book that your uncle gave you."

Misha stared into his lap and thought of his talk with Captain Daniels on the way back to Montana. He had felt so good during that conversation. But with all the stress and the intrigues that were going on the past little while, he had lost that feeling. And whenever his mind turned to God now, all he could think about was why God would allow all of these terrible things to happen. "I don't understand either one of those books," he said. "They both seem to be full of fairy tales and nothing more."

He looked back up at her to see her reaction, but she just turned her head away from him and put the book back on the little table. Then she looked into his eyes. "I believe in both of these books, Misha. And I believe that there really is a God, and that He is watching over us, and that if we will trust in Him, He will help us."

There was a tension in Misha's chest when she said these things; it was a feeling of irritation, of impatience, of frustration. "I don't understand how you can believe in such things," he said. "We have seen so much death and suffering in the Soviet Union. We have lived in fear for so long. If we were to tell the world what has occurred in our country during the past twenty years, no one would even believe us because it is more horrible than any sane person could imagine. And now you're telling me that there is a God who loves us. If He's so loving, then how could He allow the communists to come to power? How could He allow the largest nation on earth to crumble into pieces at the hands of lunatics and murderers?" He felt angry all of a sudden, and he wasn't sure if he was angry at God or his wife. "It's the good people who have suffered, Larisa, while the evil people are the ones who have benefitted since the communists took over. How can you explain that and tell me that there is a God? My uncle always believed in God and told me that I should, too, but look what his faith did for him."

"Your uncle was a good man, Misha, and now he's in a better place."

Misha let out a sarcastic, cynical laugh. "He's rotting in the ground somewhere. All because of his faith." He surprised himself with his tone. He hadn't meant to sound so caustic. The stress had taken a greater toll on him than he had realized.

Larisa put a soft hand on his. "Misha, I know you, and I know you don't mean what you're saying. Don't lie to yourself. Don't look for scapegoats and excuses. That's what the Party does." Larisa's voice was calm and self-assured, and her confidence intimidated him.

The anger and irritation and tension was changing inside of him, turning into something else, but he didn't know what. It was as though all of his emotions had wadded up into a ball and melted, and were now a glowing, burning mass inside of his soul that was expanding and rising up into his throat.

Larisa put her hand on his arm. Her hand was small and delicate, her skin smooth, her fingers slender. "Misha," she said almost in a whisper. "What would your uncle do if he were here?"

The image of his uncle filled him with guilt. His wife was right. He had to hang in there.

Misha put his hand up to his forehead and shook his head

back and forth. "I'm afraid, Larisa. I've been playing cat and mouse games with the Party for so long that it has become a way of life for me. But I can't do it any more. I'm making mistakes. They're on to me again, and this time I don't think I'll get away as I did last time."

"Misha." Her voice was soft and calm and soothing. The confidence in her voice was no longer intimidating; now it was strangely reassuring. She put her hand on his shoulder, then started slowly rubbing his back. "You're a good man, and you're strong. You must not let them break you. Don't you remember what your uncle used to tell you about faith and integrity and living by good principles? I remember how you used to talk about him all the time when we first got married. How much you admired him. How much you missed him."

Misha thought of the forest and the vortex and the rolling fields of grain and the empty church and his uncle vanishing. "My uncle left me," he said.

"Your uncle was taken from you."

He swallowed hard and wiped his eyes and ran his hand through his hair and cleared his throat. "I'm not coming back, Larisa. They're taking me to my death."

"Why can't you call Rose Petersen right now? Couldn't she take us to safety before you leave for Montana?"

He shook his head. "It's not possible."

"Why not?"

"Because of Nikolai. I think he's still alive. Semerov said he's probably at the Soviet Purchasing Commission in Washington, D.C., and that he'll likely be on this transport plane with me."

"Can't Rose Petersen arrange to take Nikolai, too?"

"No. Semerov said Nikolai is under suspicion, which means they'll be watching him there. They won't let him out of their sight, and the FBI can't jeopardize relations between the US and the USSR over one or two Soviet agents who don't want to be spies any more."

"Do you know for sure that Nikolai will be on that plane?"

"No," he said, and he paused to think about it for a second.

Could he make a run for it right now? But if he did . . . He shook his head. "No, I have to be on that plane tomorrow. It's my fault that Nikolai's life is in danger, and if I don't show up tomorrow, he'll be repressed for sure. I have to be on that plane. For his sake."

He felt Larisa's hand squeezing his arm, and he looked at her face. He could see in her eyes that she understood. This was not the same Larisa that he had once known. This was not the same woman who years before, panicky and desperate and afraid, had pleaded with him to run away. It was still Larisa who sat before him, yet somehow it was a different Larisa. She was calmer, more mature. "I think we'll be okay, Misha. I think God will take care of us."

Wishful thinking. "I hope you're right," he said. His only hope now was that Rose Peterson would somehow be able to get him and Nikolai out of Montana.

Malkov sat across the table from Agent Howard and watched the large, serious face as the American leaned forward. "Well," Howard said, "was I right?"

Malkov nodded slowly. Yes, Howard had been right. Malkov now had all the information he needed on Rose Petersen. He knew exactly what she was looking for, what she was suspicious of, whom she was doing surveillance on. He even knew her life story now: schooling, hobbies, family, prior relationships. He knew her real name. He knew enough now to know how to stop her cold, but even better, he knew how to bait her, deceive her, lead her down false trails, give her wrong impressions, guide her to inaccurate conclusions. The only piece of the puzzle he didn't have was who the two traitors were.

Semerov was such a fool, trying to transfer him. No, he wasn't going back to Moscow. He had his contacts within the Party. He was going to stay right here, not under Semerov's direction, of course, but foreign intelligence was his key to more power, and now he was about to receive some information that was going to make him more valuable to the Centre than Kostrin ever was.

If only he had received it sooner. Then he could have uncovered Kostrin's clever lies about Rose Petersen. He could have shown Semerov who was the more valuable man at Amtorg. He could have avoided the blow-up with Semerov and the game-playing that he had to do over the phone with his contacts back in Moscow to keep him on foreign assignment.

He pushed these thoughts aside. It didn't matter. The important thing was Howard's information.

Malkov smiled at Howard. "Everything checked out, just as you said. And how about your deposit? Did it arrive as you expected?"

Howard's stone cold expression didn't change. "The money's in the bank. Now I'm ready for the final installment."

Malkov continued the cordial smile. "Well, then. Let's have the other half of the story."

Howard pulled out a file folder and laid it on the table in front of Malkov. "It's all here. Photographs, reports, dates, names, times and places. All spelled out."

For the next twenty minutes, Malkov greedily sifted through the documents and photographs while Howard explained the FBI's activity against Amtorg, the Soviet Purchasing Commission, the Soviet embassy in Washington, D.C., and the Soviet consulate in New York City. The revelations astounded him. The FBI was good, very good. It knew details about Soviet personnel and operations that Malkov would never have guessed the Americans possessed. Yet at the same time, the big picture was still eluding them. The Americans had no idea just how deeply Soviet intelligence had penetrated their organizations, their personnel, and their secrets. It made Malkov proud to think about it. If only Howard knew what Malkov knew about the depth of Soviet espionage against the United States. Would he be telling him all this?

Howard finished his story. Malkov closed the file and held it in his hands reverently, then looked up at the surly American across from him.

"Are you satisfied?" Howard asked.

Malkov reached down to his left side and picked up a satchel. He set it on the table and slid it over to Howard. "Yes," he said. "And if you're interested in making an extra ten thousand, I have a small errand that you could run for me."

Howard unzipped the satchel and glanced inside, running his hands through the piles of bills, then zipped it closed. "What kind of errand?"

"It's very simple. All you have to do is bring Kostrin's wife to Amtorg after he leaves New York City."

"And you'll take me straight from there to the cargo ship headed for South America."

"Precisely. I've arranged passage for you on a cargo ship that's heading down to Argentina in the next few days," Malkov said. "I'll contact you."

Howard agreed to do it, then left, and Malkov made his way back to Amtorg. He couldn't wait to drop in on Semerov with this file. What he wouldn't give to see Semerov's face as he realized he was wrong, that Malkov had been right about Kostrin all along.

Once back at the office, Malkov found a small room with a phone and closed the door, making sure that he was alone and out of earshot. He dialed the number to Montana and waited until the gruff voice of Comrade Vorlakov answered on the other end of the line.

"I have good news," Malkov said.

"You've confirmed it?"

"It's not just Kostrin and Ryzanov. Kostrin's wife is in on it, too."

"Did you tell Semerov?"

"Not yet."

"When will we have them?"

"Tomorrow. Once that transport leaves the ground, they'll be in our hands."

"And Kostrin's wife?"

"She'll be delivered to Amtorg after Kostrin has left for Montana."

"Excellent."

Malkov hung up the phone, then picked up the file and headed for Semerov's office.

THIRTY-TWO

The past several days in the United States had flown by like a whirlwind. It was hard for Larisa to get used to a new land when all she could think of was the possibility that Misha would soon be in a torture chamber somewhere in the belly of the Soviet Union, somewhere in a dark basement room with strong cruel men bearing into him, beating him, interrogating him, threatening him. And finally exterminating him, as if he weren't a man at all, but some kind of insect, some kind of filthy vermin that the Party had to cleanse itself of if it were to perpetuate its own pure existence. She also knew that if the Party exterminated her husband, it would exterminate her and her baby, too.

But in spite of the fear, she had taken walks with Misha and alone with Kolya during the past couple of days and had seen her neighborhood. She had visited shops and diners and public parks, had overheard numerous conversations about the war and the weather and President Roosevelt's health, had listened to the different accents and dialects of immigrants from abroad and Americans from other parts of the United States.

America was nothing like the Soviet Union. She was surprised by how optimistic and industrious the Americans were. Only the war weighed them down. Their work ethic impressed her. They reminded her of the old Russian and Ukrainian farmers who worked for themselves on their own land, before collectivization began. The Americans worked hard, she thought, because they worked for themselves and were not plagued by the paranoia of constantly wondering what the government might do to them next.

America was religious, too, with churches and synagogues everywhere. She had entered a church once with Kolya asleep in her arms, just to see what it looked like. The ceiling had towered above her and there were pews and white walls and stained-glass windows, and someone was practicing hymns on an organ. It was so peaceful and quiet and bright that her heart melted inside of her and she felt like crying.

Larisa took out Elya's necklace, knelt down at the sofa, and prayed that she and Misha and Kolya would be able to stay here. This was the first time she had ever prayed out loud. In her thoughts she had prayed many times during the last couple of years since she started reading the little black book, and she believed that God was listening. She knew He was listening.

At that moment there was a knock at the door. Strange, she thought. Rose Petersen wasn't supposed to be this early. She went to the front door. "Who is there?" she asked in English.

She was expecting a woman's voice, but a man's voice answered, and such intense panic gripped her that she didn't understand what he said. But then she realized that whatever he had said was in English, not Russian, and that he sounded like an American, no Russian accent at all.

"What do you want?" she asked.

"I'm looking for Larisa Kostrin," he said. "Is that you, Mrs. Kostrin?"

It was definitely an American.

"Mrs. Kostrin, please don't be afraid. I'm here to help you. Rose Petersen sent me."

Rose Petersen. He knew Rose Petersen. But she thought that Rose Petersen herself would come. "Where is Rose Petersen?" she asked through the door.

"Mrs. Kostrin, I'm here to help you. I know about your husband, and I'm trying to help him, too. I wanted to bring Rose Petersen with me, but she was called away on another assignment just a few hours ago. You're going to have to trust me. Please."

She peered out through the peep hole. A tall, burly man in a dark brown suit towered in front of her. His face was stern and serious, and his eyes gazed steadily forward through the round glasses that he wore.

"My name is Agent Madsen," he said. "I'm with the FBI. You

and your husband are in grave danger. I'm here to help, but you need to come with me right now. We don't have much time."

"Wait just a few minutes," she said. "I need to get my baby and a few other things." She went to the bedroom and grabbed her purse, then picked up Kolya from his crib. She was about to open the front door, but before she did, she stopped in the living room and set Kolya on the sofa. She reached into her purse and pulled out the little piece of paper with Rose Petersen's information on it that Misha had given to her yesterday.

She looked at Kolya. Then back at the front door. Then back down at the piece of paper.

☆

Mark Daniels exited Colonel Griggs' makeshift office at Gore Field and walked across the air strip until he stood next to Paulsen, who was watching the new Russians. There had been an unexpected change of plans—they were flying out tonight instead of tomorrow morning. Two Russians supervised the loading of the silver C-47, one tall and solid-looking who stood over six feet tall, the other thin and wiry, probably about five eight. "What do you make of those two?" Mark asked.

"Those two are creepy, captain. I don't know who they are, but I don't think they're regular Soviet military."

Mark could feel his revolver holstered at his side beneath his flight jacket. "Neither do I," he said. He turned to Paulsen. "Go tell Burns that we're leaving in a couple of hours. And make sure you guys don't forget your sidearms."

"Yes, sir." Paulsen tightened his cap above his forehead and trotted off to find their radio man.

Mark watched the two supervising Russians for a couple of minutes. All he could see was the back of them, but even from that angle they looked different than the regular Russian workers who were loading the crates and black suitcases onto the plane. Their stance, their movements, their gestures all reeked of a dark, self-assured sense of authority. The big man looked around once and caught Mark's eye. They stared at each other from about fifty yards away for several seconds, then the big man turned to face the plane again, unaffected by Mark's gaze.

These are the guys that are going to be on my plane, Mark thought. I'm going to have to keep a close eye on them.

Paulsen was right. This whole operation did stink. Why this sudden rush to fly out tonight, when the flight was originally scheduled to head out tomorrow morning? It made no sense. That FBI woman had called him the day before and said Boris and Alfred would be on this flight, and he wondered if they had something to do with the change in departure time. Did that FBI lady know about this schedule change? He rummaged through his pocket and found the little notebook, which he pulled out and looked at. There on the first page was Rose Petersen's contact information.

He stared at it briefly, then watched the two creepy Russians for a few seconds. He looked behind him at the colonel's office and thought of the telephone sitting on the desk. Griggs had left at the same time Mark had, so the office was empty.

He looked back down at the little notebook in his hand. A gentle wind rustled the page.

THIRTY-THREE

Karen Jones threw the door open and dashed inside, rushing down the corridors as fast as her dress shoes would allow her, clopping rapidly all the way. She zigged and zagged around desks and corners, then up the stairs, around a couple more corners. She didn't bother to knock. She grabbed the handle and turned; the door was unlocked. She barged inside and shut the door behind her, then turned to see the Chief rising from his chair.

"Karen—"

"Where's Howard?" she asked.

The Chief looked startled. "He's on assignment. Said he had a contact to make. And you've got two messages."

"Contact? What contact?" She was breathing heavily. Her collar felt tight around her neck.

"Didn't say."

"I have to find him. Now."

"Karen, you look worried. What's wrong?"

Where could Howard be? A dozen possibilities flashed through her mind before it hit her. "I know where he is," she said, holding her finger up in the air. "I have to go, Chief."

"Who? Where?"

"Howard." She turned around and grabbed the door handle, swinging the door wide open.

"Hold on, Karen," the Chief said from behind her, and his tone made her stop and turn around. "Before you go anywhere, you'd better check out these two messages that came in for you while you were out. One's from Boris's wife, and the other's from that captain out in Montana."

Her heart sank. "Boris's wife?"

"Yeah. Called about ten minutes ago. And that captain called about five minutes later."

"What did Boris's wife say?"

"She said an FBI agent was at her door to pick her up and that she was going with him. She said she was nervous and wanted you to be there. I told her you should be back in a few minutes, and she said she'd tell the agent to wait for you to arrive. Then she hung up before I could get anything else out of her."

Karen looked down at the floor. "Howard," she whispered, too inaudibly for the Chief to pay attention.

"Now who do you suppose would be picking her up?" the Chief asked. "I thought you were going to do that."

She looked up. "It's Howard, Chief."

"Howard? You wanna tell me what's going on?"

"No time, Chief. Come with me. I'll need some backup. We've got to find Agent Howard." She turned and walked out the door. Within a few seconds she heard the Chief's door close, and the Chief's footsteps caught up to her as she descended the stairs.

"Karen, you've got to tell me what's going on," he said as they trotted down the steps, and Karen could hear him struggling to breathe and talk at the same time while he hurried after her. "I haven't even told you what that captain said in his message."

Karen didn't slow down. "You can tell me on the way, Chief," she said as they burst out of the front doors onto the street. She climbed into the driver's side door of a black government car, and the Chief crawled in on the passenger's side. She started the engine, barely glanced over her shoulder to check for traffic, then slammed her foot on the gas pedal.

Ten minutes. That was too much time.

Larisa set down the receiver and looked over at Kolya. A sickening hollowness filled her chest, but she was too afraid to cry. She clutched her bag in her hands and sat down on the couch, staring at Kolya while he slept, wondering what she should do.

There was another knock at the door, this one more urgent. "Mrs. Kostrin?" The man's voice sounded impatient. "Mrs. Kostrin, are you there?"

She got up and walked to the entryway. "Hold on," she said.

"Mrs. Kostrin, we don't have time. We have to go right now."

"You'll have to wait for a few minutes," she said without opening the door. "I need to get some things."

"We don't have time."

She said nothing and waited. Another minute passed in silence, and then he was pounding at the door again.

Where was Rose Petersen?

"Mrs. Kostrin, please open the door. Maybe I can help you pack some things so that we can get out of here faster."

She knew she couldn't hold him up too long. What if he was legitimate and she refused to go and he had to leave? She might be missing her only opportunity. She should have asked that FBI man on the phone who this Agent Madsen was. Stupid. But she was nervous and frightened and wasn't sure if she could trust the man on the phone, either, because Misha said that she should only speak to Rose Petersen. Should she call the man back?

The man pounded on the door again. "Mrs. Kostrin, please open the door. I know you're frightened, but I'm here to help you. You have to trust me."

She dialed the number again, but no one answered. She set down the receiver, then went back to the door. "I want to wait for Rose Petersen," she said.

"Mrs. Kostrin, please. I'm telling you, she was called away on a special assignment this morning and no one knows for sure when she'll be back. I'd stay here with you and wait for her if I could, but we don't have time. The Soviets could be here any minute, and if they arrive while we're still here, they won't let you out alive. Mrs. Kostrin, please."

She opened the door a crack but left the chain intact and looked into the man's eyes. He seemed genuinely concerned.

"Mrs. Kostrin, I'm sorry," he said in a quieter voice. "I've been watching the Soviets for a long time, and I'm taking a huge risk already of exposing my identity to them by standing here talking to you. My orders are to bring you out safely, but if you refuse to go with me, then I'll have to leave you here. Neither of us wants that. I wish Rose Petersen were here, but she's not. Now are you going to trust me?"

His voice reflected a controlled desperation. His face looked pained, concerned. He seemed sincere. Just trying to do his job. And he wasn't trying to force his way in.

"Can't you wait just a few more minutes?" she asked.

She could see the tension around his eyes as he answered her. "Mrs. Kostrin, you're putting us both in serious danger. We have to go now. Otherwise I'm going to abort this mission and leave you here to fend for yourself. Do you understand?"

If he were a Soviet agent, he would have forced his way in by now. And he wouldn't be threatening to leave her. "All right," she said. "I'm coming. Just let me get my baby."

☆

"What did Captain Daniels want?" Karen asked as she drove through a red light, first checking to make sure there was no cross-traffic. Out of the corner of her eye she saw the Chief gripping the sides of his seat.

"He said there were several new faces among the Soviet personnel at the airfield in Montana, and that they had moved the departure time to tonight. Even gave me a couple of names that you should be familiar with—Vorlakov and Malkov."

"Tonight? But we won't be ready until tomorrow morning."

"I know. He said they were guarding the plane extra close and wouldn't let him near it until just before takeoff. Said he hadn't seen Boris and Alfred yet, but he suspected they were being held somewhere near the airfield."

"What did you tell him about Vorlakov and Malkov?"

"I told him they were very dangerous men and that they were planning to take Alfred and Boris back to the Soviet Union to be executed for treason. I explained that we had a rescue operation planned for tomorrow morning at Gore Field, but that our agents wouldn't be in place until sometime during the middle of the night. I told him not to let that plane take off."

"And what did he say?" She turned a corner tightly. The Chief's hands were on the dash and the door.

"He said there's no way he can stop that flight. Not even his commander can. Said this is a real special shipment and that only the War Department can override the order."

"The War Department," she said with disgust. "They'd never delay that shipment. What did you tell him to do?"

"Nothing."

"Nothing?"

"It's out of our hands, Karen. I can't risk our own agents or our operations for the sake of two Soviets. You know that."

She felt the heat rising up the back of her neck. "We can't just abandon them, Chief. Not after all that we've been through already. You must have told that captain something."

"I told him that if he couldn't delay the takeoff, then he was on his own to prevent Alfred and Boris from getting on that plane, and that if he didn't, they were dead men."

"That's all you could think of?"

"What else could I have told him, huh?" The Chief sounded angry and irritated. She had questioned his judgment, a big no-no with Director Robinson. "If you want to save those two Russians, you can fly out there yourself if you think you're so smart. And while you're at it, you can call the War Department and tell them all about our little operations against Amtorg, and you can tell the Soviets, too. Don't cross me, Karen. If we stick our necks out too far for these two Russians, we'll get our own heads chopped off. I know you've grown attached to them, but as far as I'm concerned, they're expendable. Understand? Sure, it would be nice to get some information out of them. I'd love to help them out if I could. But in case you've forgotten, the Soviet Union is officially an ally right now, and I can't risk an international incident over two measly Russian accountants. You got that?"

"Yes, Chief." She bit her lip. She should have kept quiet.

"I know you're a woman, Karen, but you can't put your heart before your head. Not in this job."

Her blood was boiling, but she bit her lip harder. She hated that kind of patronizing condescension, but she knew the Chief didn't mean it. She knew how he was when he got angry. He said a lot of things he didn't really mean. She had brought it on herself for crossing him.

"I'm sorry, Karen. I didn't mean that."

She let out a deep breath and calmed herself. "I know, Chief. We're just under a lot of stress, that's all."

"Are you going to tell me where we're going?" he asked. "And what's this business with Agent Howard?"

"He's working for the other side."

"Agent Howard? Working for the Soviets? Are you sure about that, Karen?"

"Positive."

She drove past the building where Boris and his wife were living, and her gut told her not to stop. Ten minutes was too long. Howard would have been gone by now, especially if Boris's wife had told him to wait for Rose Petersen.

"Where to?" asked the Chief.

She looked at the surrounding buildings and read the street signs. "Amtorg."

THIRTY-FOUR

Larisa sat in the back seat on the right side of the car with Kolya cradled in her arms, her single bag resting on the floor between her feet. Her stomach was gnawing at her. Her knees felt weak. A slight tremble momentarily shuddered through her body. At least the baby was quiet.

She looked out the window at the buildings and stores and apartments, the people walking along the sidewalks, the cars around them. The neighborhood looked familiar.

"Where are we going?" she asked.

Agent Madsen sat with his left hand firmly wrapped around the steering wheel, his right arm slung behind the passenger's seat. She could see the right side of his face. Cold. Serious. Tight. As he drove, he turned his head slowly from side to side as he scanned the road for traffic and pedestrians, and she wondered if he might also be looking for something else. Soviet agents, most likely.

"I'm taking you to a safe house," he said. "An old apartment building where you and your son can stay for a couple of days without worrying about Semerov sending for you. Then we'll get you out of the city and reunite you with your husband."

The content of his words should have been comforting, but his tone was so professional. So calculating. So—distant.

Where was Rose Petersen? And why would the FBI send only one agent for her if the Soviets really were after her? Shouldn't they have played it safe? Sent three or four agents in a couple of cars? But maybe sending one agent was the safe thing to do. Maybe to attract less attention.

The car passed smoothly through another intersection, and Larisa saw a middle-aged man sweeping a sidewalk outside the entrance to a building. He wore a white apron on top of a blue shirt. The top button was undone, revealing the neckband of a white T-shirt underneath, and she wondered how he could possibly be wearing so many layers of clothing on such a warm day in the middle of June. He looked up at the car as it passed by, and her mind took a snapshot of his face. Dark hair, bald spot on top of his head, large nose, rough olive-colored skin. Very Mediterranean looking.

She had seen this man before, a few days ago when she had walked through this area with Misha. What had Misha shown her? Yesterday they had spent most of the day at home. The day before that they had gone to a park. And the day before that . . .

She leaned forward. "Where is this safe house?" she asked.

Madsen's face remained cold and serious, but she noticed tightness around the corners of his mouth and eyes that gave her the impression that her question irritated him. He turned his head a little toward her, but kept his eyes on the road. "We're almost there," he said. "Just a few more blocks."

She looked out the windshield and peered ahead. A variety of buildings on both sides of the street. Curbs and sidewalks and pedestrians. She thought of the man in the blue shirt and apron, and suddenly she remembered. Of course. Misha had brought her here to show her the office building where he worked. It was straight ahead of them, maybe two or three blocks away. But why would they be driving along this street?

The stoplight ahead turned red, and the car slowed to a stop. A gloomy, depressing sensation settled over her, as if a heavy blanket had slowly descended around her and was pressing down on her shoulders. She looked at Agent Madsen. His lips were pressed together, and his jaw muscles rippled beneath the skin, clenching as if he were chewing gum. Both of his hands gripped the steering wheel, and he was rubbing it with his thumbs. His shoulders were tense.

In her left arm she held Kolya, whom she had wrapped in a soft white blanket. His weight rested on her left thigh. She repositioned her arm so that her left hand was under him, and his little leg made a good handhold. Could she do this with one arm? She lifted up. He was heavy for a two-year-old, but she felt his small body rise up off of her leg. Yes. One arm would work.

She kept her eyes fixed on Madsen, who waited impatiently for the signal to change and had his eyes ahead of him, away from her. She leaned forward cautiously and reached down with her right hand, her eyes still glued to Madsen, until her fingers found the handles of her handbag. She grabbed it, leaned back in painstaking silence as she slowly picked it up and rested it gently on her right leg. She slipped the straps beneath Kolya's leg until they rested between her left hand and Kolya's thigh, and she held the handbag tightly. Her right hand now free, she took her eyes off of Madsen for a second and checked to make sure the door was unlocked. It was. She glanced at the door handle. She moved her right hand over to the handle and delicately wrapped her fingers around it, then gripped it firmly.

Could she make it?

She looked back at Madsen, who still paid no attention to her and was waiting for the light, his head shifting back and forth as he observed the cross-traffic and the pedestrians in the crosswalk. She waited for him to turn his head further away from her. The seconds ticked away with agonizing slowness. He was looking toward the right front corner of the car. What was taking him so long?

A woman in a sharp skirt and a light blouse stepped off the curb into the crosswalk and strode smartly in front of the car. Larisa couldn't see the woman's face from the back seat, but Madsen's head turned slowly from right to left, following the curvaceous figure as the woman crossed the street. Larisa watched the woman for a few seconds until the figure had passed completely in front of the car and was crossing the on-coming lanes. Then she looked at Madsen. All she could see was the back of his head.

Now!

Larisa was close enough to the edge of panic to enable her to maximize her speed and agility, yet just far enough back from that edge to allow her to stay in control. With the fear of a young mother who knew it was now or never and whose child was in her arms, she pulled up on the handle and pushed on the door with a single motion. She lifted both her legs at once and swivelled her body ninety degrees to the right, pressing Kolya against her bosom and ducking her head as she planted her feet on the street and leaned forward head-first, trying not to crush the frail bundle that she held in her left arm.

"Hey!"

She couldn't see Madsen, but she knew his head had whipped around and that he was reaching for her. She closed her eyes for some reason and grabbed the doorframe with her right hand and pulled herself out of the car, then pushed against it as she stood up and opened her eyes again, and she felt Madsen's fingers scarcely swipe the back of her blouse as she bailed out of the automobile.

She clutched Kolya and her handbag and ran, heading back in the direction from which they had come.

She had a couple of seconds. He'd have to put the car in gear before he could get out of it, and then he'd have to run around the car before he could take off after her.

"Mrs. Kostrin!"

When the sound waves hit her ears, a sickening tension gripped her sides and stomach as she pictured him on her heels, ready to reach out and grab her. But then she realized that the voice was not close. She could tell by the sound that he was standing back in the street, the car still between them. Good. That was good. She was putting more distance between them.

She knew he was running now, and she pushed herself to run faster.

Unlike the intersection behind her, full of pedestrians, the sidewalk ahead was discouragingly bare. The only person she could see was the middle-aged Mediterranean-looking man who was sweeping the sidewalk up ahead of her. She ran and ran and ran, panting and gasping and gulping air, bouncing little Kolya until he started to cry.

"Help me!" she cried as she approached the man. "He's going to hurt me!"

She didn't bother to watch the man's reaction or even to wait for it. She dashed past him, past the windows of the man's store, across the intersection, which lucky for her had the traffic traveling parallel to her now, the cross-traffic stopped at the light.

When she reached the other side, she saw that the brick building on her left had its front door ajar, so she turned, pushed it open, and went inside.

She stopped. Blackness. Dust. Boxes. The building was dark and abandoned. She looked back, but realized instantly that she didn't have time to go back outside and find another building. She rushed into the room, almost tripping over several boxes as her eyes struggled to adjust to the dim light, and she rubbed Kolya's back and whispered softly to him not to cry and that everything was okay, and by some miracle the little boy calmed down and stopped his crying.

The building was like a maze. Boxes and construction materials were piled in numerous rows, and several doors exited the main room into the other rooms beyond them. She chose one, went through it, closed it behind her. She wound through a couple of corridors, through more piles of boxes, then found a space in the corner where a stepladder with a tarpaulin wadded up on top of it leaned against the wall.

She slung her handbag over her right shoulder, and with her free hand pulled the tarpaulin open and draped it over the stepladder. She crouched down in the corner, pulled the stepladder toward her until the tarpaulin covered her like a small tent, and held Kolya close to her, trying to keep him calm.

Agent Howard ran down the sidewalk, his dress shoes slamming against the pavement, sending an uncomfortable shock through his knees and hips. Eight years with the agency and he had never bothered to get himself in shape. The last thing he needed right now was more complications. Why had she run?

He saw Mrs. Kostrin about half a block ahead of him. She didn't slow down at all for the curb at the intersection, but hurdled it as if it weren't there and jumped out into the middle of the street, still running as fast as she could. She didn't seem to be running very fast, but it was fast enough to stay ahead of him, and he saw her duck into a small brick building on the corner. He should have known something like this would happen. Nothing ever worked out the easy way. If only he had kept himself in shape.

He hadn't been paying attention to the shopkeeper with the broom, but as he got closer, he noticed the man watching him, staring at him as if he were waiting for him. What was he looking at? Well, it made sense. A guy in a suit running down the sidewalk after a lady with a baby in her arms—who wouldn't take notice? But the man wasn't just watching. As Howard ran past him, out of the corner of his eye he saw the man's leg kick out in front of him, catching Howard's left foot in mid-air and sending him plunging forward toward the pavement.

He put out his hands to catch himself, and once they touched the sidewalk, he crumpled his right arm up against his body so that he rolled over onto his shoulder to disperse the force of the landing. The next thing he knew he was lying flat on his back, and his heels hit the pavement. He sat up, but before he could get back on his feet, something hard whacked him on the back of the head, sending an explosion of pain throughout the back of his skull. He got to his feet and felt another blow on his right shoulder as he arose, and then the shopkeeper was on his back with a strong right arm around his neck, trying to put him into a headlock. Howard heard the man's broom clack against the cement when it hit the ground.

Before the shopkeeper could get a good hold, Howard grabbed the man's wrist with his left hand, then reached up behind him with his right until he felt the man's shirt, which he seized hold of in his fist. He stepped backwards with one foot into the shopkeeper to shift the center of gravity and displace the man's balance, then he bent forward and pulled down with all his might, and the man flipped over Howard's right shoulder, slamming into the pavement on his back. Howard heard a dull sickening thump. The man had hit his head on the ground.

Howard still held the man's wrist in his left hand. He pulled up on it to keep the man's arm straight, and the man, obviously delirious, tried to raise his head. Then Howard pushed his right knee down hard into the man's chest, evoking a brief gasp, and reared back with his right fist. "You stupid idiot!" he shouted. With one swift, direct punch he landed a powerful blow square to the man's face, and the man's head snapped back, striking the pavement again, knocking him out cold.

Howard stood up and released the man's hand, which dropped to the sidewalk at the man's side, limp and motionless. Howard got up and started running. He had to wait another fifteen or twenty seconds at the intersection for the light to change, then he darted across. When he reached the front of the building, he paused. He put his left hand on the door, and with his right he took out his revolver. He slowly pushed the door open and cautiously peered inside.

Karen slammed on the brakes and the car skidded to a screeching halt, the tires squealing as they slid along the street, the wheels locked. The Chief threw out his hands in front of him to protect himself, but hit his head on the dashboard anyway. In half a second Karen took the car out of gear, put on the parking brake, and killed the engine. Before she had her fingers around the door handle, through the windshield she saw Agent Howard's head turn and look in her direction.

She threw the door open and jumped out of the car. Long strips of black stretched out on the road behind the car, and a pungent smell of burned rubber filled her nose. "Agent Howard!" she shouted.

Howard turned away from her and ducked inside the building. The door slammed shut behind him, but bounced back open a foot or two. It slammed shut again, but again propped itself back open. The door, ajar as it had been, stopped moving. At least he couldn't lock her out.

She drew her weapon and glanced back through the windshield into the car at the Chief, who was still conscious, but was holding both of his hands up to his forehead. She didn't have time to ask him if he was all right. Clenching her revolver in her hand, she ran toward the building.

She stopped when she reached the entrance and leaned against the doorframe. Her heart was racing, thumping so hard within her chest that she could hear the beating inside of her ears. Her stomach was tight and nauseated, her palms were already starting to sweat, and even using both hands it was hard to hold her weapon steady. She took a few quick, deep breaths through her mouth, then nudged the door open with her foot.

From where she stood, everything inside looked black, but her eye caught hold of something moving. Suddenly a bright orange flash of light lashed out from somewhere ahead of her, off to the right. A thunderous boom accompanied it, and the doorframe a few inches above her head exploded into a shower of splintered wood and chips of stone that sprinkled her hair with a layer of fine particles. She smelled dust and the metallic scent of smoke.

She crouched down reflexively and hurried inside, hunched over, her arms still extended in front of her with her weapon drawn, only now it was pointing at the floor. Her eyes hadn't yet adjusted to the darkness, but she made out several piles of building materials and boxes that she crawled behind. She held still and waited, wondering if Howard had seen her come inside.

From somewhere against a wall on the other side of the room, she heard a door handle turn. A door opened, then closed. Click. She listened. She waited.

Silence.

Larisa was hardly breathing. She had never felt fear like this. The only time she had ever felt anything close to it was the night before Misha went back to the Lubyanka, when their neighbors across the hall had been liquidated. She remembered Misha's arms around her, her right ear covered by his hand, her left ear pressed into his chest.

Tears streamed down her face involuntarily. Kolya was making barely audible noises, as if he wanted to cry, and she was praying in her heart that he would be quiet. She rocked him gently, slowly, silently. She kissed him softly on the forehead. Please, Kolya. Don't cry. We'll be all right, but you have to stop making those sounds. She rotated his face toward her blouse, hoping his blanket and her body would muffle his quiet whimpering.

She heard Madsen's footsteps. It sounded like he was on the other side of the long table that she had seen when she came in here. He was only a few meters away.

"Mrs. Kostrin."

The voice sent a cold shiver down her spine. She closed her eyes tightly and pressed her lips together.

"Mrs. Kostrin, where are you?" Madsen was speaking quietly, in a voice just above a whisper.

Kolya tried to turn his head, but she pushed him against herself.

"Mrs. Kostrin, please. The Soviets must have seen us. They're right behind me. I don't think I can hold them off. If you'll come out right now, we might be able to make a run for it out the back door."

The stress inside of her was mounting, rising up, preparing to burst. She couldn't control herself now. The fear was too great. She sobbed hard and heavy, but they were dry, silent sobs. And sitting here on the floor, curled up in a little ball with her baby in her arms, not knowing if she could trust the voice or not, believing that she couldn't, made the panic swell within her. What would she do if he got closer? Calm down, Larisa. Think. Think!

Howard stopped and listened. No noise at all came from the other room where he had fired at Agent Jones. But there was definitely someone in this room. Even when he couldn't explicitly hear her, her baby was making just enough noise that on a subliminal level he could sense her presence.

But where exactly was she?

His revolver was pointed down toward the floor, and he raised it up to the side of his face so that it pointed toward the ceiling. Easier to walk that way. Too much clutter in this room, too easy to bump things next to you. He took a carefully placed step forward, letting his weight gradually transfer from his back foot to his front. Then he lifted his back foot off of the floor, moved it forward through the air, placed it softly on the hardwood floor. He transferred his weight again. No creaks. That was good.

He stopped. Something had definitely perked up his ears. But where exactly was it? He held his breath. He looked around the room, surveying the area with a panoramic sweep of his eyes. Rotating his head that way helped his ears pinpoint the direction, and the visual inventory of the room helped him eliminate places where a woman with a baby could not possibly fit.

Yes. There it was again. He hadn't been imagining it. A gentle rustling, as if two pieces of cloth were just barely rubbing against each other. And something similar to breathing, only not as smooth. Not adult-sounding, either. It was a baby. Sniffling? No. Whimpering. Just barely. And it was coming from the right, on the other side of the table.

He scanned the wall from corner to corner. The right corner was too stacked with heavy pieces of wood. The middle of the wall was more likely. Only boxes there. She could have moved those. But then again, she only had a minute on him. Probably not enough time. But the left corner was ideal. The only thing there was a stepladder leaning against the wall with a tarpaulin conveniently draped over it. Who would put a tarpaulin on a ladder like that?

He heard a noise behind him. Vague. Indecipherable. It came from the other room, so he decided to ignore it. Jones wasn't a threat as long as she was still in that other room, and he wanted to get to that stepladder before Jones got to him.

He took another step forward.

Something moved on the floor next to Larisa. Not out where Madsen was, but here under the stepladder, right next to her. She tensed up even more and held Kolya tighter. She slowly rotated her head to the right and almost fainted. The tail was long and pink, the fur brown, the sharp bucked teeth white, the black eyes menacing. And the size of the thing. It was as large as a small cat.

It was right next to her, not looking up at her face, but examining her skirt, sniffing. A bead of sweat streamed from her right temple down the side of her cheek, and now she could smell the thing. Musty, dank, dirty. The wall behind her, the floor beneath her, boxes to her left, the adjacent wall to her right, Kolya smashing her from the front, the tarpaulin blanketing her from above, darkness and dust and fear all around her, only a little light from some distant window on the other side of the room making it to where she sat all scrunched up in the corner, illuminating the room just enough for her to see the color of that hideous fur.

Madsen's footsteps were coming closer now. He was around the table. She could see his shoes through the tiny space between the tarpaulin and the floor. He was right there!

Suddenly the tarpaulin flew off of the stepladder, and she looked up. Madsen stood towering over her, revolver held up next to his face, his expression dark and cold and mean, a glint in his eye. She felt a sharp, piercing pain in her thigh where the rat had been sniffing, and she knew that Madsen's sudden motion must have startled the creature so badly that it had to fight or flee, and it had chosen to attack.

It was too much. The physical pain of the rat bite, the emotional fear of losing herself and her child, the dreadful helplessness. The world was spinning. Madsen's face was swirling around and around and around. Everything was turning gray.

She pressed her eyes closed and inhaled quickly.

Then she screamed.

Karen was on her feet, standing in front of the closed door, and based on Howard's voice from the other side, which she had actually been able to hear thanks to a large crack between the wall and the door frame, she knew approximately where he was in the other room. She peered through the crack just in time to see Howard's large shadowy figure pull away some kind of blanket or sheet off of an object in the corner of the room, and now the bloodcurdling scream filled her body with an adrenaline rush so intense that she felt like she was charged with electricity from head to foot and that her shoes were no longer even touching the floor.

The door was flimsy. She could do it. She stepped back, cocked her leg, and kicked hard right below the doorknob. The latch tore through the old, thin wood, and the door burst open. Karen's foot planted itself immediately on the floor, and her weapon was pointed, aimed, ready to fire.

"Howard!"

His head turned away from the floor in the corner and he looked back at her. There was a strange glint in his eyes, a flash or gleam that told her he had been surprised only momentarily, and that now he had made a decision. The hand holding his revolver twitched.

She got off one round before another bright orange flash answered back, and she felt a hot, burning pressure slice through her upper left shoulder.

She squeezed the trigger again.

Another orange flash answered back. Fire all across her scalp. Her head arched back. The ceiling was in front of her, but she knew she was still standing. She couldn't see anything, but she felt that her shooting arm was still level.

She squeezed the trigger again. And again. And again. Now she was falling backward, and the floor wasn't pressing against the soles of her shoes any more, and the whole world was floating, and she suddenly felt an exhilarating warmth come over her, a calming, soothing, peaceful warmth that made her almost euphoric as she floated off to an unknown world.

Then everything went black.

THIRTY-FIVE

The cargo hold was familiar, as was the aircraft. Dusk was falling and it was still light outside, but darker inside the cargo area, which was illuminated by a single light bulb suspended from the ceiling. Fifty black suitcases bound with white cord and sealed with red wax were stacked neatly in front of Misha to his left, and directly in front of him stood about fifteen wooden crates carrying the latest shipment of uranium chemicals.

Dima, short and stocky with a scraggly beard, just as Misha remembered him, pointed to the little metal bench against the wall with the seats attached to it. "Sit here," Dima said. "Don't move." Dima waited until Misha had sat down, then exited the plane.

Misha looked around at the shadowy cargo hold; he was completely alone. Only the distant noise of another C-47 taking off reached his ears, and that sound quickly dissipated into silence. So this was it. He leaned forward and put his elbows on his knees, then rested his forehead in the palm of his right hand.

He thought of Larisa. He pictured her silky brown hair flowing around her shoulders, her soft brown eyes sparkling with reflected light, her smooth white skin glowing. The most beautiful woman he had ever known. The only woman he had ever loved. His best friend.

He thought of Kolya. The baby knew who he was now and responded to his voice. Kolya wasn't afraid of him as he had been in March back in Sverdlovsk. And now Misha was leaving him again.

Finally he thought of his uncle Konstantin. All he had to do to fulfill his uncle's last wish was to pick up a little black book and read it, and he hadn't done it yet, even after eleven years. And those crazy dreams—what could they mean?

There was no way out now. Four armed Soviet guards

surrounded the plane and made sure that no one went in or out without Vorlakov's permission. More guards would be waiting for him in Alaska. But he couldn't leave Nikolai, even if there was a chance he could outrun the guards. His fate was sealed.

He rubbed his forehead with his right hand. He closed his eyes. "God," he whispered quietly, "if you're really there, please help me. I'm sorry that I was angry with you. I promise I'll read the book. Please let me be with my family again."

At that moment a clanging sound came up the stairs to the door of the cargo hold. He sat up and turned to see Nikolai's tall, slender figure enter the plane. Nikolai's shoulders drooped, and he stared at the floor. Dima entered the door behind him and pushed him over to where Misha was sitting. Dima pointed. "Sit there," he said. The lanky figure sat down next to Misha on Misha's left side, and Dima again exited the plane.

Misha turned in his seat, and his heart leapt within him. "Nikolai!" he said. "You're alive!"

Nikolai sat hunched over, still staring at the floor, but he turned his face to acknowledge Misha, and the corners of his mouth turned upward into a gentle smile. "Amazing, isn't it?" he said. The voice was tired; the eyes were full of apathy.

"When they sent me back to New York alone, I thought for sure that you were dead."

Nikolai shook his head and stared at the floor again. "No such luck."

"You have to tell me what happened."

There was a long, silent pause. Nikolai clasped his hands and started rubbing them together, then he looked straight ahead at the wooden crates for a couple of seconds, and then he stared back at the floor. "It was late at night," he began. "We were in the Lubyanka. Vorlakov took me and another man down to a small office that reminded me of a waiting room. It had a small desk where Vorlakov sat down and filled out some paperwork, and a few wooden chairs. The guy that was with me was young, maybe twenty-five. Handsome kid, too. Tall and thin with a healthy face. Blonde hair. Crystal blue eyes. Name was Stepan. Vorlakov left the room and I asked the kid if he was married, and he said no.

"A few minutes later Vorlakov came back, and this time another man was with him. Not very tall, but he had a large head and was sneering all the time, and he wore a tiny pair of thin spectacles that were too small for his face. Said his name was Malkov. I guess you know him."

Misha nodded. "He'll be on the flight with us tonight."

Nikolai continued. "They motioned for Stepan, so he got up and followed them into the hall. The door was still open, and I was so nervous after they left the room that I got up and tried to hear what was going on from just inside the doorway. I heard Malkov say something like, 'What about the other one?' And then Vorlakov said that Colonel Braginski had just received a phone call from Comrade Semerov. Vorlakov said, 'We're not going to do the other one tonight. He's going back to the United States.' And then Malkov started complaining about it and said he wanted to do it tonight, but Vorlakov told him to calm down. I heard footsteps, so I sat down again, and then Vorlakov appeared in the entrance. He told me to wait there and that he'd be back in a while, then he locked the door with a key and closed it so that I couldn't get out.

"After that everything was quiet for a long time, but then I heard shouting coming from somewhere down the hall. Then there were all these thumping noises, banging and yelling, and a scream that made me shiver because I recognized Stepan's voice. Then there was silence again for a couple of minutes, and finally I heard a loud bang, like a pistol fired inside a closed area, and I knew that Stepan was dead.

"Vorlakov came back a few minutes after that and unlocked my door. He looked like he had been sweating, but his breathing was back to normal and I couldn't see blood anywhere on him. He smiled and looked very friendly all of a sudden and told me that I had been reassigned and that I should follow him. My knees were so weak and shaky that I could hardly stand up, but I forced myself to walk behind him, and after a few minutes I got my strength back.

"The next thing I knew we were standing in front of Colonel Braginski, who also smiled and seemed friendlier than he should have been, and he told me that I was going back to the United States to continue working on industrial espionage, only this time I would be working out of the Soviet Purchasing Commission in Washington, D.C. I could tell that something was wrong. They were all smiling and trying to be cordial, but it was too contrived. They were almost as tense as I was. Braginski filled out a couple of forms and sealed them in an envelope, which he gave to me. Then he told me to wait out in the hallway.

"I paused once I stepped out into the hallway, and during that brief moment I could barely hear Braginski whispering something to Vorlakov. He sounded angry and called Vorlakov an idiot and said, 'You almost eliminated one of our best accountants.' When I heard that, I hurried down the hallway to get away from the room, and Vorlakov showed up a few seconds later, still friendly and smiling as if nothing were wrong. He took me to an empty apartment where I spent the night, and the next morning I was on my way back to Kuybishev.

"Since then I've been in Washington, D.C. At first everything was normal, but after about a month I noticed that people were watching me all the time, following me around, just as it was before our last flight home. Then I was assigned to work only on financial transactions and administrative paperwork. No intelligence work at all. That's when I knew they were on to me." Nikolai looked over at Misha and flashed a fake smile. "And here we are again."

That explained the guards around the plane. The Centre had made a big mistake last time, and they weren't about to repeat it. "Who was Stepan?" Misha asked. "Why did they kill him?"

Nikolai let out a sigh. "I don't know much about him. He worked as a courier at the Soviet consulate in New York City. Rose Petersen had been meeting with him, too. I guess someone observed him meeting with her and reported on him."

Misha felt a pang of guilt. "Just as I did to you."

Nikolai looked over at him again, then back at the floor. "It's behind us."

"So, what are we going to do?" Misha asked.

"What *can* we do? The plane's guarded. It'll be guarded once we get to Alaska. We're dead already."

"Do you think there's any possibility that we'll be alone on this flight, that Malkov and Vorlakov will get on another plane?"

"Not a chance."

"We'll have to make our move after takeoff, but before we reach Alaska."

"What do you mean, make our move? Do you have a plan?"

Misha looked to his left and stared at the door that opened into the cockpit. "It feels like we've been in this situation before," he said.

Misha glanced at Nikolai, who stared at the cockpit, too. "But the pilots aren't up there yet," Nikolai said. "Once Vorlakov and Malkov are on board, they'll be watching us the whole time. I don't think either of us could take out Vorlakov."

"We don't have to take him out," Misha said. "All we need is for one of us to get to the cockpit. It's a long flight. We can wait for a moment when Vorlakov and Malkov aren't paying much attention, then you could make a run for it. If they try to chase you, I'll be back here to slow them down."

"That will only give us a couple of seconds."

"Take a look at how close that cockpit door is," Misha said, nodding toward the little door at the front end of the cargo area. "A couple of seconds is all we need."

Mark stood next to Paulsen about fifty yards away from the silver aircraft and watched the Soviets finish up their loading operations. The sun was setting, but there was still enough light outside that Mark could see a couple of the Russians' faces. He saw Misha and Nikolai as they boarded the plane, and he asked Paulsen if he recognized them.

"Sure do," Paulsen said, nodding. "Only this time they look

more like prisoners than couriers."

That's because they are prisoners, Mark thought. "I'm going to check out that plane," he said without looking at Paulsen.

"But the colonel said——"

"I don't care what the colonel said."

Mark walked toward the aircraft, and he got over halfway there before any of the Soviet guards took any notice of him. One of the guards spotted him approaching the plane and yelled something in Russian over to the big man that Mark had made eye contact with earlier. The big man looked up, turned around, and walked toward Mark. "Hey!" the big man shouted.

Mark ignored him. He was about fifteen yards from the aircraft when the big man intercepted him. Up close the man was even larger than Mark had realized. The guy had a big round meaty face and enormous hands, a thick neck and broad shoulders and a solid build, and stood at least six and a half feet tall. The big man stepped in between Mark and the plane and rested a massive hand on Mark's shoulder, stopping him dead in his tracks. Mark could feel the power in that hand, and it sent a cold wave of intimidation throughout Mark's shoulders and chest. Mark looked up at him. The Russian's eyes were cold and determined. There was an unnerving sense of confidence about the man, probably born of his sheer physical power. But it was more than that, too. He had the confidence of a man with absolute authority.

"Where are you going?" the big man asked in English. The voice was deep and rich. He spoke with a thick Russian accent.

"I'm going to inspect my plane," Mark said, staring into the big Russian's eyes.

"Nobody gets on this plane until I say so," the man said.

"Oh yeah?" Mark said. He did a good job of sounding firm and tough, but inside his kidneys were pumping away. The authoritative approach wasn't going to work with this guy, but Mark decided to try it anyway. At least the gorilla would know where Mark stood. "What's your name?" Mark asked.

"Vorlakov."

Mark reached up and pushed Vorlakov's hand off of his shoulder, stepped closer until only a couple of inches separated them, and looked up into Vorlakov's eyes. He then pushed a finger into the Russian's massive chest. "Now you listen up, Mister Vorlakov, or whatever your name is. This is my plane and I need to inspect it before we take off."

Mark could see that Vorlakov wasn't intimidated a bit. The massive head stooped down a few inches and came so close to Mark's face that he could smell the man's evaporated perspiration. "You'll get on this plane when I tell you to," Vorlakov said in a calm, authoritarian voice. "If you don't like it, talk to your colonel. His orders."

Mark spoke calmly, more quietly, but held his stance. "All right, Mister Vorlakov, you win. But once that plane leaves the ground, I'm in command. Got that?"

Vorlakov stepped back and seemed to lighten up. His shoulders loosened up a little, and his face broke into a warm smile. He slapped Mark on the shoulder. "Relax," he said. "I'll call you over in five minutes."

Mark didn't return the smile. Vorlakov's face and voice were friendly all of a sudden, but there was something dark and foreboding about Vorlakov's eyes, as if they had little chunks of black coal in them. No light in them at all. Mark turned away and walked back to Paulsen.

"Well, Captain, how did it go?" Paulsen asked. Burns was standing next to him.

Mark looked at his co-pilot carefully. Paulsen was a good guy. Joked around sometimes, but trustworthy. He looked at his radio man. Burns was quiet, unassuming, timid. But also trustworthy. "You guys have your weapons?"

"Yep," Paulsen said. Burns nodded.

"Good."

THIRTY-SIX

From the back of the cargo hold, Misha sat still and watched the American crew come aboard. A wave of relief swept through him when he recognized the pilot. Captain Daniels didn't look over at him, but Misha suspected that the young American pilot knew that he and Nikolai were the two men in the back of the plane. Captain Daniels entered the plane, immediately turned left, and headed to the cockpit followed by his co-pilot and radio man. Misha looked at Nikolai.

Nikolai looked back, and Nikolai's eyes told him that he had seen Captain Daniels, too. Nikolai's face was softer somehow, brighter. There was hope.

Malkov followed behind the three Americans, only he turned right when he stepped inside and walked toward Misha and Nikolai, his perennial sneer glazed with arrogant smugness. The momentary feeling of joy that Misha had just experienced when Captain Daniels came on board vanished. Malkov looked directly at Misha, and Misha felt a cold, dismal emptiness swell inside of himself. Malkov's horrid face revealed everything. There was no doubt about it. Misha and Nikolai were dead men.

Malkov walked up to Misha and smiled. "How very nice to see you this evening, Comrade Kostrin."

Misha felt the anger starting to jell inside of him, but he stayed calm. He said nothing.

☆

Vorlakov came on board and turned around to pull the door shut behind him. He looked to his left and saw Malkov's back. Malkov turned around and started heading toward him. Vorlakov glanced at Nikolai and caught him stealing a quick glimpse of something toward the front of the plane.

Vorlakov looked to his right. The American pilot had already come back out of the cockpit and was approaching him.

"Just making sure the door is properly secured," the American said.

"I closed it," Vorlakov said, and he stood up straight and tall and stared down at the little American boy to give him the hint that it was time for him to turn around and go back to the cockpit.

The American kept walking. "All the same," he said, "I'd like to double-check it."

Vorlakov backed up to let the American have access to the door, but he watched him carefully and made sure that he kept himself between the American and the two prisoners behind him.

The American fiddled with the door a little, but Vorlakov had shut it properly, and he could tell that this American pilot wasn't really checking the door as he said he was.

"Looks secure," the American said, then turned around and headed back toward the cockpit.

Vorlakov followed him.

When they reached the cockpit, the American pilot turned around briefly. "By the way, Mister Vorlakov," he said, "you can call me Captain Daniels."

Vorlakov clenched his teeth. These stupid American kids were all the same. Brash, arrogant, haughty. Thought they knew it all. Captain Daniels entered the cockpit and sat down in the pilot's seat, and Vorlakov reached in and pulled the cockpit door closed. When he turned around, Malkov was standing right behind him.

"I don't trust these Americans," Vorlakov said, keeping his voice down. "Did you see the way Ryzanov looked at the pilot when he came back to check the door?"

Malkov shook his head.

"And when that pilot was checking the door out, I could tell he was trying to get a better look at Ryzanov and Kostrin out of the side of his eye."

"Do you think they know each other?" Malkov asked.

"I don't know," Vorlakov said. "But this whole mission is making me feel uneasy. We're going to keep an extra close eye on these two. I don't want them to have any contact at all with the American crew, even if one of those pilots comes back here during the flight."

Malkov nodded. "Do you want to start softening them up on this flight, or should we wait until we have a Soviet flight crew?"

Good old predictable Malkov. Always eager to start interrogating and torturing people. But now that Vorlakov thought about it, it wasn't such a bad idea. It would make it easier to keep Kostrin and Ryzanov under control. "I suppose we can scare them a little on this flight," Vorlakov said. "We can only rough them up, though. They were both working on the most sensitive intelligence operation of the war. The Centre wants them at the Lubyanka alive."

"I don't think it would matter if they died on the flight out of Alaska," Malkov said. "They know less about their espionage work than we do, and if there's anything we don't know yet, I'm sure you and I could get it out of them. It would save a lot of time and hassle at the Lubyanka when we arrive."

Vorlakov almost couldn't believe his ears. Malkov truly was a sick little man. Whenever it came time to torture and interrogate, Malkov's brain turned off. It's like a fever came over him, a blood-lust that overcame all of his reasoning powers. Vorlakov enjoyed torturing people, too, but not like Malkov did. That's the one thing Vorlakov didn't like about Malkov. He was good at what he did, but he lacked self-control. "Our orders are to bring these two back alive, Comrade Malkov. And that's what we're going to do. We only have permission to use deadly force if they try to escape or make contact with the Americans. Is that clear?"

"What about the American crew?" Malkov asked as if he hadn't paid any attention to what Vorlakov just said. "We can't let them see us back here roughing up Kostrin and Ryzanov." Malkov's eyes were glossy. Astounding. Intoxicated already, just by the thought of it.

"We'll move them to the other bench, the one at the back of

the cargo hold that faces forward. It's not visible from here."

Malkov's head turned and looked toward the back of the plane as if double-checking the veracity of Vorlakov's statement. "Good idea," he said.

They walked back to Ryzanov and Kostrin, who looked tense and nervous and frightened out of their minds. That was good. The fear of anticipation always made it easier. "You two go sit over there," Vorlakov told the two prisoners, pointing at the other bench, which sat against the back part of the cargo area and was perpendicular to the one that he and Malkov would sit on. The two men got up and moved.

"Have a seat, Comrade Malkov," Vorlakov said. Malkov was standing straight and rigid, his attention fixed on the two men seated on the other bench. "Comrade Malkov."

Malkov turned around and looked at him as if he hadn't heard him the first time. "What?"

"I said sit down. We can't get started until after the plane is in the air, anyway."

Malkov sat down but kept his eyes on the two prisoners, gaping at them with the voracity of a wild animal about to consume its prey. Knowing Malkov, the fact that Ryzanov and Kostrin were helpless probably made it all that much more pleasurable for him.

Mark looked over the dials and gauges and switches, checking and double-checking while he listened to the monotonous drone of the Skytrain's two engines as they revved up for takeoff. Paulsen was going over the checklist as well.

"Tower says we're cleared for takeoff," Burns said.

Mark released the brakes and throttled forward, and the C-47 was soon lifting off of the runway. He brought it to a comfortable cruising speed and altitude, then told Burns to turn off the transmitter to make sure that what he was about to say wouldn't be heard by anyone other than Paulsen and Burns.

"Well, gentlemen, I'm afraid there's something I need to tell you," he said. "How good are you guys at finding ways out of tricky problems?"

Paulsen looked over at him with a big smile. "I just fly the plane, Captain. I thought it was your job to figure out ways out of tricky problems. Isn't that why you have two bars on your hat and I only have one?" Mark looked back at him but didn't smile, and once Paulsen paid attention to Mark's face, he stopped smiling, too. "What's on your mind, Captain?" Paulsen asked.

"Are you awake, Burns?" Mark asked.

"Yes, Captain."

"Well, guys, I have a tricky problem for you. But first, I need to make it clear that I have no authorization from anyone to tell you what I'm about to tell you, so I might be risking a court-martial. But I'm in a real pickle and need you guys to give me some ideas."

Paulsen stared at him, examining his face as if looking for some indication of how serious Mark really was. "Is this some kind of a joke, Captain?" he asked.

Mark shook his head. "You know those four Russians back there? They're all spies, and they're spying against the United States. But two of them are good guys and two of them are bad guys."

"How does that work?" Paulsen asked.

It took Mark about fifteen minutes to relate the story of what he had talked to the Russians about on those two flights back in March, how Nikolai and Misha were a couple of accountants who had been recruited to work for Soviet intelligence, how Misha's wife and child were in New York City right now, how Rose Petersen from the FBI was trying to find a way for these two men to stay in the United States so that they could give the FBI the scoop on Soviet intelligence against the United States government. Hearing it come out of his own mouth was surreal. He wasn't sure if he believed all of it himself.

"But something's gone wrong," he concluded. "I talked to a man from the FBI earlier today, and he told me that these two Russians are being taken home to be executed for treason, and that the two guys with them are both professional killers working for the Soviet secret police. He said if I wanted these two accountants to stay alive, I was going to have to figure out a way to save them myself, because the FBI can't intervene for them. So that's where we are, gentlemen. The lives of those two men back there are now in our hands."

"I'm not sure how to put this, Captain," Paulsen said, "but isn't that none of our business? I mean, we have our orders, and our orders are to fly this airplane to Alaska and hand it over to the Soviet flight crew that's waiting for us there. The stuff you just told us about—that's, well, I mean—Griggs himself doesn't even know about it, right?"

"That's right," Mark said.

"And Colonel Griggs is our superior officer, the only authority we answer to, right? As I understand it, the FBI has no jurisdiction over us. That FBI man can't order you to interfere with those Soviets back there, especially when we have a direct order from our commanding officer to leave them and their cargo alone. Correct me if I'm wrong, Captain."

"Everything you're saying is absolutely true, Paulsen," Mark answered. "If we do anything at all, it will be out of our own initiative."

"And in violation of a direct order."

"That's correct."

Paulsen shook his head. "I don't like it, Captain. It goes against everything we've been taught and trained to do. I thought the mission always comes first, even before our own lives, right? If our lives aren't as important as accomplishing the mission is, then why would the lives of these two Russians be more important?"

"He's right, Captain," said Burns, who was usually so quiet that the fact he said anything at all made both Mark and Paulsen listen up. "The Soviets are our ally in this war. If we interfere with this mission, we could create an international incident. We'd be court-martialed for sure. We'd spend the rest of our lives in a military prison."

"And if you think about it," said Paulsen, "we don't even know who these two guys are. You said yourself they're Soviet agents, and that they've been spying on us since before the war began. And we are at war, Captain. People die in war. Do we really care what happens to them?"

Paulsen's words stabbed Mark to the heart, and he began to regret having spilled his guts about Misha and Nikolai. A part of him wanted to get angry, to yell at his two subordinates for not seeing things his way and for being cowards, but another part of him knew that they were right. Griggs had given specific orders. This was an unusual shipment of highly sensitive materials that as far as he knew had been approved by people at the highest levels of Lend Lease and the War Department, people who knew a lot more than he did and could see the big picture with a bird's-eye view. He had his orders. And everything he knew about being a good soldier told him that he had to follow those orders whether he liked it or not.

But there was something in the back of his mind, something that lurked in the depths of his soul, something that flickered in the far places of his heart like a candle placed on a window sill on a dark stormy night, beckoning to lonely travelers to come find shelter and safety. He couldn't be angry at Paulsen and Burns. They were absolutely right. But they hadn't talked to Nikolai and Misha the way he had. They hadn't looked into the eyes of those two men, seen the fear and the panic and the sincerity. They didn't fully appreciate what was at stake.

And as for the War Department and Griggs and his orders—well, maybe they were wrong.

"I care what happens to them," Mark said in a calm, quiet voice. "And I want you both to know that I'm not going to sit idly by and allow those two men to die."

"Captain, think about what you're saying," Paulsen said. "Are you willing to risk your career and everything that you've worked for, all for two strangers from another country that's probably going to be our enemy once this war is over?"

Mark stared at the dials in front of him and thought about

his father on the platform at the train station. He thought of his brother who looked up to him and wanted to be like him. He thought of his family and the years he had spent working and training to become a pilot. He thought of the possibility that if he just wouldn't mess things up, he might still see action in this war.

Burns's quiet voice came over the headset. "I can't support you in this, Captain. Our orders are to deliver this plane and its passengers and cargo to the Soviet flight crew in Alaska, and if you violate those orders, then I will report you."

"What are *you* thinking, Captain?" Paulsen asked.

"What are you thinking?" Mark replied.

Paulsen's face was tight and focused on Mark. His lips were pressed together and he was squinting slightly, and then his eyes broke contact with Mark's and he looked over at the console. Several seconds passed, and finally he looked back up at Mark, and his eyes told Mark that he was wavering. "You wanna know what I'm thinking, Captain?" he said, and he started to nod his head a few times as he tried to reassure himself. "All right," he said, putting his hands up. "Let's just assume for a minute that we decide to help these guys out. What could we possibly do?"

"I can't believe I'm hearing this," Burns said.

"Well, whatever we do, we'll have to do it in flight," Mark said. "Once we land in Alaska, there are going to be Russians all over us. There's no way we could get them out in Alaska."

"What if we snuck them out in some of those crates back there?" Paulsen asked.

"But what about the two guys guarding them?" Mark asked. "What would we do about them?"

"Maybe we could overpower them," Paulsen said.

"What are you talking about?" Burns asked. "Didn't you look at that one guy? He's a Goliath. A Frankenstein."

"Well, there's five of us and two of them," Paulsen said.

"What do you mean, five of *us*?" Burns said. "There are *three* of us and *four* of them, and don't forget that if the captain's right, then two of those guys have guns and are professional killers."

"No, we can't sneak them out in crates," Mark said. "The crates are all staying on the plane, remember? The only thing that's supposed to come off of this plane is the three of us, and that's what the Russians are going to be looking for. If anything else leaves this plane, and I mean anything at all, they'll get suspicious and check it out."

"So it has to be in flight," Paulsen said. He looked disappointed.

"I can't believe you guys," Burns said. "We're talking about violating a direct order here. This is treason."

Paulsen's eyes brightened up. "What if we dressed the two Russians up in our clothes? Then they could walk off the plane right past the Soviet guards in Alaska, and we could put them on the next flight back to Montana."

"Oh, that's really bright, Einstein," Burns said. "And what about us? What are two of us supposed to do? Hide in a crate in the back and hope that the Russians send us back home when they discover us somewhere over Siberia?"

"Well, maybe we could dress the Russians up in our flight suits, and two of us could put on their clothes," Paulsen said. "They're wearing flight jackets too, you know. We could tie up the two guards and hide them in the back, then the two of us in the Russians' clothes could bail out. One of us would land the plane in Alaska and walk away with the two Russian accountants, and we'd be scot-free."

"You're crazy!" Burns said, and he was visibly becoming more and more irritated with each sentence that Paulsen spoke. "Everything you just said is madness!"

"We can't tie up the two guards," Mark said. "Their job is to escort the two accountants to the Soviet Union, and the Soviets in Alaska will be expecting them. If we show up in Alaska without them for any reason, there'll be big trouble."

"What if we knock them out and put parachutes on them and throw them out of the plane?"

"No good, Paulsen" Mark said.

“I guess we can’t kill them, either,” Paulsen said.

“Kill them?” Burns’ face was white as a sheet. “Now you’re talking about murder.”

“All right, all right,” Mark said. “This isn’t getting us anywhere. Now let me explain the situation one more time. Tomorrow morning this plane is going to land in Alaska. When it does, three Americans have to get off, and four Russians have to stay on. No matter what we do, that’s what has to happen in Alaska.”

“What if we turn the plane around and go back to Montana?” Paulsen asked. “Or some other airfield?”

“The problem with that is that no one will give us permission to change our flight plan. Not even Griggs has the authority to alter our mission. This whole operation comes straight from the War Department. If we go to some other airfield, or even back to Montana, the Russians will know about it, and they’ll want their people back. The point is not to avoid landing in Alaska. The point is to save these two Russian accountants. Can you see the contradiction? On the one hand, the only way to avoid suspicion is to stay on this course and deliver the Russians to Alaska, but on the other hand, if we’re going to save them, then that’s also the one thing we have to avoid.”

“Captain, I’m not trying to be insubordinate,” Burns said. “But I think you’re risking your career for nothing. I know you want to help those two men back there. Maybe I do, too. But it’s not within our authority to do so. And there’s nothing we can do about it, anyway. The internal politics of the Soviet Union are none of our business.”

“What if we pretended to have engine trouble?” Paulsen asked. “Then we wouldn’t need someone higher up to change the mission plans. We could land somewhere and sneak the two accountants off.”

“Still no good, Paulsen,” Mark said. “That’s a nice idea, but the logistics of it are too complicated. We can’t pretend to have engine trouble, because once we’re on the ground, the Army will learn that there was nothing wrong with the plane and that we made the story up. Besides, we're flying a C-47. This is just about the most reliable aircraft in the Army Air Corps, and this particular plane has had special maintenance work done on it because of its sensitive cargo. Any excuse involving mechanical problems would be very suspicious. And think about what we'd have to do once we're on the ground. How would we hide and smuggle two Soviet agents to safety, all by ourselves? And even if we did, we can't grant them political asylum. That's something the government has to do. If we're going to save these two Russian accountants, we have to come up with something better, something that at least has a chance of working, even if it's a long shot."

A gloomy malaise settled over the cockpit, and no one spoke for a full minute or so as they contemplated the plight of their passengers. Finally Paulsen broke the silence. "Burns might be right, Captain," he said. His sudden enthusiasm for helping out the two Russian accountants seemed to have waned as quickly as it had germinated. "It's impossible. No matter how you look at it, it's impossible."

Mark had been thinking about this all day and had come to the same conclusion. Over and over again he had hit the same dead end—there was nothing he could do. It was maddening. "I just can't bear the thought of letting those two men die," he said.

THIRTY-SEVEN

The plane had been in the air for only a few minutes. The humming drone of the engines filled Misha's ears with an irritating buzzing, and neither he nor Nikolai had said a word since takeoff. He sat to the left of Nikolai on the short bench at the back of the cargo hold, where they were both out of the line of sight from the cockpit, which he figured was probably why Vorlakov had told them to sit there. Misha didn't want to think about Vorlakov's reasons for keeping him and Nikolai out of the Americans' sight. It could only be a bad thing.

He allowed himself to look over to his left, where Vorlakov and Malkov sat side by side on the other bench, the one that was bolted into the left wall of the cargo hold and faced toward the right side of the airplane. It was only a few meters away.

Malkov was still staring at them, just as he had been continuously ever since he and Vorlakov had returned from the cockpit door together. The sneer was there on the wide, fleshy face, but the smile was gone. The expression on Malkov's face was austere, yet steady and focused. His eyes looked glazed over, as if he were slightly inebriated, and although he stared deliberately at Misha and Nikolai, his mind seemed to be concentrating on something else, as if he knew the secrets of their future and wanted them to know that, but had no intention of revealing what those secrets were. Malkov's skin was gray and colorless and had a sickly, shiny quality to it, as if it were moist. Yet Malkov did not appear to be sweating.

Misha stared at the floor. His heart was beating fast, and his breathing was short and shallow. This flight was the nightmare of denunciation all over again. For years he had avoided it, brushed up close to it on a couple of occasions, but now, finally, the nightmare was catching up to him. And this time it looked like there would be no miraculous last-minute deliverance.

He looked at Nikolai. Nikolai slouched in his seat, but his shoulders were tense, and his face looked fretful. His eyes shifted from one thing to another but didn't focus in on anything, and every now and then he reached up with his right hand and rubbed the back of his neck in a nervous ritual of controlled panic. The flight ahead of them stretched out into eternity. This was no way to pass the time.

"Nikolai," he said, waiting to make sure he had his attention.

The gaunt, tired face turned; the hollow eyes stared through him. For a second it seemed that Nikolai wasn't really there, that his spirit had left his body and was somewhere else, and that Misha was gazing upon an empty shell of flesh and bones that used to be a man. But then a spark of intelligence returned to the vacuous eyes, and Nikolai looked like he was again cognizant of his surroundings.

"Nikolai, are you listening?" Misha asked, just to be sure.

The ghostly image nodded, and Misha saw the Adam's apple rise in the throat as Nikolai swallowed. Some color returned to Nikolai's face. "Yes."

"If we're going to do something, we'd better do it soon," Misha said.

Nikolai shook his head. "We can't. They're sitting between us and the cockpit. We'd never make it."

Misha looked at the floor again, but out of the side of his left eye he took a quick glance at the two men on the other bench. Then he turned back to Nikolai. "Vorlakov is sitting on Malkov's right side."

"So?"

"So Malkov is sitting between Vorlakov and the cockpit door. That means Vorlakov will have to get around Malkov before he can chase anyone in the direction of the cockpit, and it's Vorlakov that we have to worry about. If we move fast and charge them, we could reach them on their bench before they have a chance to stand up. I could jump on them and hold them for a second, and you could rush past them and have a clear shot at the cockpit."

"It won't work, Misha. Even if we surprise them, we can't get to them quickly enough. And they have guns."

"They wouldn't shoot us in here."

"How do you know?"

"Because that would alert the Americans. They aren't stupid."

Nikolai looked over the top of Misha's head and glanced over at their escorts. "I don't know, Misha. They look like they're up to something. And Malkov looks crazy."

"Put your head down," Misha said. "You'll make them suspicious."

☆

Vorlakov rested calmly against the back of his seat, watching his two prisoners carefully. They were too frightened not to know what was going on. They had figured it out. And now they were talking to each other, glancing in his direction from time to time. They were nervous, panicky. A bad sign. Two desperate men who knew that torture and death awaited them. That made them two desperate men with nothing to lose.

He turned his head to the left. Comrade Malkov's face reminded him of a gargoyle. "Well, Comrade Malkov," he said in a relaxed tone of voice. "What are you thinking?"

The corners of Malkov's lips turned downward, adding depth and texture to the ghoulish sneer that had become a permanent fixture on Malkov's face. "They're plotting something," he said, and he anxiously licked his lips once the words had fallen from his mouth. Malkov was a wolf, Vorlakov thought as he looked at him. Time to sic him on them.

"Are you ready?" Vorlakov asked. He already knew that Malkov was more than ready. Malkov was even more than eager. Vorlakov asked this to prompt Malkov, to give him the signal that their work was about to begin.

"It's time," Malkov said. "We have to do this now, before they finish their plotting." He almost drooled as he said this.

Vorlakov looked around Malkov and stared down the narrow

corridor that led to the cockpit door between the wall of the plane on the left and the wall of heavy wooden crates on the right. No sign of movement from the Americans. Usually the Americans waited a few hours before checking the cargo and the Soviet couriers, anyway. He had plenty of time. He'd soften the prisoners up a little, then stand guard and keep his eye on the cockpit while Malkov did the psychological stuff and took care of the finer aspects of inflicting physical pain. That's the way it always was. Vorlakov did the rough, heavy work, and Malkov touched up with the mind games and gave the physical suffering his own stylish signature. A sick little man, but good at what he did. Vorlakov looked at the prisoners again. "Let's get started," he said.

Out of the corner of his eye, Misha saw Vorlakov and Malkov stand up, and he knew immediately that he and Nikolai had waited too long. An awful, morbid nausea pervaded his belly. His tongue and throat dried up, and his mouth felt like it had cotton in it. He sat up straight, as did Nikolai, and he felt a shaky, nervous tremble run down his right arm. At first he thought it was his own arm that had trembled, only to realize that it was actually Nikolai's left arm, which was pressed against his right, that had shuddered. Wonderful. It was bad enough to be on the brink of panic himself, but to have someone next to him who was even closer to panicking made it almost impossible to rein his emotions back from that abysmal edge where fear dropped off into insanity.

Vorlakov came first. He walked casually. A broad, warm smile stretched from ear to ear across his round, beefy face. The friendliest guy in the world, Misha's old chum. The eyes even twinkled a couple of times, but Misha saw the empty blackness behind the glitter. Vorlakov's enormous frame loomed before him, approached him, portended his impending doom. Vorlakov represented power and deceit, inspired uneasiness and fear, and that's why the Party valued him. The ogre of the Lubyanka.

Malkov followed closely behind Vorlakov, and looked like Vorlakov's opposite. Malkov had a massive, fat head, but it wasn't boyishly round and disarming like Vorlakov's. Malkov's features were sharp—his nose, his forehead, his eyes and glasses—except for his cheeks and chin and neck, which were covered in a fatty, leathery layer of skin. He was breathing hard and fast through his nose, and looked ecstatic. Misha thought of his visits to the doctor when he was a little boy, how the anticipation was usually more intense than the actual pain, and he wondered if the same might be true for a warped miscreant like Malkov. The eager gleam in Malkov's eyes answered Misha's question. For Malkov, the anticipation was obviously sweet, obsessively so. But Misha knew by looking into that face that for Malkov, the real pleasure was yet to come. Malkov stopped at about the halfway mark between the two benches.

"How is your flight so far, Comrades?" Vorlakov said as he stepped around Misha and stopped in front of Nikolai. He leaned forward, put his left hand on Nikolai's right shoulder, and looked into Nikolai's face, still smiling cheerfully. "How about you, Comrade Ryzanov? Are you enjoying your flight?" Vorlakov's tone was friendly, but out of place. Obviously he could see how frightened Nikolai was, yet he still kept on smiling, just as he had with Misha four years earlier in the lieutenant's office at the Lubyanka.

Nikolai looked up into Vorlakov's face, but was too paranoid to answer. He sat with his hands clasped in his lap, docile as a lamb.

Within a fraction of a second, Vorlakov's entire body shifted, moved in a way that Misha didn't quite perceive. His right hand formed a massive fist, and his arm shot forward with speed and power and efficiency. He stepped forward a little, too, putting all of his weight behind his arm as the fist slammed into Nikolai's abdomen. The bench shuddered from the colossal force of the blow, and Nikolai let out a quick, sharp gasp as he doubled up around Vorlakov's fist. The sucker punch took a fraction of a second, and happened so quickly that the startling shock wave that passed through Misha as his nervous system reacted to the imminent threat of danger was more of a delayed response, striking him just as Vorlakov was pulling his fist back out of Nikolai's mid-section.

Nikolai sat completely bent over, gripping his stomach with both arms, his face bright red, his eyes ready to pop out of his head, his mouth wide open. But he wasn't breathing. He was trying to, but he couldn't. A portrait of agony covered his face, a frozen snapshot of exquisite pain captured briefly in Nikolai's stunned expression.

Vorlakov wasted no time. He immediately stepped in front of Misha and looked down at him, but he wasn't smiling any more. The blackness had snuffed out the glimmer in the eyes, and the deceitfully pleasant round face had now mutated into its true form, the grisly, morose, calloused face of an experienced executioner who enjoyed the absolute power inherent in the sadistic, morbid duties of his job. A crazy thought passed through Misha's mind at that moment, and he felt a hint of gratitude to Vorlakov for this sudden mutation. Strike me, torture me, kill me if you must. I don't care. But thank you for getting rid of that smile.

The thought passed quickly. It was a stupid thought. Why did he always think these stupid thoughts at times like these? It must be a defense mechanism, he decided. A way to brace himself for, or rather distract himself from, the unknown horrors that lay ahead.

Vorlakov leaned forward and reached out with his left hand toward Misha's right shoulder, but didn't rest it there as he did with Nikolai. Instead, he grasped Misha's flight jacket and lifted up and back to keep Misha sitting erect. Misha felt the powerful hand pushing against the right side of his neck, and he strained his head to the right to push back against it. Then Vorlakov moved in the same manner that he had when he punched Nikolai, and Misha instinctively scrunched up, snapping his arms in to cover his abdomen.

His speed paid off. Vorlakov's iron fist plowed into Misha's right forearm, which lay across his stomach at the base of his ribs. The horrendous blow surprised Misha with its utter power, and in spite of his measures to protect himself, it thoroughly knocked the wind out of him and crumpled him up. Sharp pain shot through his stomach and sides and around his back, and when he opened his eyes, he was staring at Vorlakov's shoes, which were about a meter in front of him. He was amazed that he felt no pain in the arm that took the force of the blow, but he knew the arm was merely numb from the shock of it, and that it would soon have a large, throbbing bruise from elbow to wrist. He hoped that it wasn't broken.

Vorlakov then grabbed Misha's hair at the back of his head and pulled up a little, then quickly brought Misha's head down. Misha knew what was coming and rotated his head to the right, so that when Vorlakov's knee made contact, it missed his nose and crashed into the left side of his eye socket. Pain streaked through his head like lightning through clouds. He was dizzy and stupefied, but still conscious and alert. He coughed and gasped a couple of times, but he managed to start breathing again, and when he opened and closed his right hand a couple of times, he knew that his arm was not broken.

Misha sensed Vorlakov stepping back, away from him and Nikolai, and even above the drone of the engines he heard Malkov's heavy breathing come closer. Malkov must be some kind of animal to get so much excitement out of this.

"Sit up, Comrades." It was Malkov's voice. Malkov was trying to sound calm and steady and self-assured, like Vorlakov, but he was breathing too heavily. The voice quivered, revealing the uncontrollable delight that Malkov was trying to hide behind his sneering, glowering exterior.

Misha sat up slowly and opened his eyes. His stomach hurt and his head was aching, but it wasn't as bad as he thought it would be, and the pain was already subsiding. Nikolai, however, was still hunched over, moaning in short little spurts as he started to breathe again after Vorlakov's punch. Vorlakov had stepped off to the right and was standing on the other side of

Nikolai a couple of meters away, watching them.

It took Misha a second before it hit him. Vorlakov had stepped off to the right, which meant he was not standing between Misha and the narrow aisle that led to the cockpit door. Only Malkov was.

Malkov walked over to Nikolai and slapped him hard across the side of his face. "I said sit up."

With Vorlakov Misha felt only fear; but with Malkov, the fear was transforming into anger. The rage was jelling inside of him again, gathering, congealing, coagulating, materializing into a hot, tangible substance that started deep in his gut and boiled upward, outward, spreading throughout his torso and limbs, seething up until a cushion of heat enveloped his scalp. And with it came that feeling of invincibility, of wholesale disregard for himself that engendered a wild, frenzied confidence, except that this time he stayed in control and diverted it away from the dark, depraved realm of vengeance. This time it wasn't about his own hatred of Malkov. This time it was for Nikolai, for Larisa and Kolya, for Captain Daniels and Rose Petersen and the mighty nation that he had come to love. This time it was a matter of justice, of doing the right thing to save an innocent man.

Nikolai sat up and looked over at Misha, who returned the gaze, and when their eyes met, the world stood still for a brief moment, and there was no Malkov and no Vorlakov and no transport plane and no Soviet Union; only Misha and Nikolai, two acquaintances who had become friends, two friends who were now brothers, and Misha's only desire was to atone for his betrayal of Nikolai and to again be worthy of the respect of his wife and son, regardless of what price he might personally have to pay. Misha gave a slight nod to Nikolai to let him know that it was time to move, and in Nikolai's weary, hopeless eyes, Misha saw understanding. Then the brief, suspended moment passed, and Misha and Nikolai were on the airplane again, with Malkov and Vorlakov threatening their lives, and an American crew up front who might intervene to save them if only one of them could reach the cockpit door.

Misha looked up at Malkov, who was smiling and sneering and glaring down his nose with contempt at them, soaking in the pleasure of his long-awaited success at bringing about Misha's demise, and he was getting himself ready to speak, to degrade and humiliate and insult. But the anger inside of Misha was flowing through his veins, surging within him like a flooded river, seeking a target to direct itself at, a valve through which it might escape; and Misha decided in that moment that Malkov had no right to speak, no right to live.

In one swift move, Misha hopped to his feet and grabbed Malkov by the throat with his left hand, gripping and squeezing as he extended his arm and shoved Malkov backward into the stacked wooden crates behind him. Malkov was taken by surprise and lost his balance, making it easier for Misha to pin him against the crates. Misha couldn't see Nikolai right now, but felt the slender figure slide past his back toward the left side of the plane, and out of the side of his right eye Misha saw Vorlakov reacting, rushing toward his fleeing hostage. But as Vorlakov reached the small bench and tried to run behind Misha's back on his way to catch Nikolai, Misha reached back with his right arm and managed to land his right hand on Vorlakov's flight jacket near the shoulder.

Misha was now facing the right side of the airplane. With Malkov pinned solidly against the wooden crates, Misha braced himself with his left arm against Malkov's neck and shoved Vorlakov with his right with all the strength he had. Vorlakov was an enormous man, but Misha hit him hard enough to knock him toward the back of the plane, and when Vorlakov's legs hit the front edge of the little metal bench that Misha and Nikolai had been sitting on, Vorlakov lost his balance and fell to the floor, landing hard on his right side.

During that split second, Misha had been watching Vorlakov and hadn't paid attention to Malkov whatsoever. When Misha turned his head back around, he barely caught a glimpse of Malkov's right hand as it pulled out a revolver from inside his flight jacket and pressed the end of the barrel into Misha's upper abdomen, and a sickening, hollow emptiness permeated Misha's stomach as he reached for Malkov's hand.

Vorlakov landed just in front of the metal bench that was bolted into the left wall of the plane. Stunned only momentarily, he instantly got up onto his hands and knees, unzipped his flight jacket, and reached in for his revolver. He whipped it out and glanced behind him, only to see Malkov pulling out his own revolver and pointing it at Kostrin's stomach.

Vorlakov looked toward the cockpit. Ryzanov was already at the door, pounding on it, struggling to pull it open. It was too late to keep the Americans out of this now. In all his years with the NKVD and the NKGB, he had never let a prisoner escape, and he wasn't about to start now. He jumped to his feet and dashed forward.

He reached Ryzanov a couple of seconds later and wrapped his left arm around Ryzanov's neck, putting him in a solid headlock. Ryzanov struggled to breathe and was unable to scream, and he clawed at Vorlakov's arm, but with no effect. "Calm down," Vorlakov told him. "You don't really think you can escape, do you? You have nowhere to go."

Misha's free hand moved like lightning, grabbing Malkov's wrist and shoving it downward. A sharp cracking sound exploded from below and reverberated in Misha's ears, and fire erupted in his left thigh, a new fire, a fire of physical pain, different from the river of burning rage that had filled him a moment before, and he sensed immediately that his strength was draining out of him. He didn't have much time.

He grabbed Malkov's hand and pushed the revolver downward, away from himself toward the floor, and Malkov squeezed off another round, which blew a small hole in the cargo deck. Misha tightened his grip around Malkov's throat with his left hand, digging his fingers into Malkov's thick neck, hoping to close off the windpipe or cut off enough blood circulation to render him unconscious. Misha could feel Malkov weakening, but he was still putting up a strong resistance, and as Misha twisted Malkov's hand up so that the revolver came between them, Malkov managed to get off a third round.

By this time the revolver was at about chest level, caught in the few centimeters of space between the two men, pointing to Misha's right and Malkov's left. The barrel of the gun belched forth its blaze of reddish-orange fire, singeing Misha's flight jacket as it propelled a bullet through one of the windows on the right side of the airplane. The window blew out of the cargo hold with a violent purge of glass, and a gust of wind rushed through the hole.

The pistol fired again, this time hitting a small wooden crate against the right wall, not far from the blown-out window, and from inside the crate came the distinct sound of shattering glass. A clear liquid poured out of the bullet hole and spread across part of the floor, followed by a blue flame that suddenly flowed out after the liquid and engulfed the box. The flames changed to red and orange, and black smoke billowed out of the burning crate.

Malkov was steadily getting weaker, but so was Misha. Misha leaned his weight into Malkov to keep him pinned against the crates, and finally Misha felt Malkov's finger slip off of the trigger, which Misha now felt against his own. Malkov's hand was still gripping the revolver, and Misha's hand was wrapped around Malkov's, but with a forceful shove Misha twisted the gun away from himself so that it pressed into Malkov's chest.

He pulled the trigger. Another explosive crack bit into Misha's ears, and Malkov's body went limp. Misha's leg was burning and he felt a trickle of blood running down past his knee underneath his trousers, and he couldn't support Malkov's weight. His legs buckled, and both men collapsed to the floor.

Mark still hadn't thought of anything good, but had decided

to go back and check on the Russians anyway to see if he might figure something out. He had barely turned the controls over to Paulsen and gotten out of his seat when the relative calm in the cockpit was pierced by a loud pounding at the door and the desperate shout for help from someone on the other side. Then came the unmistakable sharp popping noises of gunfire from somewhere back in the cargo area.

All three of them froze with disbelief, and Paulsen and Burns both looked over at him with blank expressions on their faces. "Was that gunfire?" Paulsen asked.

Mark found his holster and pulled out his weapon, then cautiously opened the door and peered out. Vorlakov had Nikolai in a headlock in one arm and a pistol in the other. He was dragging Nikolai backwards and was about halfway between the cockpit door and the back of the plane. Mark extended his shooting arm and locked his elbow, leveling the Colt in the direction of Vorlakov and Nikolai. He stepped out of the cockpit into the cargo area, still pointing his weapon forward, cupping his left hand under the butt of the pistol to stabilize his right arm as he aimed for Vorlakov's head. He had no clear line of fire. The target was too small, and with Nikolai in the way, he didn't dare risk it.

Black smoke curled around the ceiling and filled the cargo hold with the acrid, pungent odor of burning chemicals. He couldn't see the flames yet, but the smoke was coming from the starboard side of the airplane, off to his left up ahead of him.

"Drop your weapon!" he shouted. Nikolai's body was rigid, his eyes closed. But Nikolai's hands were still clawing at Vorlakov's arm, and his feet were still kicking.

"This matter is not your concern," Vorlakov shouted back over the noise of the engines and the wind that was rushing through the plane. "Go back to the cockpit."

Mark shook his head and slowly began moving forward, keeping his aim level and steady with each step. "Put down your weapon and let him go!"

Several thoughts raced through Mark's mind. This was

insane. What went on back here? And if that idiot doesn't put his gun down so we can get that fire out, we're all going to be in real trouble. He silently cursed the War Department and the Lend Lease program for allowing these Russians to haul cargo on his plane without telling him what was in it. For all he knew, these crates might be loaded with high explosives. And where were the other two Russians?

Mark had no clue what to do as Vorlakov kept stepping back other than to keep moving forward slowly with his own weapon pointed straight ahead. Please help me out here, he prayed. Just let me get out of this alive.

As Vorlakov came within a couple of feet of the end of the row of cargo, Mark saw a single hand holding a revolver extend out from around the corner of the crates where Mark couldn't see, and then the hand pointed it at the back of Vorlakov's head.

Startled, Mark took his eyes off of Vorlakov and looked at the hand with the gun, then realized his mistake and looked back at Vorlakov. But the error was made. Vorlakov had seen him looking at something, and now turned his head to see what it was.

Misha held the gun less than a meter from the base of Vorlakov's skull, and in his heart he thanked the NKVD for the small arms training he had received after he was recruited. There was no way he could miss. How ironic. How appropriate. Him ending Vorlakov's life in the same way that some executioner had ended Ivan's—with a bullet to the back of the head. Was it you, Vorlakov? Are you the monster that killed Ivan? His finger was wrapped around the trigger. He had one shot left. The desire to squeeze was overwhelming.

But he couldn't do it. Something inside of him stopped him. He stared at the back of Vorlakov's head and hesitated. If I pull the trigger, I'll be no different than him.

Suddenly Vorlakov's head turned around, and Misha was looking down the short barrel into the big man's eyes. There was no fear in Vorlakov's face, only surprise. Vorlakov paused, and his expression relaxed. The deep blackness of the cold, soulless eyes sparkled, and Vorlakov smiled.

Vorlakov was fast. He rotated his body to his right, bringing Nikolai around in front of him as a shield, and he lowered his right arm as he attempted to take aim and fire at Misha before Misha could fire at him. But he wasn't fast enough.

Misha pulled the trigger. Vorlakov's head jerked back violently and his body fell backward, striking the floor with a sickening thud and cushioning the blow for Nikolai, who immediately rolled to the side and rubbed his neck with his hand, gasping for air.

At that moment Misha heard a loud explosion from the other side of the cargo hold, and he knew that the fire had spread to the other box containing combustibles. The aircraft rocked and tilted violently, throwing Misha and Captain Daniels off balance, and they fell to the floor. For several seconds the engines whined at an uncomfortably high pitch, the sure indication that they had gone into a dive. Then the plane leveled off, shuddered for a moment, and finally stabilized. The engines were louder now, and the wind rushing through the cargo area strengthened. Misha stood up using his good leg and hobbled around the back of the crates, Captain Daniels close behind him.

Misha stopped abruptly and held out his arm to his side to keep Captain Daniels back, and the two men stared. Several shredded wooden boards were burning along with some other packing materials at the back of the cargo area, and the fire had spread to the piles of black leather suitcases toward the front, which were now burning ferociously. And in the middle section of the cargo area, just behind the starboard wing, a wide, gaping hole had blown out of the side of the plane, and the engine on that side was spewing thick gray smoke out into the air.

"Parachutes!" Captain Daniels shouted as he pulled Misha back toward the door on the left side of the plane. Captain Daniels ran to the cockpit.

"I can't hold her, Captain!" the co-pilot shouted.

"We've got a massive fire in the cargo hold," Misha heard Captain Daniels say. "Get your parachutes and bail out!"

Captain Daniels returned to the cargo hold and helped Misha and Nikolai with their parachutes while the radio man wrapped a tight belt around Misha's leg. "I'll take the medical kit with me," the American told him. "We'll dress the wound right once we're on the ground."

The airplane was full of thick gray smoke, and everyone was choking. Captain Daniels opened the door and told Misha to stand in front of it. Misha stood at the precipice and stared down into blackness, and before he was ready, Captain Daniels had shoved him out into a sea of nothingness. Every muscle in his body tightened up. He wanted to scream, but he couldn't even breathe, and his stomach was up in his throat. His parachute jolted him as it opened automatically, and he floated down in the most profound silence, a stark contradiction to the chaotic clamor he had left just seconds before.

The moonlight was not strong, but it shone just brightly enough that he could see four other parachutes above him, off to his right side. The silence was brief, punctured suddenly by the horrendous whine of the airplane engines as the transport fell into a steep dive. There was a muffled crunch as the airplane punched a hole in the surface of the earth, and off in the distance below, Misha saw a brief fire ball rise from the ground, then vanish.

THIRTY-EIGHT

Karen was at the bottom of an ocean, down in the dark blue depths where vision is blurred and sounds are murky and the weight of the water presses all around you. And somewhere far above her, above the surface of the water, a voice beckoned her to rise. Now she was ascending, gliding upward, honing in on the beacon that called to her.

She opened her eyes. Blinding whiteness stared back at her.

"Karen."

She blinked repeatedly until things started coming into focus. Never had she felt so groggy in all her life, and it took a few more seconds before she could see clearly.

She was sitting in a hospital bed in a reclined position, wearing a white gown, with a blanket draped over her legs. A bright light hung suspended above her head against the backdrop of a pure white ceiling. The Chief was sitting on a chair next to her bed.

The Chief's warm expression and bald head were comforting. She couldn't help but smile. "Chief," she said. It was strange to hear herself speak, because her voice didn't seem to be her own. It came out weak, almost like a whisper.

"Hey there. How are you feeling?"

She cleared her throat, and this time her voiced sounded normal. "Terrible," she said. "What happened?"

"Don't you remember?" the Chief asked. "You were shot twice. One bullet hit your shoulder, and the other tore off a small piece of your scalp, but was deflected off of your skull. You're lucky to be alive."

The fog was clearing. The sky was beginning to shine through. It was coming back to her—driving the car with the Chief in the passenger seat, Howard running into the building, the shootout inside.

"Where's Boris's wife?" Karen asked.

"She's safe. I found her hiding in the corner of the room where you were shot. She was crouched down on the floor with her baby screaming in her arms, and she was in so much shock from the shooting that I don't think she was even lucid at that point. Poor lady was even bitten by a rat."

"But she's okay?"

"Oh, yeah. We had a doctor check her out, and he said she'll be fine. No problems at all."

"What about Howard?"

The Chief pulled his glasses off of his face and carefully folded them in his hands. He stared into his lap. "Agent Howard is dead."

She stared up at the lamp on the ceiling for a second, then closed her eyes.

"I had some of the boys from the office investigate the shooting. They went down to the building and checked it out, then talked to Boris's wife. You fired a total of five shots, and Howard got off three. Your first two shots hit him in the torso, but Howard is such a big guy that I guess he absorbed them and managed to return fire. His first shot hit you in the shoulder, and his second shot hit you in the head. His third shot hit the wall behind you. Your third shot hit him square in the face and killed him instantly. Your fourth shot hit the wall behind him, and your fifth shot hit the ceiling, so you must have been firing while you were falling backward."

"I remember that," she said. She opened her eyes.

"You want to tell me what you found out about Agent Howard?" the Chief asked.

She had a new contact at Amtorg, she explained, and was meeting with him the morning that she was to pick up Mrs. Kostrin. This new contact told her about Malkov's meetings with Howard. He said that Semerov didn't trust Howard, so Semerov had some of his agents check out Howard's background. It turned out that Howard had an ex-wife who committed suicide a few years ago. Howard started drinking and accumulated huge gambling debts in New Jersey. His creditors had ties with organized crime and started making threats.

Howard sold information to a German agent for a while, then he went to the Soviets and offered to tell them who their moles were. At first he told them about a young man at the Soviet consulate named Stepan. Later he told them everything about Karen, and finally he told them about Alfred and Boris. He planned to flee to South America.

“But why would he shoot at you?” the Chief asked.

Her head was pounding. “I guess he figured he had nothing to lose. He was just minutes away from succeeding, and I was the only thing standing in his way.”

The Chief shook his head.

She wanted to sleep. “One question, Chief. Why did Boris’s wife run from Howard? How did she know not to trust him?”

The Chief stood up and looked down at her serenely. “Good instincts, I suppose. She told our agents that she just had a dark feeling come over her and that she knew she had to run. That’s all she said.”

Karen closed her eyes. Her body felt like it weighed a ton, and it was sinking back into the hospital bed, ready to plunge back down into the ocean. The Chief patted her on the hand. “Get some rest, Karen.”

THIRTY-NINE

The courier handed Semerov a sealed packet. "This just came for you, Comrade Semerov. Highest priority."

Semerov opened it. It was an emergency message. The aircraft carrying the recent shipment of uranium chemicals had crashed in Montana, and all seven men aboard had been killed. Just an hour earlier, he had been told that Comrade Kostrina had disappeared. So had Rose Petersen and Agent Howard. No sign of them anywhere.

Just a coincidence?

He walked to the window and looked down at the street below. "Very clever, Comrade Kostrin," he muttered quietly to himself. The FBI was very good. Just when he's on the brink of cracking their operations wide open, all the doors slam shut and he's back to where he started. A million possible scenarios flashed through his mind as to how the FBI had pulled it off. The only good news he had received today was that his men had found Agent Howard's safe deposit box and had recovered most of the money that Howard had been paid.

"Have our agents in Montana confirmed this?"

"Yes, Comrade Semerov. Our people have seen the crash site. It was likely a mechanical failure or an explosion on board."

"Have they recovered any bodies yet?"

"No, Comrade Semerov. The crash site is radioactive, so the Americans won't let anyone near it. They're handling the matter with the utmost secrecy."

"So we'll never know what really happened."

"Probably not, Comrade Semerov."

Very clever indeed.

"The Centre wants to know if you believe we should investigate these two reports to see if they're related," the courier said.

Of course they were related. Kostrin and Ryzanov were alive

and well, he was sure of that. Probably in FBI custody, soon to be free. And Kostrin's wife with them. But an investigation would be pointless. There was no chance of finding them.

"No investigation will be necessary," he said. "Report to the Centre that the airplane crash was a legitimate accident, and that our four comrades are all dead. Kostrin's wife was either kidnapped by the FBI or she ran away, but she knows nothing and can't possibly damage our operations here, and therefore is too insignificant a person to waste valuable resources on."

"Yes, Comrade Semerov."

Colonel Griggs visited Mark in a small, isolated room at Gore Field to fill him in. Mark, Paulsen, and Burns were all being transferred to the Pacific to see some action and get as far away from the Russians as possible. Misha and Nikolai were in good shape. Misha's leg was expected to heal completely. As for Griggs, he was heading to England to help prepare a fleet of gooney birds for a future invasion of the mainland.

This plane crash would be one of the best-kept secrets of the war, Griggs told him. He was not to discuss it with anyone. The Soviets thought everyone on that plane perished, and that's how the War Department wanted to keep it. As for the accident itself, records were being fudged everywhere. The purchase of chemicals never took place. The airplane never existed.

"What's going to happen to Misha and Nikolai?" Mark asked.

"Well, we can't exactly give them back to the Soviets, can we? Now that they're dead and all." Griggs chuckled. "Once the FBI is through with them, they'll be given new identities and set free. Who knows—maybe Uncle Sam will even find jobs for them. It wouldn't surprise me one bit."

The FBI man stood up from the table, closed the file in front of him, and left the room. Misha and Nikolai sat quietly. The past few days had been full of long debriefing sessions and interrogations with various FBI personnel. Some sessions were friendly, others harsh and confrontational. They were in Washington, D.C. They had cooperated fully with the Americans, and now they were on the threshold of freedom.

"It's hard to believe we actually made it," Misha said.

Nikolai nodded slowly. "It's a miracle."

"Where do you want to live?"

Nikolai shook his head. "I don't know."

Misha knew. "I think you should come with me and my family."

"Oh? Where are you going?"

"Southern California."

FORTY

A gentle breeze rustled the branches and leaves of the orange trees, spattering the ground with alternating spots of sunlight and shade as the trees swayed softly. A bright sun shone above, blanketing the orchards with a layer of life-giving warmth. Earlier that morning an overcast sky had sprinkled the ground with a light rain, but now the gray clouds had moved off beyond the horizon, leaving a pure expanse of blue in all directions. The air was fresh and pure, cleansed by the shower of falling raindrops, and Misha filled his lungs. The tree branches arched over the unpaved lane where Misha and Peter Daniels walked, filtering the sunshine enough to keep them cool, but allowing enough of the sun's rays through to warm up Misha's skin now and then with intermittent beams that percolated through the canopy above and flashed blinding whiteness across his eyes.

They walked over to the left, where a white fence stretched alongside the path. They leaned against it. "Beautiful day," Peter Daniels said in his deep, robust farmer voice. "How's your wife and kids?"

"Good," Misha said. He had four kids now: Kolya, Ivan, Olga, and Sasha, ages eight, five, three, and one. He and Larisa devoted all their time to them.

Peter Daniels turned sideways, still resting his right arm on the fence, but now he faced Misha. "Have you been reading the papers lately?"

Misha shook his head.

"The Soviet Union just tested an atomic bomb."

Tension passed through Misha's stomach, as if a weak current of electricity had just flowed through his body from head to foot, pausing in the center of him to stimulate his kidneys and stir up an anxiety that he hadn't felt for a long time. Misha shuddered. In the few seconds that it took Peter Daniels to say those words, Misha's entire picture of the world had suddenly changed. "I didn't know that," Misha said.

"Do you think that's what you might have been hauling out of Montana during the war?"

Misha thought of Semerov and Malkov and Vorlakov and all the other demonic servants of the Party, with old Uncle Joe, as the Americans called him, perched at the top. It was bad enough when all that the Soviets had were troops and spies and secret police armed with conventional weapons. Now it was hard to imagine what the world was becoming. "I didn't know what uranium was back then," he said. "I suppose I'm partly responsible."

"After the war ended and Mark was allowed to speak about his missions, he told me all about you guys flying those transport planes. Hard to believe our government could be so careless. It's too bad we couldn't just stay out of the whole thing."

Misha nodded.

Mark was coming home next month, Peter Daniels said. Mark was now a major and was flying C-47s again. He had helped out with the Berlin Airlift and had spent the past couple of years in Europe. "He told me over the phone that he would stop by France on his way back." Peter Daniels became quiet all of a sudden. "He plans to visit Kevin's grave."

"How long has it been?" Misha asked.

"Oh, let's see," Peter Daniels said softly. "Kevin was shot down in September of forty-four, about a year after you came to live with us."

"Five years ago this month."

Misha watched Peter Daniel's face. The big man's jaw tightened and his eyes squinted a little, but he would never show any more emotion than that. That's just the way he was.

Peter Daniels looked back at Misha and smiled as he put a strong hand on Misha's shoulder. "You know, there's something I've been meaning to tell you for a while but haven't quite been able to say it." Peter Daniels put his head down for a few seconds so that Misha couldn't see his face, then looked up again. His lips were tight and the crow's feet at the sides of his eyes became deeper as he squinted, and his nostrils flared slightly just before he started to speak. "I was pretty bitter about life when Kevin was killed," he said. His voice was low and quiet, but steady and calm. "But there was something about having you and your family here that made life bearable, especially when little Ivan came along, right after I got the news that Kevin had been shot down. My second son had just died; your second son had just been born.

"It wasn't until after the war, when Mark came home and told us the whole story about how you and your wife came to us, that I realized why I found so much comfort with your family during those difficult months following Kevin's death." Peter Daniels smiled, and his eyes were warm and full of light, a window to the soul of a genuinely good man. "When I thought about what you and your wife had been through in the Soviet Union, and then when I saw how happy you were here, raising your family and living your lives and doing the normal things that I had always taken for granted—that's what made me realize that the sacrifice was worth it. And all of this," he said, stretching his arm out and turning around. "Our homes, our religion, our country, our families—they're all worth it. You and your family helped me find meaning in Kevin's death." Peter Daniels' eyes were shiny, but he kept his composure. His voice dropped low and quiet again. "Thank you for that, Misha."

Misha felt pressure in the bottom of his throat. He thought back to the time a decade ago when his life had been so empty. Now he had his little house in the country where the government and the rest of the world more or less left him alone. He was raising his family and living peacefully, and in death his uncle Konstantin had led him to a new faith that had given him more than his uncle ever could have given him in life. What had always been impossible had now come to pass—Misha was a happy man. The emptiness had been filled.

He smiled. "After Mark gets home, I want you all to come over to my place for dinner. Larisa can make that Russian soup that you love, and I'll invite Nikolai and Karen and their little girl. We'll eat and talk and watch the kids play around, and Mark can tell us about Europe."

"Sounds good," Peter Daniels said.

Misha patted Peter Daniels' shoulder, then the two men turned away from the fence and walked down the little unpaved trail toward the Daniels' home.

ABOUT THE AUTHOR

AARON JORDAN is a native of Salt Lake City. He received a bachelor of arts degree in history from Weber State University and is pursuing a degree in law at the University of Utah. In addition to fiction writing, his interests include playing the piano and studying Russian literature and the Russian language.

9 26575 76992 3